How to Marry a Viscount

The Cinderella Society Book Three

Alyxandra Harvey

Dragonblade Publishing, Inc. is an imprint of Kathryn Le Veque Novels, Inc.
P.O. Box 23
Moreno Valley, CA 92556
ceo@dragonbladepublishing.com

Produced in the United States of America

First Edition October 2022
Trade Paperback Edition

ARE YOU SIGNED UP FOR DRAGONBLADE'S BLOG?

You'll get the latest news and information on exclusive giveaways, exclusive excerpts, coming releases, sales, free books, cover reveals and more.

Check out our complete list of authors, too!

No spam, no junk. That's a promise!

Sign Up Here

www.dragonbladepublishing.com

Dearest Reader;

Thank you for your support of a small press. At Dragonblade Publishing, we strive to bring you the highest quality Historical Romance from some of the best authors in the business. Without your support, there is no 'us', so we sincerely hope you adore these stories and find some new favorite authors along the way.

Happy Reading!

CEO, Dragonblade Publishing

Additional Dragonblade books by Author Alyxandra Harvey

The Cinderella Society Series
How to Marry an Earl (Book 1)
How to Marry a Duke (Book 2)
How to Marry a Viscount (Book 3)

Chapter One

D ESPITE THE CREAKING, Tamsin was reasonably certain her front parlor wasn't haunted.

Not *entirely* certain, it had to be said.

Especially considering some of the relics she kept in the house. There was a two-hundred-year-old skull in that same parlor who could only be described as dodgy. Never mind the black glass scrying mirror said to have belonged to Queen Elizabeth's astrologer John Dee, or the big toe salvaged from a botched mummy dig that her friend Persephone had saved for Tamsin on her honeymoon.

But surely a haunting would involve a cold draft of wind, a disembodied voice, some kind of mist. She knew how to sort out an uninvited spirit—a stern command, salt. Throwing a Bible, preferably a heavy one with a wooden binding. Not that she would do any such thing without serious provocation, of course. She had no idea if ghosts gossiped. People were terrible gossips when they were alive, so she supposed that probably didn't change much just because someone became a bit hazy.

She'd been desperate to see a White Lady or a Green Lady, or any kind of dead lady in any color of dress, since she was eight years old. And although every castle in Britain appeared to be haunted, she'd had no luck. Yet. Therefore, she wasn't about to start offending one if they came to visit.

Spirits were perfectly welcome in her parlor, so long as they had manners.

Verdict was out on that skull, though.

But if the suspicious creaking in a dark, empty house at midnight was not a ghost, and not a servant, as they had been given the night off, nor the kitchen cat who was currently lounging on her bed, then there was one other option left.

Someone had broken into her house.

Again.

Anger kindled in her belly, colliding with the champagne she'd drunk at the theatre. She had only stopped at home to change her gown, having spilled said champagne on herself in order to avoid the attentions of Lord Eaton. Now here she was, stuck on the stairs, and wondering if she remembered how to throw a punch. Henry had taught her and the other Cinderellas when they were twelve, but not only had that been a long time ago, he'd only just learned himself and wasn't terribly good at it yet.

Another creak.

The anger and the champagne bubbles made way for nerves. A smart, sensible woman would not call attention to herself in this situation. She would creep out the back door and call for help. Or, at the very least, hide until the intruder took himself off.

With her treasures.

Not bloody likely.

Tamsin Bell might be the daughter of the Duke of Chester, but she was also the daughter of his first marriage, and he hadn't looked her way since her mother died twenty years ago. Certainly not since his marriage to Lady Chester, who had two daughters on the Marriage Market and, more importantly, a young son who was heir to the duchy. Tamsin was encouraged to leave the Grosvenor Square family mansion when more suitors appeared at the door with her name on their lips than the names of her stepsisters.

At least Tamsin had a tidy allowance, and this small but fashionable house on Bruton Street, and her collection of "macabre knickknacks," as those of the *ton* who knew about it called it.

She'd be damned if she was going to let her house be

breached, or her collection pilfered.

Antiquarians and collectors were an odd lot to begin with, never mind the type interested in skulls and crystal balls and folkloric curses. It was more than possible for any of them to break into her house. She wouldn't put such actions past her own dear friends.

After all, hadn't they, as the goddaughters of the Duke of Pendleton, a noted antiquarian, cleared Henry Talbot of an accusation of treason with the use of an ancient Egyptian forgery? Well, mostly Persephone. But Tamsin had pitched a rock like a cricket ball and taken out Lord Fairweather. And then hadn't Meg proceeded to find a hidden cache of Tudor and late medieval art, after having a knife held to her kidney by a treasure hunter? Encouraged by Lord Eaton again, that rotter.

You simply could not trust a historian of any kind.

Luckily, Tamsin was not so much a historian as she was a collector.

Truth be told, that was much worse.

A fact that she was happy to share with the blighter currently rummaging through her things. A reckless, dangerous, and quite possibly foolish decision. But there it was.

Wielding a gold candlestick holder, she crept toward the parlor. She paused just outside the doorway, taking a peek inside. She might be hasty, but she wasn't *stupid*.

And there was definitely someone inside her parlor.

She could only see a silhouette, barely discernible with the hazy light from the moon and the gas lamp on the street outside her front door. The intruder was slender, and not particularly tall. Not very wide, either, which boded well for her chances. But they did not smell particularly nice.

They were also holding the skull. Negligently. Which was just insulting. Really, that blasted skull should have some dignity and at least *try* to protect itself. If there was better time for a ghost to appear full of unholy wrath, she was not aware of it.

And then the housebreaker reached for the black mirror.

"Put that down!" she screeched, hurtling forward, brandishing the candlestick. She'd never killed a man before, but the night was young. And she would have liked to say that she snapped out an icy command powerful enough to stop all ne'er-do-wells in their tracks, but it was a screech. She might have damaged her own eardrums.

And it wasn't even worth it.

The bloody thief yelped, tossed the mirror at her, and then threw himself out of the open window. She dove for it, catching it before it hit the ground and shattered. A ripping sound came from her dress. The candlestick hit a table, knocking over a hideous porcelain figurine of a simpering shepherdess given to her by her stepmother. Shepherdesses were meant to be fierce, fighting wolves and all manner of weather. This one looked as though she couldn't fight a bowl of oatmeal. A worthy sacrifice in lieu of the black scrying mirror.

She could have let the matter drop. She had her relics.

But she also had her pride.

Not to mention a fair amount of rage.

CAPTAIN HENRY TALBOT, now Viscount Stirling, had been back on English soil for a total of six days.

Already London was too crowded, too loud, too much. It had taken all of six minutes before he wanted to turn around and head straight back to the docks. They'd wanted to hang him here, not so long ago. And now they would want to fete him and parade him through the ballrooms and drawing rooms and gaming hells as a war hero. Again. He'd left when they tried last year, even though his father was thrilled at the attention.

To say that he and his father did not agree on much was an understatement.

Henry had no desire and no intention of being a prop or a puppet.

He'd had enough of that in the Navy when Lord Fairweather tried to frame him for treason. Henry was back, because he had to be back. He had an estate to run. Friends to take care of. Notably Persephone, Tamsin, Priya, and Meg. They'd saved him. The Cinderella Society.

They were a bloody menace. They always had been.

He'd missed that. Them.

And so, London. For now.

Every night, when sleep invariably eluded him, he read until his eyes blurred and then walked the dark streets. The fog settled over the cobblestones as the gas lamps struggled to send golden light through the haze. Cats darted into the shadows. Candlelight and music spilled through open windows; carriages clogged the streets in Mayfair, filled with aristocrats who were themselves filled with wine. It was tempting to follow suit. To drown his memories in claret and madeira and whiskey.

But a man who was foxed was too easily outfoxed.

And he couldn't afford that.

The scrape of a boot on pavement reminded him of such.

The first man came at him from the darkness of a doorway. He was roughly the size of an ox. His companion lunged from behind Henry, smaller, but armed to the teeth. Henry would have sighed if he had the time. It was always the same.

"You're going to want to pick someone else's pocket," he said, despite knowing full well that they would not listen. They saw a lord of some kind, walking alone at night, and history would suggest that Henry ought to be foxed, easy picking. That he wouldn't know how to defend himself outside of Gentleman Jackson's boxing ring.

They'd be wrong.

As they were about to find out.

It wasn't just his time in the Navy that assured him a fair fight, but his promise, after that last of his father's beatings, that he would never be easy pickings again. He'd found other ways to avoid a fist to the face. He'd always excelled at hiding. But he'd decided it wouldn't be the only tool in his arsenal. Not again.

These footpads didn't know that, though. They thought they'd found themselves an easy mark, some coin and a tale to take back to the pub.

The ox barely made a sound when he swung a fist the size of a Christmas goose. That in itself was impressive.

It wouldn't be enough. Not by a long shot.

Henry didn't even realize he was grinning as he ducked the

blow. It had always unnerved the other men on the ship. When you grew up skinny and weak, you learned to make do. You made weapons out of nothing.

He didn't bother with a return punch; it would be expected. Instead, he kicked out viciously, his boot cracking into the ox's knee. He stumbled back, grunting in pain and surprise. Henry whirled to block the cane whistling at the back of his head. It bit into his arm. He grabbed it with his other hand and slammed the end into the ox coming up behind him.

"I did warn you," he said pleasantly, even as he heard the crunch of a broken nose. Blood spattered. Knuckles grazed his ribs, too close for comfort. Then a direct hit, right to the kidney. Pain seethed through his side, all teeth and iron. But he laughed, flipping his hair out of his face as he straightened, and they exchanged a glance. "Nobody told us you was a nutter," the ox mumbled.

It was all Henry needed to get in a solid punch, enough to bruise his knuckles, enough to buy him a moment to dance out of the reach of a long, not particularly clean, dagger.

He recognized that dagger.

Not your average cutpurses, then.

In fact, they hadn't demanded money or even the silver engraved buttons off his coat. Not his boots, his hat. Nothing at all.

So this was something else. Something all too familiar.

It had taken all of six days for his father to find him.

He wasn't quite quick enough to evade the next hit, and the force of it reverberated through his shoulder. He staggered, cursing. He dropped low, extending his arms and slamming them hard into the backs of their knees. They pitched forward, the strike too sudden to give them a chance to catch their balance.

"Oi, there!" a coachman called from the top of a carriage as they scrambled to regain their footing. "I'm calling the watch."

The ox and his friend swore before taking off. Henry nodded his thanks to the coachman, tossing him a coin. He knew all too well how hard it could be to interfere, even when you knew it was right. Right wasn't the same as not dangerous. The men could easily have turned on the driver.

Henry wiped at his face and then wrapped the handkerchief around his raw knuckles. The ox had had a jaw made of rock. He should go home. Or back to the docks, to the country. Anywhere but where he found himself, night after night.

Outside her door. Tonight, covered in blood.

Lady Tamsin Bell, daughter of the Duke of Chester.

She'd think him daft for not knocking on the door. For having waited six days to let her know he had returned. But he needed a moment to find the kind, easygoing Henry she knew from their childhood. Not this version, who spent too long peering into shadows, who slept too little, remembered too much. She deserved a man who could blend in at a dinner party, in a ballroom. Not whatever version of himself he had become in the last year, more feral than elegant. He hadn't even called on Persephone, his oldest friend, because she saw him too clearly and would know instantly that something was amiss. Her recent marriage to the Earl of Northwyck wouldn't change that.

And so he walked the dark streets, comfortable in his solitude. He craved it, after being on a ship for so long with so many others. A captain's quarters was a boon, to be sure, but no captain who remained in those quarters for extended periods of time also remained as captain. He hadn't thought he would miss the sea, but he did. The constant sounds of it, the sway under his boots, the salt in his mouth. Now it was smog and beeswax candles and perfume.

There was a light burning in an upstairs window of Tamsin's house, but he could not see her. Sometimes he could make out her silhouette passing between the glass and a candle, and it was torture to look away. She'd always been pretty, but now she was beautiful. Delicious.

He'd only been back to England once since leaving to fight Napoleon as a lad, and that had been to clear his name. He'd spent most of his time hiding in the worst parts of London. He'd thought he'd return to forthright Persephone, clever Priya, quiet Meg, cheerful Tamsin.

And though Tamsin might still be cheerful, she was also made entirely of delectable curves, golden curls, and saucy smiles.

And he'd known instantly that he wouldn't survive her. He'd left London within days.

And now here he was.

Back outside her window like a stray cat begging for a saucer of milk.

Annoyed, he made to turn away.

Something moved at that window then shot over the steps leading down to the kitchen entrances. The front door slammed open, and Tamsin filled the doorway. "Stop! Thief!"

Fury slammed into him like a careening carriage.

Chapter Two

T AMSIN HADN'T EXPECTED anyone to hear her shout, but it was the principle of the thing.

And anyway, she'd already recognized the red patches on the threadbare sleeves of a worn coat. She knew exactly who had tried to steal from her. Again.

Just as she knew the man currently standing on the front walkway.

"Henry?"

She might have thought she'd imagined him, conjured him up through the power of her will alone. She'd thought of him too many times since he went away—again. He was always going away. But there he was with his hard, lean body, his dark hair, wary shoulders so much broader than they'd been when she last saw him, still half-starved and hunted by the Crown. He'd stayed a little while after his name was cleared. Not long enough.

Never long enough.

She might need years to convince him he was the one for her, and she was the one for him.

And that was so much easier to do when he was in the same bloody country.

His expression was hard, calculating. So different than the gentle boy she had grown up with, always up for a laugh, pockets always filled with lemon drops because she'd once told him they were her favorite, but her stepmother had decided she was too old for candy.

"I'll catch him," Henry said, turning to chase the thief.

"Never mind." Tamsin sighed, eyes still narrowed. "I know exactly who it was."

"I can still catch him."

"He's all of twelve years old." She raised her voice. "But mind yourself when *I* catch you, Jack Nimble."

A laugh floated from a nearby rooftop.

"That little tosspot," she muttered. She eyed Henry. "Speaking of which."

"I beg your pardon?" He raised an eyebrow. He wore a simple black coat, a simple cravat. The bare minimum expected of a viscount. And viscounts were unaccustomed to being called names. But he'd definitely been away too long if he thought that made any difference at all.

"How long have you been in London?" she demanded.

He tried to not to wince, but she knew the turn of his mouth. "A few days."

"A few days! How many?"

Definitely a wince. "Six."

"*Six days?*" She smacked his shoulder hard. "Six days and you haven't come to see me? Any of us?" The other ladies in the Cinderella Society would have told her. They shared more than a common godfather in the Duke of Pendleton; they were closer than sisters, certainly closer than she was to her own sisters.

"I needed to get my sea legs under control first."

She made a rude sound, completely at odds with the elegantly coiled curls and the sapphires at her throat. "Excuses."

She hugged him tightly, despite the scandal of it. One did not hug a man in the middle of the street at night. But she'd weathered worse, including swimming in the Serpentine in her best ballgown under the stars on her twenty-first birthday. Her father had not been impressed. Mostly because she'd received two offers of marriage that night and turned them both down.

"I'm not sure I forgive you, actually."

She would always forgive him, but he certainly didn't need to know that.

She'd forgotten how warm he was, all coiled strength and steadiness.

She hadn't forgotten.

She thought of him far too often.

And now the feel of him made her tingle, made her want to snuggle into his chest. He'd think she'd lost her mind. His arms moved around her, hesitant, then firm. But brief. He never touched her for long.

It was infuriating.

He went still. His muscles went harder, if that were possible. "Why is your dress torn?" His voice was silk and snap, all teeth.

She pulled back slightly and looked over her shoulder. "Blast."

"Tamsin." All that dark intensity focused on her. Finally. She fought back a delicious shiver. "Why is your dress torn?"

"It's nothing," she assured him. She scowled. "Well, not *nothing*. I had to dive across the parlor to save the mirror. And Jack will pay for *that*, mark my words."

When she glanced at him, Henry's expression was composed again. Solemn, alert, calm. It was almost enough to distract her from the cut on his sleeve, the blood on his cuff.

She lunged at him, grabbing his hand. "You're bleeding!"

"It's nothing," he said quietly, echoing her words back at him.

She shot him a look that had once made a suitor's poodle pee on the floor. Poor thing. She'd much preferred the dog. It had deserved an apology. The suitor had deserved a kick in the bollocks, which Meg delivered before Tamsin could think of it.

"It's not nothing," she insisted. "Why are you bleeding?" When he didn't respond, she rolled her eyes and curled her fingers around his wrist. She tugged when he didn't immediately follow her. "Come along."

"You'll get blood on yourself."

"This dress is already ruined, so come along already," she said cheerfully.

He gave a short sigh but followed her into the house. "This is not appropriate."

She laughed. "Nothing fun ever is."

"You have a strange idea of fun."

He had no idea. She wanted to climb him like a slightly broody, complicated, delicious ship's mast. She wanted to curl around him and never let go.

It was unseemly.

Embarrassing.

Also, true.

Worse still, he'd never let her. There were too many battles being fought inside his head. She could see it, even if he didn't mention it. It made him keep her at arm's length, even when she was standing too close. None of which was important at the moment. The fact that he was trying not to bleed on the black and white stones of her hallway was. It was the only thing that mattered.

"Where's your butler?" he muttered.

"I don't have one."

"Footman? Housekeeper?"

"Everyone has the night off. They won't be back until dawn, so you can stop fretting about your reputation." He, like her other friends, knew that her staff had been hired by her father and reported to him, however fond they might be of her. They could be bribed, when necessary, but her stepmother's bribes were always better. She was a duchess, after all.

"I'm not fretting. It's not safe for you."

She laughed. "You're not actually suggesting that you're a danger to me?"

He paused. She didn't like that pause. Didn't like what it implied. Didn't like the secret thrill it sent shooting up her thighs.

Oh, very well, *that* part she liked.

"I meant it's not safe for you to be alone at night." His tone turned dry. "Someone might break in."

She shrugged one shoulder, keeping her voice light, like spun sugar. One of his battles was moving behind his eyes. "I have you to protect me, Captain Talbot."

"Tamsin, I'm not—"

She absolutely would not let him finish whatever it was he was going to say. Instinct suggested it was not flattering. To him, or her. "And I'll remind you that I am the one who took out Lord Fairweather, may the devil burn his balls every day, with a rock to the head."

Henry blinked. "That's a powerful curse you've got there."

She smirked. "I've been practicing."

"The soul shudders."

"As it should. Did you know they have found more Roman curse tablets in West Hill? Most of them call for the punishment of thieves." She tilted her head. "With the liquefying of internal organs and such."

He smiled faintly, just a small twitch at the corner of his mouth.

Too many people, when confronted with her macabre interests, shivered. Smiles froze. Disgust replaced polite interest. She'd grown accustomed to it, and, in fact, bringing up gruesome facts was a wonderful way to rid oneself of unwanted guests. But Henry never looked down his nose at her, never suggested she find a more suitable hobby, never told her she was prettier when she smiled. It was one of the many reasons she loved him.

In fact, she'd loved Henry Talbot since the day after he left to fight Napoleon.

Truthfully, she'd always loved him, but that was the exact moment she knew love could sharpen and deepen when you least expected it.

It was terribly inconvenient.

She'd prayed for his safety at St. Paul's Cathedral, in Little Barrow's country church, everywhere. She'd tried everything: dropping silver coins in a well, making St. Brigit crosses with red yarn, dropping a tiny silver ship pendant in the Thames the way the druids had done. She didn't know which of them worked, or how, and she didn't care. It was enough that he was alive.

But it had been months now.

She wanted him to be hers.

Hope and hopelessness tangled inside her chest, the way they always did when he was near. It was better when she had something to focus on: a waltz, the theatre. Blood dripping on the floor.

She pulled him faster down the hall and the steps into the kitchen area. Coals glimmered in the hearth, and smoke darkened the wall above. The light from her candle bounced off the copper pans, the iron pots, glazed clay bowls. The worktables were scrubbed clean but laid out with bowls of covered bread and fruit, in case she got hungry overnight.

"Sit down." She shoved Henry onto a stool before he could protest. "Take off your coat."

He shrugged out of it as she went to fill a large bowl with water from a pitcher. She tried not to watch as he stripped down to his lawn shirt. He was built like a captain: all sturdy muscles and lean strength. He could handle anything thrown his way.

She'd like to throw herself his way.

Tamsin rolled her eyes at herself. Honestly, this obsession was getting worse. She should probably visit Priya for some kind of purging tea. An herbal remedy for the flush working up the neckline of her dress.

"What happened?" she asked when he reluctantly placed his arm on the table.

"Footpads."

She sucked in a breath. "You could have been killed."

He shrugged slightly. "They weren't very *good* footpads."

She frowned at his ruined cuff when she rolled it up, and then at the cut beneath it. It wasn't terribly deep, but it was raw and jagged. It had to hurt. "That wound says otherwise."

"I've had worse climbing the rigging."

She could picture it perfectly. Damn it.

She cleared her throat. "It will need a vinegar rinse."

"The hell it will!"

"You're not going to try to tell me that they stopped to wipe their dagger clean before stabbing you?"

He opened his mouth then shut it abruptly. "No."

"Well, there you have it, then." She washed the skin around the cut with a towel that Cook would scold her for ruining. "It seems to have stopped bleeding." She wiped again. "Mostly."

"I put pressure on it. I do know how to deal with a little stab wound, Tamsin."

"Well, la dee dah, Captain Talbot."

He smiled at that. "You haven't changed."

She decided that discretion was the better part of valor and did not ask him to elaborate. Was that a good thing? A bad thing? Did it even mean anything at all?

"Are you ready?" she asked, lifting a small cup of vinegar.

"Hell no."

"Close your eyes and think of England."

He turned slowly, eyebrow rising. She refused to meet his gaze. She'd just quoted very bad advice given to virginal girls on their wedding night. And he knew it. It had just slipped out. They'd always been frank with each other. But it was one thing to flirt at a ball; it was expected—certainly of her. She was invited to entertain, to make people smile. But it was something else entirely to say such a thing to Henry in a dark kitchen with no one nearby at all.

She probably ought to let him get settled back into life in London before she propositioned him.

She splashed vinegar into his cut. If the muffled curse that forced itself through his clenched back teeth was any indication, it was a satisfactory distraction. *"Fucking hell."*

She dabbed at the extra liquid running down his wrist. The cut was red and angry, but clean looking. "It looks better."

"It's terrified not to." He drew back slightly. "Are you finished torturing me?"

"I suppose so." Not even close.

The candlelight gilded the curl falling over his forehead, partially obscuring the notch in his eyebrow. She brushed it aside. "What's that scar from? It's new."

"Cannonball," he replied, ripping off the clean end of the towel and wrapping it around his arm. He used his teeth to tighten the knot. She tried not to stare. It shouldn't have made lust curl in her belly. It very much did.

Oh, she was in trouble.

She'd hoped these feelings would fade.

But back to the matter at hand.

"A cannonball?" she burst out. "What do you mean, a *cannon-*

ball?"

"It happens." He shrugged again. "Splinters, shrapnel."

"You could have lost your eye." He could have lost *everything*. Something tightened in her belly. In her chest.

"A few of my men did."

She blinked, horrified. *"Henry."*

He blinked back. "I'm fine. Hurt less than your vinegar rinse, in fact."

"I thought the war was over."

"It is. But there are still tensions. Not to mention pirates."

"Are you home for good now?"

A muscle twitched in his jaw. "Yes."

"Good," she said fiercely. She wasn't sure why she felt so ferocious all of a sudden. Like she might cry, but also might murder someone.

"My father does not agree."

"Your father is a jackass," she pointed out. She didn't give a fig if he was an earl and well respected in Parliament.

That ghost of a smile again. "True."

There were few people on earth, alive or dead, whom she hated as much as she hated his father, the Earl of Culpepper. She would cheerfully stab him in the kidney and then carry on with her supper. Twice.

She remembered the bruises, the haunted look on Henry's face. There were many ways to be haunted.

"Tam, why are you strangling that pitcher?"

Tam. He hadn't called her that in years. It warmed something inside of her the way even a perfect summer's day could not achieve.

She hadn't realized she was taking her anger over his father out on the jug of water. She must look like a madwoman. Especially when her dress gaped open at the side and sleeve. She glanced down, having forgotten about it. No wonder he never took a second look at her: she was wearing a gown stained with champagne and ripped at the seam. *Not* very attractive. And certainly, it was no way to arrive at the annual May Ball.

When Henry wasn't around, she was generally considered to

be a diamond of the first water. Even as a twenty-eight-year-old spinster.

"You're going to have to help me change into a new gown," she said.

He stared at her. He looked scared for the first time on a night where he'd been physically stabbed, and she'd been robbed.

Something purred inside her.

"Like hell I will," he blurted out.

She smiled.

Something was definitely purring.

Chapter Three

"TAMSIN BELL, YOU can't be serious."

"Tamsin Bell," she echoed, teasingly. "How very formal of you. Next you'll 'Lady Tamsin' me and I shall be properly chastised."

"I would if I thought it would do any good," he grumbled. He was behind her, climbing the stairs to the upper floor toward her bedroom, despite his scandalized protests. Who knew a ship's captain could be so prim?

She should not find it charming.

No surprise, she absolutely did.

"How much champagne have you had tonight?" he demanded.

"Not enough." She wasn't even muddled. At least not by drink. Henry could achieve that all by himself, unfortunately.

"Call for your lady's maid."

"She has the night out and won't be home until dawn. I've told you that."

He groaned. "Then stay home tonight."

"Don't be ridiculous." She hated rattling around an empty house alone. It reminded her too much of the years after her mother's death. And though she'd been banished from the family home, she hadn't been banished from society. And she had no intention of staying home and missing a perfectly lovely evening.

She might have considered it if she thought Henry would stay with her. But the way he was sputtering put an end to that daydream rather abruptly. She knew she could only push him so far, and she was flirting with the line as it was. He never used to be so unmovable, so sure of his own power. Not that he'd been a pushover exactly, just that his father was a monster, and his best friends were four wild girls very used to getting their own way.

"We did run you ragged," she murmured.

"Pardon?"

"The Cinderellas. We did like to boss you about."

"That was fine. It's right at this very moment that you are running me ragged."

She would choose to take that as a good sign.

"And we're not children anymore, Tam."

He really shouldn't growl things like that, his voice silky across the back of her neck. She nearly stumbled. Where was her aplomb, her ability to flirt and tease until she had the high ground? It had utterly escaped her. And he wasn't even trying to discombobulate her.

She might not get many moments like this, alone with Henry, despite her attempts. She would enjoy every delicious, stolen second.

"Here we are," she said, pushing open the door to her chambers. It was a large room, decorated in a dark, stormy blue, with velvet settees and silk curtains around the bed. There were silver candlesticks, and a small fire burning in the grate, the mantel painted with mermaids by Meg's own hand.

"So this is your bedroom," he said quietly.

She wasn't sure why she was nervous about what he thought. He already knew she wasn't the type for pale yellows or classical austerity, as fashion demanded. She wasn't demure. She'd tried once, when she was young, but when her father paid no more attention to her than usual, she'd abandoned it. It was hardly entertaining.

"It suits you."

She smiled at him, brightly enough that he blinked.

"I'm still not undressing you."

Her smile dimmed, but she refused to let him see it. He was

being a gentleman. And she was being a goose. "Of course you are—how else will I get changed?"

She opened the doors of an armoire painted with forget-me-nots. They had been her mother's favorite flower. Inside were three more ballgowns, the options her lady's maid had steamed and brushed clean for tonight. A red one, a green one, and a blue one with silver beads. Any of them would do well enough for the fete. Perhaps not the green one. Any lady not forced to wear debutante white might well wear green to a spring fete. She had no intention of blending in. She never did.

She held out the other two. "Which one?"

"Which one what?"

She raised her eyebrows. "Which one should I wear?"

A very brief, very faint suggestion of panic crossed his features. "How should I know?"

She grinned. "You have to choose."

"You choose. It's your body!"

"Hmm," she said, fully invested in teasing him, just as she had when she was a girl. Well, not just *like* that. She mostly did not want to deliver him a facer anymore. And he was being adorable, the war-hardened captain trying not to squirm. She should probably put him out of his misery.

Not a chance.

"The red one," he finally said, tightly.

She nodded. "I happen to agree." She laid it carefully on the edge of her bed. The candlelight caught the beaded stitching around the neckline and at the hem. Henry stared very attentively at the desk over her shoulder. She turned her back to him. "If you please."

"What?"

"You need to unhook my dress." Just saying it sent a hot shiver through her.

"Tamsin."

"Henry."

"This is monstrously indecorous, even for a Cinderella."

"The Cinderella Society is very proper, I'll have you know."

He snorted. "You forget who you're talking to."

As if she could.

She wriggled her shoulders. "Do hurry. The champagne stain is getting rather clammy."

There was a beat of silence and then the soft brush of his shoes on the polished floor. The sound of his closing in behind her made her mouth go dry. His dark presence at her back, his breath across the nape of her neck. "There are hooks in the middle; they—"

"I know how they work."

Of course he did. This couldn't be the first time he'd undressed a woman.

She waited for a pulse of jealousy.

Mostly, she was just even more eager. He would know what he was about.

Really, when had she become so desperate for his attention?

Many, many years ago, on the exact day after he left to fight Napoleon. Right.

And here he was, just as unaffected now as he had been then. He'd barely replied to her letters, had been here six days before seeking her out, and even then, had he really sought her out? Or had he merely been out for a walk?

She really ought to get a grip on herself.

And then his fingers brushed her skin. She could swear she heard him swallow. Perhaps he wasn't entirely unaffected after all. She could work with that. She was used to shining a little too brightly in order to be noticed. A little patience, while he regained his land legs, as he'd said. There were worse things than teasing, building tension.

She'd waited this long.

Still, when he touched her again, she had to bite back a tiny, embarrassing moan. His hands were warm and strong and gentle, efficient as he unhooked her dress, carefully, slowly. The only sounds were their breaths, the flickering of the candles. A carriage rumbling outside her window. The dress released, dropped to pool at her feet.

As scandalous as it might be, she was still wearing a petticoat over her stays and chemise. Still wore her stockings with the red ribbon garters, her jeweled dancing slippers. It was the illusion of nudity.

But it was a very good illusion.

"Now the petticoat," she said, trying to pretend this was all very ordinary. As if her heart wasn't racing in her throat.

"*What?*"

"It's damp."

He muttered something under his breath.

"It's only a few laces," she encouraged him.

"That's hardly the point," he grumbled, but he obliged her, untying the laces and pulling the thin cotton over her head until she stood in her stays and chemise and stockings.

She shivered, and it had nothing to do with the cool night air sneaking around her knees.

"There, that wasn't so hard, was it?" she said, trying to sound cheerful instead of tortured. Her voice was a little too hoarse, a little too raspy as she reached for a clean, dry petticoat.

"Let's just get this over with."

"You make me feel like a leper," she said, poking her head through the neck opening and shimmying the petticoat down into place over her stays.

He made a noise in the back of his throat. "You have adoring masses paying you compliments whenever you leave the house. You don't need me."

Except that she did need him.

And she worked hard for those compliments. To be remembered. Considered. But it wasn't her, not really. It was a bubblier, frothier version of herself, macabre occult collections aside. But Henry knew *her*. Certainly, more than the others. Enough that his opinion mattered.

She tried not show that her hands were trembling as she reached for the red dress and stepped into it. Henry moved to help her once she pulled it up past her waist. His fingers brushed her skin again and again as he worked the tiny hooks. She'd never considered that the act of dressing could be sensual. But she felt the faintest brush of his fingertips all the way down to her thighs. The scrape of his breath, the tickle of his hair against her neck when he bent closer.

The bodice pulled tighter over her breasts, caged her arms, wrapping her neatly back up into the form of a sensible, respectable woman.

A pity, really.

"Why were you covered in champagne?"

"I spilled some at the theatre," she said. He tilted his head, waiting. She tilted hers back. "What?"

"I know there's more to it than that."

"Why should there be?"

That eyebrow rose again, newly scarred. "You are not a clumsy woman, Tamsin. I've never seen anyone more graceful." He said it simply, like it was a plain fact.

Her cheeks went pink. They never went pink. She'd been receiving elaborate poetic compliments since the night of her coming-out at seventeen. She was pretty, daughter to a duke, an heiress. She knew compliments. Most of them had nothing to do with her.

This one made her want things. Desperate things.

"Thank you," she said instead. Polite, flirtatious, charming. All of the things she had been trained to be. He barely noticed; he was too busy stalking down the stairs as though his backside was on fire.

Hmm. She was going to choose to take that as a compliment as well. It was just easier.

If he didn't take himself right out the front door first, that was.

She should have known better.

This new Henry did not give up so easily, not without getting the answer he was waiting for.

Hell and damnation, she was trying to kill him.

When she'd stepped into her gown and bent over to pull it up, an honest-to-God sweat had broken out on the back of his neck. He hadn't been this scared when facing down French warships, cannonballs, accusations of treason. But the line of her spine, the curve of her bottom, had nearly done him in. He'd had to clench his fists to keep from reaching for her.

She wasn't for him.

God, he wished she were.

Had wished it with every letter she had written to him, still locked in a box in his house, parchment soft as butter. Those letters had seen him through the worst of the war, through the stink of blood and rotten fish, through hunger, through everything. The first had taken him by surprise, and then he had grown to rely on them. They connected him. Persephone's letters kept him grounded and alive, but Tamsin's letters gave him hope that coming home might be worth it. Not that he deserved her or would presume to present his suit—only that she was alive in the world, and that was somehow enough. It made a difference.

Until she'd asked him to undress her.

And then nothing was enough.

Not the glimpse of her back, the knowledge of the shape of her under all of those layers, the warmth of her skin. The fact that she smelled like roses and mint. That there were tiny roses embroidered over her stays. It had taken considerable willpower not to lower his mouth to the soft spot of her nape. To scrape his teeth over her, to lick her until she begged for more.

Not for him.

Not for him.

And even with the blood draining out of his head at an impressive speed and the discomfort of too-tight pants, he knew she hadn't answered his question, and that she had done so deliberately. He'd only been in London and Little Barrow for a brief time after being cleared of the charges of treason, but it had been long enough to see how little the world understood her.

They fell for her smiles, her charm, and never saw anything else. Oh, they tutted and whispered about her strange collection of relics, but when half the aristocracy had dead bodies in their drawing room, it was easily overlooked. The craze for all things Egyptian, especially mummies, made her even more fashionable even as it infuriated Persephone. Persephone had very clear notions about ancient Egypt and the treatment of its historical relics. He had received roughly six hundred letters on the matter.

Tamsin picked up her pace suddenly, darting into the drawing room. "I'd nearly forgotten, what with all of the blood." She touched her candle to the others, illuminating her treasures. He used to think of her a magpie, but after watching her burst out of the house in a rage, he amended the comparison to a dragon. "If Jack managed to steal something, I will feed him to my horses. Slowly."

She probably wouldn't. She had a soft spot for the lost and the lonely.

Probably.

Her collection had grown since he'd last seen it. The light fell on beautiful painted tarot cards, spheres of crystal, elf arrows he remembered digging for when they were children, an impressive number of Egyptian scarab beetles and statuettes. An opened crate sat at the edge of a chair embroidered with unicorns with bloodied horns. He'd bet his left arm Meg had done the needlepoint work.

Tamsin ignored the crate. "I've only just bought that. It was delivered an hour ago, and I haven't had time to sort through it. If he stole from there, I'd never know it."

Henry turned and paused in front of an entire wall of poppets. Some were sewn from rough burlap and stitched with red thread, some formed from clay, others crowned with human hair, and a disconcerting number of them sported iron nails through their heads or limbs. "What's going on here?" he asked, as she counted items under her breath.

Her smile was dry. "They're poppets, Henry."

"I can see that."

"As a spinster, I am, of course, obsessed with having children someday, and the dolls they might need." She held his gaze long enough that he knew she had had much practice.

"No, really, what are these little things?"

Her smile was damn near blinding. He wanted to scoop her up and disappear into the private darkness of the house.

"You don't believe me?" she asked.

"There are people who do?"

"Yes, it's all very appropriate for me to pine for what I do not have. Especially matrimony. My stepmother was very clear on the subject."

"Tamsin, if you wanted to be married and have babies, you would have them."

She smiled again. "I've missed you, Henry."

It was wholly inappropriate for her to call him by his first name, despite their having known each other their entire lives. But considering the impropriety of the last half an hour, it seemed absurd to comment on it.

"They are curse dolls," she continued. "Magical poppets. Some are for luck or love or healing. Others are stuck through with pins to cause your enemy pain. I wonder if I should test one out on Lord Eaton."

The very name sent a flash of fury through him. Before he'd left for his second posting, he found out that Lord Eaton had been groping women—including all three of his friends, and Tamsin the most often. He'd chased the man clear out of Little Barrow and planned much worse before he had to ship out. He'd have done worse for any lady, but for Tamsin he'd burn the man's entire life down around him.

His back teeth ground together.

"The ones over there are meant to be love spells," she said. They were prettier, more detailed poppets, with braided hair, careful embroidery, little red hearts.

He paused in front a poppet that seemed no more than a regular doll, with embroidered eyes, and braided yarn for hair. "I remember this one."

"You do?"

He nodded. She'd carried it everywhere after her mother died. She stroked a braid reverently even now, twenty years later. "You named her something dramatic. Vanessa? Veronica?"

"Vasilisa," she murmured softly. He could see the memories touching her like mist. "My mother named her that." She hissed out a sudden breath, attention caught by the poppet next to it. "That little rotter broke the arm off this one."

It was a clay figure of a woman kneeling, thirteen pins stuck throughout her body. It was beautiful and mysterious and faintly alarming. Just like Tamsin.

"Oh, we are going to have words about this," she said. "I can promise you that."

"Was anything else damaged? Stolen?"

She shook her head. "It doesn't look like it. I must have caught him before he'd had a chance to get to work."

"About that."

She shot him a wary glance. "Yes?"

"What were you thinking, confronting a housebreaker? He might have been armed!"

She shrugged. "He's just a boy."

"You didn't know that."

"Well, there's no point fretting about it—done is done."

"Has this happened before?"

"No?"

A blatant lie. Never mind the tone, but the pretty, daughter-of-a-duke smile was a dead giveaway. "Tamsin."

She mocked his tone. "Henry."

He'd set officers quivering with fear with one look. But she just patted his arm like he was an elderly lady in need of a nap.

"I'm serious," he said.

"Frequently, yes."

He very nearly growled. She twinkled at him. There was no other word for it. She shimmered like a star.

It was no surprise that he had always loved stars. Even before taking to the sea, where they could be the difference between finding home and losing your way forever.

He sent her a look.

She sent back a grin. "You can glower at me outside. I'm expected at the Yorks'."

She retrieved her cloak, which she'd tossed over the newel post. It was velvet and satin, trimmed with roses and utterly impractical. "That wouldn't keep a mouse warm," he pointed out. He couldn't help himself.

She tied the ribbon around her neck. "It's hardly snowing outside. The flowers are in bloom, Henry. And it's May Ball."

He knew she thought he'd become fussy. But he'd seen how

fragile people were, how easily they could be hurt. And he'd be damned if he failed her the way he had failed others, war or not.

She led the way down the walk to the road where her coachman had clearly been instructed to wait. She glanced at Henry over her shoulder, the lamplight gilding her honey hair. "You could come with me."

"Definitely not."

"Spoilsport."

He hated crowds. He'd never entirely loved them, but it was so much worse now that they followed his every move, whispering, offering wicked rewards for his service to the Crown, wondering how his fame might help them. Pretending that they hadn't been equally eager to see him hang, just last year.

He caught her wrist, just as she was about to step up into the carriage. She'd nearly distracted him. "Hoyden."

She raised her eyebrows. "Captain."

"What happened with the champagne?"

"Why is it so hard to believe that I spilled it?"

"Because I know when you're lying."

She looked as though she was considering taking offense, and then decided not to with a tiny, adorable wrinkle of her nose. "Oh, very well, if you're going to insist."

"I am."

"Lord Eaton cornered me at the theatre, and it was the fastest way I could think of to escape."

Cold fury nearly snapped his bones. He was desperate for the command of a cannon again. "What do you mean, he cornered you?" His voice was soft and lethal.

"Oh, his usual games. I'd hoped he'd stopped. He was out of society for a while, but alas, all good things come to an end." She ducked into the carriage, and he released her, reluctantly. "I did consider planting him a facer, but there were too many gossips circling. Not to mention my stepmother was watching. Champagne seemed quicker."

Her family did not take care of her. His own father might have been a right bully and a bastard, but his grandparents had cared for him. Tamsin's own father sometimes forgot she existed.

It might have been easier if her stepmother did the same.

Even so, Tamsin wasn't Henry's to take care of.

He knew it.

He didn't care.

"Move over," he muttered. "I'm coming with you."

Chapter Four

THE YORK MAY Ball was a tradition of the London Season, and even those who had been attending events for weeks looked forward to it. The weather was finally reliable, and the Yorks filled their gardens with benches, torches, and a water fountain filled with wine. Four guests had nearly drowned in it last year.

Inside, the ballroom frothed with flowering crabapple branches, lilac, peonies, and tiny, delicate violets. Greenery hung from the ceiling and the chandeliers, creating a soft bower scented with honey candles. Even the musicians wore flowers pinned to their coats. Circlets were offered to the ladies as they were announced. Tamsin chose one with fat peonies and red ribbons.

She kept her hand tucked into Henry's arm, both to remind herself that he was really, safely home and also to keep him from bolting.

"Captain Talbot, how good to see you!"

"Is it captain now, or Viscount Stirling?"

Guests turned toward him as they walked, like sunflowers. Jewels gleamed; circlets of flowers scented the air too sweetly. Men bowed. There were handshakes, smiles, winks. She knew Henry hated every second of it. She smiled for him.

"Captain, do join us," a lady invited, the appreciative gleam in her eye as sharp as a knife's point. Her cleavage was predatory.

Henry's mask slipped, and Tamsin glimpsed a brief flare of

panic. She tightened her fingers around his sleeve. "I'm so sorry," she said, flashing her trademark dimple. It worked on everyone except for her family. "But I'm afraid the captain has promised the next dance to me. You know how I love the quadrille."

"Of course." The lady smiled back, then drew her fan down Henry's arm. "Later, then. Much later."

"Hmph," Tamsin said when they were out of earshot. "That was a bit obvious. She is rather pretty, though." She glanced at the twitching of the muscle in his jaw and lowered her voice theatrically. "Bet I could burn the whole ballroom down if I knocked that candle into the drapes there. Wouldn't be but a moment's work. You could jump out of the window with none the wiser."

His lips twitched. "Much obliged."

That terrible tension had eased from him, but she didn't miss the way he kept her tucked safely against him, with his back to the wall as much as possible, as though there were dangers lurking. And there were, of course, but it was the sort of danger she excelled at. Social murder, intrigue, entertaining people so they remembered you; it was still a battle. Just not the kind Henry was accustomed to fighting.

She felt the sudden snap to attention when someone shrieked, the pause, the assessment of their surroundings, and finally the relaxing of the hard muscles of his arm when he recognized who was shrieking. It was suddenly very easy to imagine him on a ship, in his uniform, shouting commands into a brutal wind.

"Henry!" Persephone darted toward them, trailed by her husband, Conall, Earl of Northwyck. He was tall, breathtakingly handsome, and attracting coveted glances from half the guests, male and female, as usual. Even as he had eyes only for Persephone.

"When did you get back?" she demanded, hugging Henry tightly, which was not the thing, and then smacking him with her fan, which was definitely not the thing. Her fan, naturally, was painted with historically accurate Egyptian hieroglyphs and blue scarab beetles.

Henry hugged her back, some of the harsh lines of his face

softening. Persephone always had that effect on him. They'd been thick as thieves since leading strings, living on neighboring country estates. "It's good to see you, Cleopatra."

The guests nearby watched them with avid curiosity, not just because of Henry's scandal, but also because of Persephone's scandal, and now her title of countess. She sighed. "I forget people can see me now," she muttered.

"I could always see you, love," Conall murmured behind her. Persephone blushed. There was something sweet about the charming earl-turned-spy being so unabashedly in love with his bluestocking wife. It was deeply unfashionable, of course. Which made it all the better.

Tamsin was starting to give up on finding such a match for herself. She had been considering something far more prosaic before Henry returned.

"How do you find it?" Henry asked, after exchanging an amused glance with Conall over her shoulder. "All of the attention?"

"It's frightfully inconvenient, actually," Persephone grumbled. She'd been relegated to the sides of the ballroom and disdainful sniffs years ago, after being discovered half-clothed in a barn with a peer's son no one could remember. Least of all her. He'd been a rake intent on seduction, and she'd been a girl intent on taking herself firmly off the Marriage Market in order to concentrate on her antiquarian pursuits. "Did you know that Lady Henderson insists on giving me her opinion on the best way to extract bone from dirt? At my own dig site? When she's never had dirt on her hands in all her seventy years?"

"Have you shot her yet?"

"Everyone says I'm not allowed to. Even Priya."

Conall grinned. "To be fair, my sister only said it was too obvious, and offered you a tonic to make her cast up her accounts at the next public event. And something about purple spots."

Persephone sighed again. "I suppose she doesn't deserve *that*." She narrowed her eyes. "Unless she touches my relics again. She left smudges on a gold cartouche that is easily five thousand years old last week!"

"Someone broke into my house and knocked over my clay poppet," Tamsin commiserated, certain of a satisfyingly violent reaction.

"Little Aphrodite?" Persephone gaped. They'd taken to naming Tamsin's poppets as her collection grew, mostly to keep them sorted. "Who? When?"

"Just tonight. It was only Jack Nimble. But he broke her arm. He's usually more careful than that."

"That little weasel."

"I know. I think I can fix it."

Conall narrowed his eyes. "Are we missing the material point here?"

"Definitely not," Tamsin and Persephone answered in unison.

"Someone *broke* into your house. And obviously more than once, since you've commented on the execution."

"Thank you," Henry muttered. "Honestly, I was beginning to think this had become normal behavior in London."

Persephone shrugged. "It can be for antiquarians and collectors." She tilted her head, and the light caught her dark hair under her circlet of lilacs. "Conall has met some unsavory types in his travels. I'm sure he can be of service. Do you want vengeance?"

Tamsin grinned. "And this is why I love you. I'm so happy you finally got to visit Egypt, but I'm even happier that you're home." She nudged Henry. "That *everyone* is home." She'd missed them even more than she'd realized. Meg was still in the country with her new husband, the Duke of Thorncroft, and although Priya lived in London, she hated socializing. She didn't often let herself get dragged around to soirees. They had a weekly tea, mostly taken in one of her greenhouses. Tamsin had come to rely on them.

"About that vengeance..." Persephone added.

Tamsin waved it away. "Jack is not dangerous. I think he's just hungry. If I can convince him to take my food, he won't need to steal my relics. Some of them are dangerous."

"Don't tell him that if you want him to stop," Henry advised. "And he's definitely hungry, at that age. But he's also sweet on you and likely showing off a bit. I'm not sure a baked potato will solve that problem."

She turned to face him. "How do you know that?"

He lifted his brows. "He's a young lad with eyes in his head, isn't he?"

She thought there was a rather lovely compliment in there somewhere.

It would have been nice to have a moment to appreciate it. Even nicer, not to have it interrupted by Lord Eaton. The oily lecher. He was rich enough and beautiful enough, with his blond curls and sharp jaw, to be forgiven most of his unseemly behavior. It was always written off—surely the lady in question had misunderstood. As if a man's hand grabbing your backside was a terribly complicated thing to analyze.

"What's he doing here?" she muttered. "I should have dumped that champagne on him instead of myself."

"Who?"

"Lord bloody Eaton."

Her friends followed her gaze. Persephone hissed. It was the only way to describe the disgruntled sound that emerged from her when she spotted Eaton leaning against the wall as though his spine was too aristocratic to bear his weight. He bowed at Tamsin, then straightened, looking at Henry. Something flickered behind his charming, arrogant gaze, something very like apprehension. Almost fear.

Delightful, really. And one of the many reasons she wanted to kiss Henry until she didn't remember her own name.

Henry went still again, his eyes narrowing, his mouth quirking in a small smile that did not bode well. "Excuse me," he said softly.

Tamsin grabbed his elbow. He only paused when her dancing slippers slid across the floor, threatening to upend her. "Where are you going?"

"To eject that blighter from the ballroom. Preferably through a window. In the attic."

"Oh good," Conall drawled. "The Season has been getting dull. I'll come with you."

Persephone poked him. "You're not helping."

"I wasn't trying to."

"Henry, you can't," Tamsin said, which was the wrong thing to say.

"I assure you, I can."

"Not here."

He frowned. "Why was Dougal allowed to punch him in the face, and I'm not?"

"Because Eaton will challenge you to one of his stupid duels."

He was known for them. Illegal in theory, secret in practice, and he'd still managed to kill three gentlemen in as many years. Never mind those he'd maimed or terrorized.

"And, if you'll recall, we went through some trouble to make sure he didn't do the same to Dougal."

Meg's husband, Dougal Black, the new Duke of Thorncroft, had punched Eaton for the same reason Henry was staring stonily in his direction. It had taken Tamsin and all of the Cinderellas to flatter and distract Eaton from his fury. She'd let him touch her waist, whisper in her ear. She would never, ever share that information with Henry. Or Conall, if the narrowing of his eyes was anything to go by.

"That's different," Henry said. "Thorncroft was a millhouse worker before he became a duke. He'd never shot a pistol or held a sword before. It would have been murder." He smiled that smile again, the one that absolutely shouldn't do such interesting things to her insides, but absolutely did. "I was in the Royal bloody Navy," he pointed out. "I fought Napoleon."

"And he's a captain now," Conall put in helpfully.

"And I'm a captain now," Henry repeated.

"Conall, honestly." Persephone pinched them both.

"Not now," Tamsin said quietly. "Not here. Not with my father in attendance. Please."

It was the *please* that stopped him. Henry knew what a scandal would do to her father. He'd blame her.

Henry's breath shuddered out, frustrated and uneven. "Fine," he said starkly. "But this isn't over."

It was definitely not over. Tamsin's father motioned to her imperiously. She muttered a curse under her breath that had both of Henry's eyebrows shooting up. "Do you talk to the queen with that mouth?"

She wanted to smile, but her father was watching, Lord Eaton was smiling at the other end of the ballroom, and her stomach was twisting.

Henry extended his arm. "You don't have to," she murmured. Conversations with her family were rare and left her feeling gray. She hated to expose anyone else to that. Not that anyone else seemed to notice. Or they simply didn't care, as long as they had the attention of a duke.

"Like hell you're talking to any of those vipers alone," Henry said.

"We'll come too," Persephone said, stalwart as ever.

Tamsin shook her head, finding her polite, vivacious smile as guests eyed them curiously. "It will make them cross."

"They are already cross."

"Persephone," Conall said.

She scowled up at him. "Oh, you can encourage fisticuffs and duels, but I can't do this one simple thing for Tam?"

He paused. "Good point." He smiled gently at Tamsin. "I'm sorry, Tamsin, but it appears as though you have an army at your back."

Tamsin's smile fit better on her face properly anchored. "The Cinderella Society never leaves a lady behind."

"Bloody right," Persephone said.

"But in this case, discretion may be the better part of valor," Tamsin added. "You know how my stepmother is when she has an audience."

Persephone bristled, then sighed. "I do not like that woman."

Tamsin wanted to agree, wanted to shout it from the rooftops, but she was still trying to convince herself otherwise, all of these years later. As if it would somehow make everything easier.

"We'll be right here," Persephone promised.

"Glowering majestically," Conall added with a wink.

Tamsin let Henry escort her to her father because it was proper. But mostly because she was stronger when he was near. She wondered if it would embarrass him to know that. His expression was calm and unreadable as they moved through the crowd.

The Duke of Chester's neglect of his daughter from his first marriage was well known, and it always drew interest when he deigned to acknowledge her in public. It wasn't that he disliked her particularly, or wished her ill, more that he tended to forget she existed. Until her stepmother voiced another grievance, of course. And then suddenly she was a problem to be fixed. Tamsin had thought that progress when she was very young. She'd needled her stepmother, hoping to be seen again, to be more than another ghost roaming the manor house.

But she was a woman grown now, and more, a woman with several severed body parts in her front parlor and a looking glass rumored to have been used by Elisabeth Bathory. She could handle polite conversation while wearing a circlet of flowers.

It surprised no one at all that the Duchess of Chester had commandeered three circlets of roses and stacked them together into a crown. Her dress was embroidered with so much gilt thread that when she moved, it resembled the sun flashing on water. They would write about her gown in the gossip papers tomorrow. And about this discussion, if it did not go well. Tamsin knew the rules: do not embarrass the family.

Tamsin curtsied gracefully. She'd learned to play cricket, to shoot pheasant and ride horses, hoping to get her father's attention. He'd only noticed her curtsies, praising them when they reminded him of her mother. He hadn't mentioned her in years, of course, but Tamsin remembered. She'd added dancing and watercolors and the pianoforte to her repertoire, in search of more recognition. A nod, a compliment. Anything.

"Father," she murmured.

He nodded over the rim of his champagne glass. He wore a perfectly curled wig, even though it was a decade out of fashion. No one dared comment.

"Stepmo—Duchess," she added. The duchess hated to be addressed by anything but her title. "Lord Willoughby."

"You are a vision, as always," he replied. He was twice her age and had offered to marry her three times that number.

"Talbot," he added. A small insult—even though Willoughby was an earl and outranked Henry, until he also claimed his father's title, he still ought to be addressed as Viscount Stirling, or at the very least, Captain Talbot. "I didn't know you were back."

"Is that…blood on your cuff?" Lady Chester tutted.

"Yes."

"He was set upon by footpads," Tamsin hurried to explain when Henry did not elaborate, and the shocked duchess fanned herself vigorously enough to create a crosswind.

"Bad luck, Talbot," Willoughby replied nonchalantly.

Tamsin narrowed her eyes, but he didn't notice. She knew he only saw shining hair and the diamonds in her ears, the dip of her neckline. "The *viscount* has only just returned to England. I'm sure we're all very grateful for his service to the Crown."

"Of course, of course. But war is such a gloomy topic on such a fine evening, is it not?"

"Indeed," the duchess said sharply. "Napoleon has been soundly routed, and that's that."

Tamsin frowned. Henry had nearly died fighting in that gloomy war, not to mention almost been hanged by his country for it. She found she did not care for his experiences to be dismissed, May Ball or not. It rankled. She was considering how to deliver a set-down polite enough to be ignored by her stepmother when Henry shifted infinitesimally closer.

"Easy," he murmured. "He's not worth it."

He wasn't wrong. But *Henry* was worth it. But since he also hated the attention, she bit her tongue. It was probably for the best that Persephone had hung back. For an antiquarian wall-flower, she was like a rabid dog when Henry was threatened. And it wouldn't bother her one bit that even as a countess, she ought to tread carefully around a duke and duchess.

Tamsin's father still had not said a word. He was distracted, nodding at acquaintances, motioning to a nearby footman for a fresh glass of champagne. Smoothing the bit of old-fashioned lace on his cravat. Her stepmother murmured to him behind her fan.

He finally turned to Tamsin. "You'll come for luncheon to-morrow," he said. "There are matters to discuss."

She knew that tone, and it brooked no refusal. She was no doubt in for another lecture, criticism on her strange hobbies, her lack of a husband. She had a brief moment of cold panic that Lord Willoughby was about to be offered up as an appropriate choice once again. "Of course."

Henry's warmth touched her, his arm brushing hers until the breath frozen in her chest loosened enough to release. He shifted slightly, standing between her and Lord Eaton, watching her over the shoulder of a debutante. His stare was steady, stony. Lord Eaton could not meet it. He only inclined his head at Tamsin. She was beginning to wonder if he realized she'd spilled champagne all over herself to escape his attentions.

"That's it," Henry said, as they walked away from her parents. His tone was easy, as though he were discussing having another scone with tea. "I'm throwing him in the Thames."

Chapter Five

NEVER MIND THROWING Eaton in the Thames—Tamsin wanted to hold his head under.

For a very long time.

She'd left the festivities to visit the ladies' retiring room, weaving through the cheerfully drunken guests to the abandoned halls. There was something melancholy about the hallways during a fete, the sounds of music and laughter suddenly distant, the air colder. A strange sort of solitude.

Usually.

She did not know why Lord Eaton was suddenly everywhere, but she did not care for it. Not one whit. Especially as he had cornered a poor maid in the shadows. "My lord, I must get back," she said haltingly. She sounded young. Scared. "Lady York is expecting me."

Lord Eaton laughed.

Tamsin revised her opinion of holding him under the filthy waters of the Thames. It was too good a death.

"You're to serve the guests, aren't you?" he asked. "So serve me."

Tamsin was certain he thought he sounded charming, seductive. The maid cringed. It didn't seem to bother him. Tamsin stepped closer. His hands were not gentlemanly. Little surprise. "My lord." Her voice cracked like a shot though the dim light.

He straightened but did not immediately step away from the

maid. She gasped, her eyes wide. She was barely twenty years old, with pink cheeks and blond ringlets. She looked exactly like a painting of a milkmaid. And she was probably just as strong as one, but if she did an earl an injury, she would likely be turned out without references. Even if he deserved it.

Tamsin, as a duke's daughter, was perfectly willing to do an earl an injury. This earl in particular. She knew just what it felt like to be groped by him, to be offered an innocent smile as his fingers roamed toward the backside. Meg had "accidentally" broken his pinky finger when he attempted it with her.

Tamsin smiled gently at the girl. "Lady York requires your attention."

"Perhaps I require it more," Eaton replied.

Tamsin pretended to pout even though it made her physically nauseated. "And perhaps I require it even more, my lord." She kept her voice light but flirtatious.

His smile grew. "I am at your service, Lady Tamsin."

She would *not* gag.

Mostly because although his glances roved over her admiringly, stopping at her breasts and her hips, he still had not released the maid. Tamsin could call for help, but she knew perfectly well that he would find a way to talk his way out of it.

She cocked one hip out. "So you say, but here we are," she murmured. "I am bored, Lord Eaton. Entertain me."

"I suppose I might be convinced."

The maid hadn't said a word; her gaze flickered between them, agitated and nervous.

"At once, if you please. I am not accustomed to being kept waiting." Tamsin lifted her chin. "I am the daughter of a duke." She raised her eyebrows haughtily to the maid. "You may go."

Lord Eaton eased away, and she bobbed a relieved curtsy and fled.

He turned toward Tamsin, all smiles. All expectation. She took a step back. "Not here, my lord," she murmured. "Anyone can see."

She led him out of the corner, into the light cast by candles and lamps. Toward the relative safety of the crowd.

"A maid?" she asked archly. "*Not* very creative."

He followed her, adjusting the curl that fell over his temple. She nearly told him there was too much cologne in his pomade. "Just a bit of fun," he said. "It's May Day, after all."

She'd like to cosh him over the head with a Maypole.

She paused, having led him to where she was safest. "The girl did not appear to be having fun, my lord."

He chuckled. "Trained to hide it, aren't they?"

Everything inside her recoiled.

"You will stop accosting the maids, Lord Eaton," she said very calmly. "You will stop accosting all women, period."

He turned toward her, all smiles and winks and perfect hair. "Jealous, are you, darling?"

She knew her role: continue to flirt, tease, appease. Abruptly, she was done with it. It had not curtailed his behavior in the past and was unlikely to do so now. Instead, she smiled back. "I am wearing a red dress, my lord, and your blood will not stain it at all."

"I beg your pardon?"

"I believe you heard me. You will keep your hands to yourself from now on."

He laughed, but stopped when he realized she was perfectly serious. "You are overset."

"Disgusted, actually."

His eyes narrowed. "You'll speak to me with respect."

"Certainly. Just as soon as you earn it."

Fury flashed in his face and was quickly banked. And it was not because of the group of ladies suddenly emerging from the retiring room in a cloud of perfume and laughter.

She did not like what replaced the anger: something arrogant, smug. Slippery. "We shall see, Lady Tamsin."

"Lady Tamsin!" one of the women called out. "Do join us."

"Thank you," she replied, relief stronger than she would like to admit. "I believe I shall."

SHE HAD NEVER welcomed the crush of guests, the too-hot air, the strong mix of flowers and perfume, the cacophony of voices and music more.

A mere moment with Lord Eaton had left her feeling as though she needed a good scrub.

And though she could not regret it, the prickling of her skin warned her she had likely made a misstep. A colossal one. The only thing that man valued more than his title was his ego. And she had inexplicably (to him) scratched it.

She pushed back another frisson of worry. She would not let him have a single moment of power over her.

"Ah, Lady Tamsin, you've returned at last." Lord Hamilton toasted her with his champagne glass. He stood with Miss Elliot and Henry, who only looked a little miserable and trapped. "As ever, you are the Season's most decorative bauble."

"One must entertain, after all." Tamsin's smile sparkled.

Henry's eyes narrowed ever so slightly. Anyone who did not know him well would not have noticed.

Tamsin noticed.

She also noticed his noticing Lord Eaton reentering the ballroom behind her.

"We must be merry," she added hastily, hoping to distract him. "What is May Day without gaiety?"

Persephone often said that she felt lonely in crowds, but it was the opposite for Tamsin. This was where she felt seen and appreciated. It might not seem like much to make people laugh or brighten their day with whimsy—she was certainly not saving lives or defending king and country. But she liked to think she made a little difference. That some other lonely soul felt connected on a night such as this one.

Especially as Persephone and Conall had already left and Henry had melted into the crush, no doubt to do the same. He'd stayed a full hour longer than she'd expected him to. He had never liked crowds, but now she could tell he also didn't relish being indoors. It must be all of that time spent with the sea air on his face.

Her father would not bother with her again, having already made his pronouncement. But she had acquaintances and friends here, in this moment, searching for happiness just as she was. She would make it enough. She always did.

"Shall we play pennies?" she suggested.

An older gentleman pursed his lips, confounded that she would suggest gambling games out loud in his presence. She twinkled at him. He fumbled and dropped his cane.

"Let's!" Miss Elliot agreed.

In the end, Tamsin found herself in the garden with four gentlemen and two ladies, all eager for distraction. The wine fountain had not yet run dry, but it was certainly far shallower than it had been at the start of the evening. Small flower wreaths hung from the trees, no bigger than teacups, ribbons dangling in the breeze. Torches burned merrily.

"A penny through the wreath," Tamsin decided. "Lord Hamilton, might you have a one at hand?"

"Certainly, Lady Tamsin."

They took turns flipping the penny in the air, and if it did not go through the wreath, the thrower had to drink. Goblets sat waiting to be filled at the fountain, and footmen gathered discreetly to watch the competition.

It was surprisingly difficult to manage with such small wreaths made of such overblown roses and peonies.

"Try again, Miss Elliot!" Tamsin encouraged her, and was encouraged in her turn.

She took the penny, fitting it easily between her thumb and forefinger. They'd played at pennies when they were children, competing for the last of the tarts. Of course, the target had been the pond.

Not small, spinning hoops made of flowers with drooping, drowsy petals. Which got in the way.

Her first shot hit the wreath and sent it spinning. At the cheerful cry, Tamsin filled her cup from the fountain and took a generous sip before trying again. This time, the penny sailed through the wreath, and she bowed majestically, like a courtier before the king.

On and on it went, until guests trickled out to join them, making wagers and drinking champagne even if they were not competing. The wine made Tamsin feel as though she were floating, just enough.

Miss Elliot, diminutive and quiet, appeared to have a constitution made of iron. She had terrible aim but drank like a sailor. She wasn't even flushed, and her posture remained exquisite. Tamsin was mildly envious.

Mr. Matthews did not have the same luck. He was three sheets to the wind and could barely stand, even with the help of a footman with violets in his wig. Lord Hamilton gave up on pennies and started to toss his crowned hat instead, which he had fetched from the house for the very purpose. Then he fell backward into the wine fountain, so much like some ancient sacrifice, dripping red, that Tamsin had to take a moment to admire it.

He sputtered and then slumped, snoring loudly. They declared him the winner on the grounds that he had not drowned in wine, and then went back inside.

The jovial din quieted when Lady York stepped on the dais, accompanied by several dramatic notes from the violin. She wore a rope of roses across her dress, like a fairy queen's military sash. Dozens of tiny diamonds sparkled and flashed in her hair. "Thank you all for joining us," she said. A perfect strawberry floated in her champagne. Her cheeks were flushed. "As you are well aware, we cannot have a May Day ball without a proper May Queen!"

Applause greeted her pronouncement, and a great amount of eager straightening of shoulders and smoothing of hair. Ladies vied for this crown, spending hours on their gowns, choosing just the right jewels, just the right touch of salve for their lips.

Lady York descended into the crowd, beginning a slow, theatrical procession through the guests, crown nestled on a silk cushion. The crown was made of tin leaves, accented with tiny paste jewels that caught the light like morning dew. Girls giggled, and women pretended not to care, especially if they cared too much.

Tamsin's stepmother lifted her chin, waiting expectantly. Tamsin could have told her Lady York would eat that crown of flowers before giving it to her. She'd insulted Lady York's sister just last month, and though it wasn't enough to risk giving a duchess the cut direct by not issuing an expected invitation, it was certainly enough for the simplest of retributions.

Tamsin could not have predicted, however, that *she* would be crowned May Queen.

For one thing, the honor was generally given to debutantes fresh out of the schoolroom, not twenty-eight-year-old spinsters who had just started a drinking contest in the back garden.

"I cannot think of a better May Queen than a lady who brings such merriment to every event she attends," Lady York pronounced, stopping in front of Tamsin. She winked. "And as she attends them all, she must be recognized for her service!"

A cheer erupted. Lady Chester had precisely the same expression she'd had the day she was served cream that had gone off in her tea.

Tamsin curtsied to Lady York and bowed her head to accept the crown.

"And this year, we have a surprise," Lady York added. She motioned for two footmen to approach. They cradled in their arms a cloak laden with spring flowers. The material was made of sheer sarsenet, heavy with roses and peonies, lilacs and violets preserved in sugar. It had taken someone hours of work to sew such delicate blossoms to the mantle. It was cold to the touch, no doubt having hung in the icehouse until the last possible moment.

And now it floated perfectly around Tamsin's shoulders, so that she was cloaked in flowers.

The strains of a waltz wound through the excited chatter. "You will lead the dance, of course," Lady York said, shooing people out of the way.

Tamsin was suddenly alone in the middle of the dance floor, candles burning above her head. She felt strangely exposed, even though she'd never minded being the center of attention. No one stepped forward to claim the dance.

And she knew exactly why.

Lord Eaton wove through the guests, whispering to the men. They stayed glued to the spot. She didn't know if he was warning them off so that she might be humiliated for her comments to him, or if he had every attention of claiming the dance for himself. It would suit his sense of self-importance. And few would dare gainsay him, especially in public. She found the gazes of friends, and their eyes lowered regretfully. One of them shrugged. "He's very tall," he mouthed.

Lord Eaton waited until everyone's attention was on Tamsin before calling out with one of his white, perfect smiles: "I will claim the May Queen."

"Bollocks to that," she said under her breath, even as the guests parted, and he closed in on her.

She'd join Lord Hamilton in the fountain first.

Lord Eaton was only steps away. She debated spraining her own ankle but wasn't sure on how to get it accomplished while standing perfectly still with hundreds of eyes of her.

"I believe that honor is already mine, Eaton," Henry said calmly, appearing suddenly in front of Tamsin.

He stood like a captain, at attention, capable, protective. So different from the young boy she'd known, constantly pulled to pieces by his father. He was still Henry—it was only that he'd found some line of iron in his soul while at sea.

Relief flooded her, making her dizzier than the wine.

"Oh, thank God," she muttered at him. "Took you long enough."

He bowed smartly, and she curtsied back. Lord Eaton sputtered but could do nothing else as the music swelled, and then Tamsin was in Henry's arms and nothing else mattered. Other couples were quick to join in, whirling like petals falling from an apple tree.

"I thought you'd forgotten our bargain," she said to Henry. At the last Cinderella ball hosted by the Duke of Pendleton for his many unmarried goddaughters, Tamsin had promised to keep the marriage-minded debutantes at bay, if he promised to dance every waltz with her. He hadn't known he was saving her from Lord Eaton's attentions at the time. It was the same night Meg's duke had punched Eaton right in the face. Not even being crowned May Queen could top that night's entertainment.

"I don't forget." Henry steadied her as they whirled, his hand between her shoulders. "I don't like the way he looks at you."

"I'm afraid I vexed him."

"That's not what I meant, but good. He needs vexing."

"I think so too." She grinned up at him, feeling warm and safe and somehow free, as if the moment was private between them. As private as when he'd helped her dress. At least now he was touching her. "He's very cross," she said. "He'll likely take it out on you."

Henry grunted. "He can try."

"You're not worried?"

"No."

Tamsin let it drop, mostly because she had no intention of letting Lord Eaton ruin this moment with Henry. She could smell his soap, and if she moved her hand just slightly, she'd be able to touch the curls at the nape of his neck. She didn't, of course, but oh, she was tempted. The warmth and strength of him was intoxicating. As was the tiny seed of hope flowering in her chest. Appropriate for a May Queen wearing a cloak of flowers.

When the music stopped, Tamsin suddenly didn't want to stay a moment longer. She wanted this to be the last thing she remembered from the night: dancing in his arms, covered in flowers. "Will you take me home?"

"Thank God," he murmured fervently. He paused, and she thought his ears might be turning red. She knew he hadn't meant it to come out so… salaciously. More's the pity.

She smiled widely. "Why, Captain Talbot, is that a proposition?"

"It is *not*."

But he said it too quickly, too darkly. She smirked at him, delight trickling through her.

He groaned. "You're a menace, Tam."

They took their leave, Tamsin trailing peony petals as she went. Her carriage waited at the end of the lane, and it took no time at all to be free of the queue. There were advantages to arriving late. They were barely three streets away from home, another stolen moment with Henry that would not last.

He sat across from her, his knees brushing hers. It provoked a delicious tickle up her thigh. "I'm glad you're home," she said. "Even if you did wait six whole days to tell me."

"I apologize."

"Magnanimously, I will forgive you," she said. "Because you saved me from Eaton."

"You should stay away from him."

She rolled her eyes. "Now, why ever did I not think of that?"

His lips twitched. "Fair enough."

"Are you going to join me at all of the balls and soirees?" she asked. "There are many, *many* waltzes you have promised me."

"As I said earlier, you could just stay home," he said. "I have several good books I could lend you."

"And as *I* said earlier, don't be ridiculous." She tilted her head as a rush of fondness and desire fought under her ribcage.

The carriage came to a stop. She was home already. She wanted to stay exactly where she was.

"You could claim a kiss, you know," she taunted him. He was so serious now, restrained. He'd have to be teased. "As a reward."

"I beg your pardon?"

She couldn't quite figure out what he thought, other than the expected scandal of it, but his pupils widened. That meant something, didn't it? She was sure she'd read that somewhere.

"I am the May Queen, after all," she added archly.

"You are the very devil," he returned, dry as tinder. And then he pushed her right out of the carriage. "Out you go."

She ought to have been insulted. One did not just push ladies out of carriages. It was not done. One put out the stepping block, offered a hand as she stepped out, an arm to guide her to her front door.

She should be hurt as well.

She'd offered him a kiss, after all. And instead, he stole her carriage.

She laughed out loud.

Better yet, she caught the flash of Henry's rare grin before he shut the door. In her face.

"Your manners are atrocious," she called out cheerfully as the carriage rolled away.

She was still smiling as she stepped inside her cozy house, over the memory of Henry's body pressed against her as they danced, his smile, the one he seemed to keep just for her. The anticipation of something blooming, some new thing being possible.

And then her nerves skittered to life under her skin.

She knew the moment she stepped into the parlor that something was wrong.

Terribly wrong.

Jack Nimble had returned, no doubt within minutes of her leaving for the spring fete. It had always been a game of sorts between them. He'd never gone so far as to break into her house, though, not really. An unlocked window, a bed hastily made in the hay of the stables. Once, a pretty red ribbon left in her carriage. It was her own ribbon, mind. Just to prove a point.

But this was something else. He'd come back when he knew she was absent. He'd actually stolen something, not moved it about to prove himself. It wasn't like him.

Worse yet, he hadn't taken anything truly valuable. Little Aphrodite was still on the shelf, the Roman curse tablet on the mantel.

But Vasilisa was missing.

She wasn't even a relic, just a replica of a poppet that had made people nervous when it was discovered stuck up inside the chimney of a rarely used bedroom on the country estate. She'd been dusty and crinkled when touched, stuffed as she was with herbs that had long since lost their scent. One of the footmen had crossed himself, and he was not even Catholic. A maid had screamed. But Tamsin had been instantly fascinated. Her mother had made Tamsin her own version out of blue muslin and lace and a glorious head of hair, complete with a single pearl-tipped pin.

They'd told each other stories about Vasilisa, about the boot and the thirteen nails also found in the chimney. Someone had been keen to protect the manor house from witches.

And a few months later, when Tamsin's mother's illness had

taken a sudden turn, she'd pressed the little doll into her daughter's hands, whispering, "Take care of little Vasilisa, and she'll take care of you."

This wasn't just petty theft.

This was war.

Chapter Six

HENRY SENT TAMSIN'S carriage back to her house once he'd stepped out of it, across from the Rose and Anchor. It was a lively pub popular with sailors and soldiers, near enough to the docks but just far enough away to feel like a vacation. He hadn't wanted to be spotted outside her house, just in case.

The Rose and Anchor felt like home. His father would disapprove—a mild word for his outbursts. Viscounts did not frequent such establishments, especially not when they were to be earls someday. Henry should be at some chophouse, or gaming hell, or a bawdy house. Preferably all three. Viscounts didn't read so much, either, or play with a horde of girls.

Small wonder that he much preferred the Rose and Anchor, with its sticky floors, chipped earthenware mugs, and slightly inebriated musicians murdering a fiddle and a drum. Dice games dominated the tables, as did mugs of ale and crumbs of meat pies. The air was smoky and close, and yet still cleaner than the mixtures of perfumes and colognes from the York May Ball. It had choked his lungs quicker than an icy wave breaking over the ship rails.

"Captain Talbot!" someone shouted from the din, even though he was no longer a captain.

"Harper." He greeted the man with the oiled and curled beard that went halfway down his chest, even braided. He was half in love with his own beard, was Harper. He'd kept it perfect even during the miserable month they'd subsisted on hardtack and limes, blown off course by a sudden storm. On Christmas he decorated it with holly.

His wife did not, by all accounts, appreciate the festive gesture.

Henry spotted several more of his men—*former* men—at the same table, and his shoulders loosened. He was more relaxed then he'd had since setting foot off his ship.

Since drawing his hand over the back of Tamsin's corset.

Though, to be fair, that had hardly been *relaxing*.

"A round on me, Tweed," he called to the bartender. Tweed nodded, and the table cheered.

"There's a face only a mother could love," a man said mildly from behind Henry's left shoulder.

Henry tensed, instantly on alert, even before he registered the voice, and the familiar stance of the Irishman leaning against the bar. "Pierce," he said by way of greeting.

Pierce Gallagher inclined his head. "I came in right behind you. You were thinking so hard I thought your head might burst like a melon."

"Not yet." It was still a distinct possibility.

"There's always tomorrow."

"Just the man I wanted to see, actually," Henry said.

"You can't know how often I hear that very thing," Pierce said drily, smirking. It was an expression he reserved for true friends, which he could count on one hand. The general public only saw a man with fierce eyes, scars, and a knife always at his belt. Henry had fought the seas and the French with him, would trust him with his life. Better, with Tamsin's life. "Though usually from a lass a damn sight prettier than you," he added.

"So you say. Do you have a minute?" Henry asked.

"Aye."

They ducked back outside and fell into step, letting the yellow smog of London at night swallow them. "Have you got a few good men on shore?" Henry asked.

"Aye, I do." Pierce shot him a sidelong glance. "Why?"

"I've a lady needs watching." Henry paused. "Two, actually."

Persephone had Conall at hand and Meg was in the country, but Conall's sister Priya lived alone not far from Tamsin.

"You *have* been busy." Pierce whistled. "We landed barely a week ago and already you have two mistresses who need watching? Didn't know you had it in you, captain."

Henry rolled his eyes. "It's not like that."

"Shame. You could do with a tumble. Or two."

"I can still have you flogged, I'm sure."

"Have to catch me first." They grinned at each other. Henry knew a moment of peace, of a good friend at his back, with the sounds of music coming from candlelit houses and carriages on the cobblestones as they crossed into Mayfair. It wasn't the swell of the sea, but at least London late at night had its own kind of calm.

When he wasn't being stabbed.

Or hunted for treason.

He'd spent weeks on the run, just last year, in and out of the rookeries, sleeping in dodgy, filthy corners, hiding his face. Stealing food.

"I'll need men at the front and back, day and night. For Lady Tamsin Bell on Bruton Street and Lady Langdon on Bolton Row near the park."

"Tamsin, is it?"

"Shut it."

Pierce gave a low laugh before going back to his usual quiet lethalness. "Spot of trouble?"

"Could be."

Pierce was the only one who knew about Tamsin, about the way her infrequent letters kept Henry's hope alive. About Persephone and how she kept him sane. Of all the Cinderellas with their irreverent talent for mischief and, frankly bloodthirsty, revenge. His father still had no idea that the majority of his illnesses, especially involving his digestive system, were not a product of nature. They were a product of the Cinderellas, and Priya's knowledge of herbs especially. She had supplied the powders, and smiling, cherubic Tamsin had dropped them in his wine. More than once.

Persephone had hidden him on countless occasions when they were children, after bruises and broken bones. Even her grandmother had once sent his father packing with a clout to the ear and a face full of pink cake.

Whatever trouble had found him would not touch them. Any of them. He didn't relish the thought of going to ground again, but he would do it without hesitation if it was the best way to keep them safe.

And she had to be safe. Everything else could burn to ashes, the entire city of London for all he cared, but Tamsin stayed safe.

There was no compromise on that score.

"Does this have anything to do with the bloody hole in your arm?"

Trust Pierce to notice the wound in the shadows and hidden as it was.

"Might," Henry admitted.

"Six days," Pierce reminded him mildly. "Six bloody days and you can't keep out of trouble."

"Footpads." Henry shrugged.

Pierce narrowed one eye. "Did you recognize them?"

"No."

"Did they recognize *you?*"

"Yes. And it was near Lady Tamsin's house."

Pierce whistled through his teeth.

"I can't take the chance," Henry said.

"Of course not. Leave it to me."

"Thank you, Pierce."

He just shrugged. "Aye. I'll take a shift, and I've just the man for the other."

"Harper?"

He shook his head. "You know how he is around the Quality."

They shared a chuckle. "Abysmal," Henry said, remembering the time Harper choked on a pasty in front of a lady on the west coast of Cornwall, all because she had smiled in his general direction. She'd had to beat him around the back with her silk parasol to dislodge the mouthful stuck somewhere in his gullet.

He'd sung her the first song he could think of, in gratitude.

Sailor's songs were not for the fainthearted. Or the rarefied.

"He goes by Crow."

"Do I know him?"

"No, he's just landed back in England. His father's people are from Upper Canada, Ojibway, I think. His mother was the daughter of a minor baron."

"Does he know what he's about?"

"They have wars enough in the colonies. And he's fought in a fair few."

As they passed pub after pub, raucous laughter spilled out from doorways. The shadows gave way to lamplight, a crowd of carriages, men holding each other up and stinking of wine and gin. St. James loomed, full of shining stone and brick buildings, glittering with wealth. Horses snorted impatiently under the lampposts.

Pierce raised his eyebrows. "Where are we going? Bit posh this, innit?"

"I thought *you* were going to see to those guards. I can't stand guard; it might draw trouble to her door."

"And I will, but not until we have done with whatever it is you're about to do."

"Who says I'm about to do anything?"

Pierce snorted. Loudly. Disrespectfully. Especially for a first lieutenant. Former first lieutenant. Still. "That's the look you always had just before you ordered the cannons."

"Well, bollocks," Conall interrupted them from out of nowhere. Hands went to knives, muscles tensed, were forced to relax again. He only waited, smirking that damn smirk. "I almost missed the fun."

"Persephone sent you." Henry sighed. "That didn't take long."

"Believe it or not, she didn't need to send me." Conall nodded to the gentlemen's club on whose sidewalk they stood. "I know Eaton's club. Unfortunately, it also happens to be mine." He shrugged one shoulder. "Gamblers like Brooks', and gamblers also like to drink and talk. It's been useful for acquiring information."

"Good," Henry said grimly. "That will save me time getting inside." He wasn't a member of Brooks', White's, or Boodles. He supposed he ought to be now that he was no longer Captain Talbot but Viscount Stirling. His father belonged to White's, and so he never would. One decision made.

Brooks' stood on the corner, a tidy Palladian building of yellow brick, the sidewalks and the street out front crowded with gentlemen eager for entertainment and women who were definitely not aristocratic. It was too scandalous for ladies to be seen on St. James after dark. Which was why he was surprised, now that he thought of it, that he'd never seen the Cinderellas marching down the way, arm in arm. Possibly waving spears. Poisoned spears.

Conall inclined his head toward Pierce. "Gallagher."

Henry was surprised. "You know each other?"

"This one knows everyone," Pierce muttered.

Conall laughed. "True."

Henry knew of course that Conall had worked for the Crown during the war as a spy of sorts, but they'd never crossed paths in that capacity. Only as fellow planets orbiting the sun of the Cinderella Society.

"Well, gentlemen." Conall flashed his famous grin. "Are we going inside, or what?"

He led the way, charming the man posted at the front door into letting them all inside, no questions asked beyond his title as an earl and membership to the club. The ground floor was neoclassical in design, opulently decorated and hazy with cheroot smoke. They ignored the front rooms and went straight to the card room. Henry knew exactly where Eaton would be.

And there he was. Lounging with arrogant indolence, wine glass in one hand, cards in the other. Men sat around the table, equally focused on the game. Gambling went on all day and night at Brooks'. Henry hoped Eaton lost his fortune. Twice.

Conversations at the table quieted as Henry approached, flanked by an earl with a cheerfully savage smile and a man who wore his scars like the aristocrats wore their cravat pins. Nonchalantly. It was late into the night, edging toward morning, which already gave everyone and everything an edge. Except for Eaton. The entitled ass.

He stood up, crowing over his hands of cards as he slapped them faceup on the green baize table. There were muttered curses, then curious silence. Too late, Eaton realized they weren't reacting to his win. Or to him at all.

He spotted Henry and blanched. It was brief, hastily covered up. But it was all Henry needed. He knew that Eaton remembered their conversation, heavy on the threats at the Pendleton ball the previous autumn. The very night Tamsin told him Eaton had groped her, repeatedly, and some of the others. She had said it so casually, as if it was common. And it clearly was. She'd made him dance with her so as to avoid wandering hands. Twice now.

As if that was the only way he could protect her.

He'd chased Eaton out of the Pendleton ball, clear out of Little Barrow, and, within days, out of London as well. But he'd been famous then. A war hero, a viscount just exonerated from allegations of treason. London merchants suddenly knew his face, and he had made it clear that Lord Eaton's business was not to be accepted. Eaton outranked him, but at that moment, Henry was far more popular, more notorious. He'd hated it until that very moment.

"Talbot." Eaton recovered his equanimity and injected even more conceit into his tone. He wobbled slightly, smelling of wine and cologne.

"Eaton," Henry said flatly. He wasn't here to play games, to threaten, or make a point.

He was here to make a promise.

And to carry one out.

He'd made it clear that if Eaton touched a woman again without her consent, he would lose that hand. And if he touched Tamsin, he'd lose his balls too. Henry was certain the Cinderellas had more devious, painful ways of retribution, but they would take time and planning. Secrecy. His only required a spot of violence he was more than happy to indulge in. Back then.

And right now.

Right fucking now.

"You're not going to touch women without their consent anymore. And if you have to grope them when no one's looking or pretend that you aren't touching them inappropriately when you are, then here's a hint: they don't you want you touching them. You could be the king of bloody England and they wouldn't want you. Now leave the fuck off."

Henry smiled once, briefly, before driving his fist into Eaton's stomach. It was a quick, vicious strike, and Eaton doubled over, gagging. Henry followed with a right hook. Wagers were shouted over the tables before Eaton even hit the floor. Which he did. He wheezed for a long moment and vomited, and then his eyes rolled back in his head.

"Goddamn it," Conall said over the cacophony. Somebody clapped enthusiastically. Several of the staff hurried in their direction. "That was barely any fun at all."

Eaton stirred and then did not move again.

Further violence would have to wait.

But that was fine. Henry was nothing if not patient.

Chapter Seven

TAMSIN WOKE EARLY.

Rudely early.

She had only managed a few hours of sleep to begin with. It was remarkably difficult to rest when anger churned in your belly. It occurred to her that she ought to maybe focus more on collecting items that promised good luck rather than morbid histories. Or something soothing, like lace doilies.

When the sun finally sent arrows of light over the houses across the street, Tamsin gave up. She swung her feet over the side of the bed and rang the bell for her maid, toes curling on the chilly floor. Sarah came to the door and paused on the threshold, eyes widening with surprise. "You're up, miss." It was barely ten o'clock and definitely not her usual time to rise.

"It would seem so." Tamsin yawned. Her eyes were gritty. "Can't say I approve."

"I'll fetch a breakfast tray."

"Thank you. And a smart dress, if you please."

"You're going out? At this hour?"

"I am," she said grimly. "I have matters to attend to."

She indulged in a second cup of chocolate, two muffins with butter and cheese, ham, and a handful of strawberries. If today went anything like last night, she should be fortified.

She might even smuggle more ham in her reticule. If only to throw it at Jack's head.

She wore sturdy boots, even though she knew her father would not approve. But he was already going to find fault with her anyway. She may as well be comfortable. And she had a stop to make before heading to the townhouse in Grosvenor Square to be served cucumber sandwiches and disaster. He'd loved her mother, she knew that, but he wouldn't understand why she'd make such a fuss over a sentimental object like an old doll.

It was the only thing she had left of her mother's. Between her father clearing out her belongings in a bout of grief and Lady Chester's refusal to have anything displayed that reminded her of the previous duchess, Vasilisa was rare. Priceless.

But only to Tamsin.

She couldn't begin to comprehend why Jack had bothered with her. Even sitting court with the other poppets, it was obvious she wasn't anything with historical or folkloric value. Although, to a twelve-year-old boy perhaps it was enough that she was prettier than the others and had sat in a place of honor.

She slipped a knife along with the ham wrapped in a napkin into her reticule. She wasn't going to stab Jack—he was only a boy, after all. But she definitely felt like stabbing *someone*.

She slipped on a necklace of amethyst beads, purported by the ancient Greeks to stave off drunkenness, and went out to the carriage. The coachman and the footman who would accompany her were both bleary-eyed. They could probably count on one hand the number of times she had risen before noon.

She might not know where Jack lived, but she had a pretty good idea of how to find him. And if not him, at least her stolen poppet.

The Cabinet of Curiosities.

It sounded very grand for what amounted to the second floor of a confectioner's shop in Berkeley Square, right by Gunter's Ices. The shop window was filled with elaborate jars of black licorice Pontefract cakes from York, sugar sculptures in the shapes of swans and roses and a smiling hedgehog.

And it was right here on the sidewalk, under the creaking, brightly painted sign reading Stewart's Sweet Shop, that Tamsin had first encountered Jack Nimble. He'd been considerably dirtier and scrawnier, and dangling from the fist of an enraged gentle-man. That gentleman was red in the face and shouting through the starched points of his cravats about how they hanged even little boys for thievery. By the neck until dead. He was very insistent on that fact.

And he wasn't wrong.

He was, also, an ass, and known for his temper and his petty revenges. Jack looked terrified, even without knowing his reputation.

Tamsin had brushed behind him, nicking the pouch of coins stuck in the back of his belt.

"My lord," she'd sung out, making sure her smile was bright and concerned, not at all edged with the violence she was contemplating. Cheerfully. "Goodness." She fluttered her eyelashes, feeling like a goose. It was, however, effective. As usual.

"Lady Tamsin, this is not a sight for a lady such as yourself."

"I should say not," she agreed. He didn't catch the tone, the implications behind it. Jack did; she saw it in his face. She held up the pouch. "I just tripped over this. Is it yours?"

He stared at her. Red crept up his neck. "What now?"

"It's very fine embroidery. I assumed it was yours."

He dropped Jack on his feet but did not let go of his collar.

Tamsin handed him the pouch. "I hate to ask, but would you see me to my carriage?" She glanced at Jack. "There are clearly ruffians about for you to be so fearsome."

Honestly, how she did not gag sometimes was beyond her.

She might have trod the boards as an actress were she born into a different family. But the world was the world, and you used what weapons you had at your disposal. She tilted her head, wondering if she looked suitably nervous. Or just dyspeptic.

"I'd be delighted, Lady Tamsin." He bowed low.

Tamsin narrowed her eyes warningly at Jack over his bent back. He'd flashed her that grin of his and scampered away into the crowd. She'd caught sight of him the next time she visited, watching from a rooftop. She'd winked at him before going inside for "cardamon sugar sweets." She'd really been in search of a curse tablet. The shop did not sell cardamon sugar sweets.

He'd shadowed her for weeks.

But not today. He was nowhere to be seen. Smart boy. Not on his favorite rooftop, not in the alley, not on the street.

"Jack Nimble," she muttered. "I'll find you yet."

Her neck prickled, and she looked over her shoulder. No skinny pickpocket with red patches on his coat, only gentlemen touching their beaver hats in her direction, women nodding, bonnet ribbons quivering in the spring wind. She still felt it, someone's eyes on her back, as she went inside the shop.

The bells attached to the handle sang a lively jingle. She was instantly enveloped in the comforting scents of sugar and lemon and joy. There were candy drops flavored with violet and bayberry, chocolate disks rolled in colorful nonpareils, marzipan fruits, sugared plums, jars of peppermint sticks.

And Mr. Stewart behind the counter, writing in his ledger as his clerks wrapped bundles of sweets with gold ribbons. They wore matching aprons, also with gold ribbons, looking as cheerful as he was dour. Tamsin had only ever seen him smile once, and that was at Pierre Marseilles, the handsome French chef whose family had escaped the Revolution when he was young. His mother had a taste for candy and passed her skills on to her son. Mr. Marseilles popped his head into the shop, smiling when he spotted her.

"Mademoiselle!" He bowed over her hand. He wore a lacy cravat, very French, and quite stunning against his brown skin.

"Monsieur Marseilles." She curtsied.

Mr. Stewart glanced out of the corner of his eye. Pierre did the same. Tamsin hid a smile.

She pretended to peruse the glass cases as they talked over some matter of business, forgot she was pretending, and bought a half a pound of lemon drops. By the time she had paid for her purchase, the shop was momentarily empty, and Mr. Stewart nodded at her.

She slipped behind a curtain, darting through the doorway and up the plain, crooked stairs. There was no hint here of the frilly confectionary and none at all as to what lurked upstairs.

Better even than the warmth of sugar was the perfume of dust and ink and the gin used to clean objects that could not be washed. Of history, secrets. Forgotten stories, like Vasilisa's namesake might have been, were it not for Tamsin's mother. The room was clean, plain. Forgettable. Except for the trunks and cases and boxes stacked along the wall, behind a long table over which reigned a middle-aged woman with a cheeky smile and eyes that could raise the dead.

No one messed with Miss Stewart.

Not lords, not ladies, not even dukes. Not if they had any interest in the items stored behind her. Treasures found in distant graves, haunted dolls, painted human skulls, beads said to have belonged to powerful sorcerers more than two thousand years ago. There were scraps of parchment with faded spells (Egyptian mostly, which was why Persephone, even as Countess of Northwyck, was barred entry. Her response to the items, from where they had been taken and to whom they were sold, had been... animated). There were nails found in chimneys, witch bottles dug up from under cottage doorways in Cornwall. Dangerous, not quite illegal, and yet not quite legal. Mysterious.

Tamsin loved it. She had loved it since the very first day she'd been granted access.

"Lady T," Miss Stewart greeted her. Names were not used inside the Cabinet—in fact, masks were sometimes worn to hide identities. It was only seven years ago that Ann Izzard from Great Paxton was by with a mob of her fellow villagers and accusations of witchcraft. They'd beaten her with clubs and scratched at her to bleed her of her powers. And she had been lucky—she'd escaped and returned to see nine of her abusers prosecuted by the local court.

"Miss Stewart," Tamsin replied. "I've brought you something."

"A bribe." Miss Stewart's red hair was caught up in a simple knot, displaying the freckles on her cheeks and throat. Her Scottish accent thickened. "Lovely." She paused. "It's not candy, is it?"

"Of course not," Tamsin said. "I shouldn't dare."

"Good, because *I* should like to keep my teeth as long as I can."

Everyone brought her candy. Tamsin had assumed so from the start. It was too easy, what with her brother's sweet shop downstairs. And so instead she brought bits of gossip, sometimes ribbons, sharp teas. Little figurines of swans. The woman was obsessed with swans.

Tamsin handed over a tea mixture that promised the bite of peppermint, the pucker of lemon, a hint of fennel.

Miss Stewart sniffed the tisane. "That's bracing."

"I thought of you."

"One day you'll tell me who your supplier is."

"But then I would lose my advantage," Tamsin pointed out. Her supplier was Priya, of course. No one else in London had greenhouses quite like hers. There were apothecaries who begged for access to her plants and herbs. She only accepted secrets as barter. "And then I'd have to bring you candy."

Miss Stewart shuddered. "Forget I asked." She put her quill down. "Now what can I do for you today?"

"I wondered if any new poppets came in?"

She shook her head. "You know I'd have sent word. I know your tastes by now."

"No dolls? Children's toys?"

"I'm afraid not."

Tamsin's shoulders drooped. Disappointment nibbled at her, threatened to bite down. She shook it off. She'd known it wouldn't be that easy. "What about Jack Nimble?" she asked. "Have you seen him today?"

"Not for a week, at least."

She frowned. "Truly?"

"Truly." Miss Stewart tilted her head. "Let me guess, something of yours has gone missing."

"Yes." Tamsin narrowed her eyes. "You *have* seen Jack!"

"No, but you are not the first to ask me about a missing artifact today."

"I'm not?"

"You're the fourth, in point of fact."

Tamsin frowned. "There is no possible way that little Jack broke into four houses last night."

"I rather doubt it."

Confusion warred with unease. "Any idea what's going?"

"None," Miss Stewart admitted grimly. "And I don't like it."

"Were they all poppets?" That would be even odder, surely.

"No, but all the kinds of items we share an interest in. And all very important to their owners."

Tamsin shook her head. "My poppet isn't even a real poppet. She's a doll."

"But important?"

She thought of her mother, the loving way she had braided yarn for Vasilisa's hair, the way she had pressed the doll into her hands as she faded. "Very."

"Well, it seems we have a mystery on our hands."

Tamsin harrumphed. "Do you know? I'm not sure I'm keen on mysteries when I'm personally involved."

Miss Stewart rolled her eyes in commiseration. "I should hope not. I've never taken you for a fool, my lady."

"Would you tell me who the other victims were?"

She shook her head. "You know I can't do that."

Tamsin sighed. "I suppose not. Would you send word to them that I was also stolen from and would welcome their calls?"

"That I can do."

A lady emerged from behind the thick curtain shielding the back of the long room. She carried a box of femurs. There was dust on her nose. "Have you ever cleaned back there? I swear I— Oh." She stopped when she saw Tamsin. "I beg your pardon."

"Lady Tamsin, this is Lady Mirabelle. She will be assisting me for the next few weeks."

They curtsied to each other. "I'm quite jealous," Tamsin said. "You never let me help."

Miss Stewart snorted. "Lady Mirabelle has no interest in these relics and is therefore perfect for the job."

Tamsin tucked her tongue in her cheek. "I believe that is not entirely complimentary to me."

Lady Mirabelle flushed. "Oh no, I'm sure that's not what she meant."

"And yet…" Miss Stewart smiled. Lady Mirabelle was aghast.

Tamsin laughed. "Miss Stewart can say and do whatever she likes, as we are all too scared to be banned from the Cabinet."

Miss Stewart nodded briskly. "Quite right." She eyed Lady Mirabelle. "If I'm to leave you in charge, you're going to have to be a lot more gargoyle than debutante."

"I'll do my best."

"I'll be away until the end of June—rather unexpectedly."

"I hope all is well?" Tamsin asked.

"A friend in Scotland needs me. Don't let them take advantage of Lady Mirabelle when I'm gone."

"I won't. And you'll send word if you hear anything? Or come across a doll wearing a blue dress?"

"Of course."

"You as well, Lady Mirabelle?"

"Yes, certainly."

"Thank you."

Tamsin went back down to the street, more determined than ever to find Jack. Someone was targeting collectors of haunted or magical items. And worse, using a young, unprotected boy to do it.

And Tamsin didn't even have the time to truly give in to her anger. To start plotting how she would track this thief down.

Because, first, she had to survive her family luncheon.

Chapter Eight

D AMN AND BLAST.

It was worse than she'd feared.

And this from a woman who slept like a baby under a painting of Anne Boleyn holding her own severed head every night. Tamsin did not unsettle easily.

The Chester townhouse was elegant and opulent, as always, dripping gold and crowded with portraits of Lady Chester. Roses and lilies covered every surface, both bold and traditional. Suitable to a duchy and a duchess who wished to set the fashion. They made Tamsin want to sneeze.

So did her stepsisters.

Carnation and Beryl were twins, though they looked nothing alike. At nineteen, with their first Season under their belt and the lackluster results blamed squarely upon Tamsin, there was something nervous about them. Then again, Tamsin would have a nervous disposition too if Lady Chester was her mother.

Being cast out of the house still stung, but there were advantages. She mustn't forget that.

Currently, Carnation, plump and blond, was dressed entirely in pink and had bathed in rose perfume, on her mother's orders. Tamsin had heard her speech on how ladies must be elegant and demure, but also noticeable. Which no doubt also explained Beryl's unfortunate pineapple hairpiece.

They were pretty, well-bred, but never shared a smile between them. Lady Chester thought showing your teeth was ill-bred.

Incidentally, Lady Chester had very few teeth of her own. Most had been collected on the battlefield at Waterloo and fitted to her mouth.

Still, she was beautiful, if sharp, and only eleven years older than Tamsin. Tamsin had so wanted to love her, had prayed for it, wished on it, dropping silver pins in wells, blowing dandelion seeds into the wind. But Lady Chester did not want to be loved, not by the girl who looked too much like her husband's first wife. Not by the girl who drew too much attention, always. And her daughters did not want a sister who made their mother cross.

And anything that was not centered on her son, the future duke, or her daughters' marriages made her cross. Tamsin had met her half-brother only a dozen times, and he was already six years old, on his birthday and at Christmas. He still kept mostly to the nursery, and Tamsin was rarely in the house for more than an hour or so.

They were halfway through a course of quail eggs and asparagus salad when the reason for Tamsin's current invitation became clear. Painfully, painfully clear.

"We've news," her father declared.

Lady Chester smiled, and it was smug and pointed, and Tamsin put down her wine glass immediately. Carnation and Beryl continued to eat, which meant they had already heard the news.

Her father cleared his throat, the most human, non-duke thing he had done in years. "I've secured you a match, girl."

Tamsin blinked. "No, thank you."

Beryl choked on a mouthful of egg. "You can't just say no."

"I'm twenty-eight years old," Tamsin said through her teeth, feeling all of eight years old with the way her father watched her.

"I won't have histrionics," he said.

Tamsin hadn't raised her voice. She'd barely spoken.

She was perfectly capable of histrionics. Ask Lord Fairweather's head after she'd hit with him a cricket ball, the traitor.

She wrinkled her nose, thinking of last night. "It's not Lord

Willoughby, is it?"

"No, though you should be grateful for this attention," Lady Chester said. "The duke has secured you an earl."

Something about the way she said it, about the serrated edge to the patently false warmth of her smile, made Tamsin tense. "Who?"

"Lord Eaton."

She went utterly cold. Something very close to panic clawed in her throat. "Absolutely not."

"Don't be ridiculous," Lady Chester replied. "It wasn't a question."

Tamsin ought to have seen this coming. Eaton had been courting her stepmother's favor for months now, had even bragged about marrying Tamsin at the Duke of Pendleton's Cinderella ball. She had been hiding in the bushes at the time and wasn't able to throw something suitably heavy at his swelled head.

She was an idiot. One should always make time to throw things at disagreeable lords.

Tamsin faced her father. "I can't marry him, Papa." Her mind raced ahead to logical arguments, begging, plots to be made.

"Why ever not? He's an earl."

"I don't even know his Christian name." It wasn't much of an argument but the only one she could currently make without screaming. She took a deep breath. Another.

"Philip Horatious Dunham," Lady Chester provided promptly.

Tamsin shook her head. "I won't marry him. He's atrocious."

"Nonsense. He has a fine country estate and speaks well when in Parliament."

"Then do either of you want him?" she asked her stepsisters out of desperation. Not that she would wish Eaton on either of them. But panic continued to flutter like crow wings in her throat.

"My girls will marry a marquess or a duke," Lady Chester announced. "Nothing else will do."

Carnation rolled her eyes. Tamsin might have missed it if her own eyes weren't permanently stuck in a state of wide alertness, much like a deer in the woods scenting a huntsman.

"That and he did not offer for us, Maman," Carnation said.

"Oh, hush, Carnation."

Tamsin pushed away from the table, already feeling trapped. Her wine glass wobbled dangerously. "He is not honorable with women."

"He'll treat you well enough." Her father shrugged. "You're a duke's daughter."

She could only stare. "What about the way he treats other women?"

"That's none of your concern. Peccadilloes are common in young men."

Peccadilloes. She wanted to scream again.

"Please, let me find my own husband. *Please.*"

"You've had ten years to do that, girl."

Unkind. Not *untrue*, but still unkind.

"You're too picky by half. I'll hear no more about it. I've doubled your dowry."

Lady Chester's eyes widened. "Darling…"

He sent her a cutting look. "I'll not have my daughter un-properly dowered. It won't do for a dukedom."

She nodded. "Of course."

Tamsin shook her head again, as if it would make a differ-ence. She had to find her way through the murk of shock that had her pulse thrumming thickly in her ears.

She needed to think.

And she certainly could not do that *here*. Not with Beryl smirking and Carnation wincing sympathetically. Her stepmother smiling so coldly. Her father not doing anything at all. He'd already returned to his asparagus and his white wine, the matter closed. His gold signet ring flashed.

She stood, forcing herself to walk, not run.

"Tamsin?"

She froze in the doorway, hope sparking. "Yes, Father?"

"You'll marry in one week."

Her shoulders drooped, then straightened again.

Bollocks to that.

HENRY CLIMBED THE stairs to the portico of the Culpepper townhouse, the columns standing like sentry guards around him. The house was enormous, rows and rows of windows gleaming like judgmental eyes. No Culpepper had ever boarded up a window in his life, and damn the window tax. Wisteria and white roses grew in very precise lines, trained and secured to discreet trellises. Everything that could be polished was polished to within an inch of its life. It was elegant, lavish, and with intent to intimidate.

He hated it.

Even now, as a man grown who had faced Napoleon and his armies, he hated it.

Almost as much as he hated the man inside.

But he didn't hesitate. He was certain he was being watched even now, and the briefest reluctance would be marked as weakness. He knocked, and within moments the family butler opened the door.

Henry handed him his hat. "Hello, Sturgeon. I'm expected."

He didn't have an appointment, but Henry had two stitches he'd had to sew into his own arm to confirm that he was expected.

"Lord Stirling, of course. Right this way."

"I know where he is," Henry said, not waiting to be led like a stranger or a little boy. The power games he hated pressed down on him, and he'd only taken three steps into the bloody house.

Besides, his father was in his library. He was always in his library, despite his disdain for Henry's book collection. It was the only room in the house where he could properly loom. The parlors were too airy, the furniture too delicate, despite his mother having died when he was four years old. He had vague memories of soft hands, dark hair, and the smell of lilac powder.

The hall was all portraits of hunting dogs and enormous cattle that looked more like hairy rectangles on legs than actual animals. There were swords, antlers, more swords. Honestly, there were army barracks more welcoming. And subtler.

He used to hate this walk, knowing exactly what awaited him at the end of it. Insults, fists. If he cried, he was scolded for being too weak. If he talked back, that was somehow worse. This hallway and the room at the end of it had taken his confidence, his love for his father. Even his favorite cat. When nine-year-old Henry had nightmares and snuck the kitchen cat into his room for comfort, the cat was chased out of the house. He'd loved that damned cat and slept like a normal child for the month he managed to keep him secret.

His nightmares were different now.

But this bloody house, and the bloody library papered with green silk and stuffed with heavy mahogany, and his bloody father were the exact bloody same.

One day, he would be the Earl of Culpepper.

And on that day, this house would be closed up tight.

Until then, he'd set foot in it as little as possible and only with urgent and good reason.

Tamsin was the very best reason.

Damn his father for putting her in danger, even for a moment. Even peripherally.

He stalked into the room. "You always did know how to welcome a person home."

His father, Richard Talbot, Earl of Culpepper, looked up from the ledgers opened on his desk. He was a handsome man, but not a kind one. And it didn't bother him one bit. "Henry," he said. "So you've deigned to visit your father."

"If you stabbed me less, I might visit more."

"Pah, you look well enough."

And that was that, according to his father. As long as his son won a fight, that was good enough. And if he didn't win, well, he clearly needed the practice.

"We're not doing this again," Henry said evenly.

"Don't be so missish."

He pushed his sleeve up, the stiches neat but the flesh swollen around them. "Your bully boys might have hurt someone else."

"Well, did they?"

"Not this time."

"Well, then, you're fussing over nothing. You need to stay sharp. Have a brandy."

"No, thank you," Henry replied through his teeth. "They ambushed me near Lady Tamsin's house."

"Oh ho." His father waggled his eyebrows like a villain in a bad gothic romance. "It's like that, is it?"

"Don't." Henry's tone was sharp, hard as a bullet. It was the voice of a man who had commanded a ship, who had watched the bodies of men float on the churning waves. Who still heard muzzily in his left ear because of his proximity to cannon fire. It was strong enough, and sure enough, to give even his father pause. "I doubt the Duke of Chester would be thrilled with the idea of his daughter being in harm's way."

The earl did not like being wrong. Especially if it meant his son was right. "Bah, he hardly bothers with the girl."

"Still," Henry said. "You'll call off your dogs."

"So you can get soft now that the Navy doesn't have you anymore?" the earl scoffed. That tone used to drive nails into Henry's confidence, shredding every morsel of his composure. "I think not."

"Not this again," his grandmother snapped from the doorway, as formidable now as she had been when she was the countess, not simply the dowager countess. She was tall and draped in gray silk. Ropes of pearls swung from her neck, as usual. She'd told them they were mermaid's tears when he was little, and that the ocean was filled with them.

"It's nothing to do with you, Mother," his father said.

"Don't be any more ridiculous than you have to be, Richard."

Henry smiled through the rage that threatened to crack his jaw. "Grandmother."

Her face softened. "My boy, it's good to see you. I've been worried."

"You always did coddle him," his father huffed.

"Yes," she returned acidly. "It's terribly indulgent of me to be happy my grandson didn't die in the war. Honestly, Richard, you never were quite right."

Henry's smile widened. "I've missed you too, Grandmother."

"Of course you have," she agreed.

His grandmother was one of the reasons he hadn't buckled under his father's abuse. She had spirited him away to the country estate in Little Barrow as often as possible. Twice a year they could not avoid the obligatory birthday visit and Christmas visit to London, but she fought every other interaction with all of her considerable temper. The earl had all of the power, but even he could not completely overrule his mother.

"What are you doing here?" Henry asked her. She hated London.

"My grandson is finally home. Where else would I be?"

"I was coming to Little Barrow."

She patted his cheek. "I know. But I'm old, my boy. I don't like to waste time."

He gave her a sharp perusal, but she seemed healthy enough. Her face was lined but bright, her hair perfectly coiled and dripping with diamonds, as was her custom. "When did you arrive?"

"Yesterday. I would have called, but a young bachelor home after being away on the high seas for months—I wasn't sure what I would find."

He wanted to remove her from this place and invite her to stay with him. But his house still only had a skeletal staff, and more importantly, he was afraid his father's men might grow careless.

"Are you well? Truly?" he asked, and she knew exactly what he meant. This house, his son. They were not welcoming or comfortable.

"She's fine," his father put in. He did not like to be ignored.

"I didn't ask you," Henry insisted coldly.

"I'm perfectly well," his grandmother assured him. "And only in town for a little while, besides. I brought some items from my drawing room for Persephone's little museum that I thought she might like to have."

"I thought you didn't like her?" His grandmother was not particularly easy on ladies with ruined reputations.

"She saved your life and cleared your name. She can have

anything she wants. Now, you may escort me to the drawing room. Let's have proper tea."

He knew what she was doing. Even now she would not leave him alone in his father's lair. It came as no surprise that when his father stood up, Lady Culpepper narrowed her eyes. "You were not invited."

"This is my house!"

Henry stopped in the doorway. "Call off your dogs," he said, once more not turning around.

Even though he knew his father never would.

Tamsin went straight to Gunter's Ices.

When her brain chased itself like an irate ferret, sweet ices helped. They helped when she was sad, when she was happy.

When she was planning bloody murder.

She took a lemon ice across the street to the relative privacy of the square. It had become fashionable for women to stay in their carriages to eat their ices, but Tamsin needed the fresh spring air on her cheeks. She pushed her bonnet back, letting it dangle on its ribbons. Damn freckles and damn propriety. She understood Henry's need to be outside. She could do with a bit of sea air herself. And maybe a ship to take her far away. In books, girls always chopped their hair off and snuck onto ships. She wasn't sure it was a particularly realistic option for her, but she wouldn't rule it out entirely.

She kept the tears burning and locked behind her eyes. She would not cry. She would be Tamsin Bell, cheerful, flirtatious, witty. Especially when she did not feel like any of those things.

Better yet, she could be a Cinderella. With a reticule full of secret and surprising weapons.

After she finished her ice, and calmed the fear nibbling and biting at her, she felt like a mouse dropped into a maze. The walls were too high, the corners too tight. And she knew exactly what awaited her in the center.

Marriage to Lord Eaton.

Perhaps, if she was very lucky, she would trip and fall into the path of a runaway carriage between now and then.

Better yet, *he* would.

Because she had the very clear impression that only death or dismemberment was likely to save her now. She'd recognized the expression on Lady Chester's face, the smugness of it. The indifference in her father as long as propriety was maintained.

She smiled at a gaggle of acquaintances, leaving them behind to seek a secluded bench on which to steel her nerves. She ran through the list of possibilities, barely noticing the sun dappling the ground, the smoothness of the plane trees, the tartness of the lemon on her tongue.

She could marry Lord Eaton.

Out of the question.

Being forced to marry was bad enough, but to marry a man who did not give a fig for the people around him was untenable. Someone who groped at the maids, who trampled on those under his care, and had no respect for any woman in any situation. She'd have to murder him on their wedding day, before they even reached the connubial bed, and she wasn't particularly keen on being hanged for murder.

Not that she would cross it off the list entirely. A lady must do what must be done, after all.

Still, probably not the best route.

She *could* beg her father to reconsider. She wasn't above the attempt, but she already knew it wouldn't change her circumstances one bit. He wouldn't be moved, not by her tears. He generally followed the path of least resistance and the one that afforded him the most honor as a duke. Her stepmother knew that and would wield the knowledge like a sword. Or a club. The ones with the pointy iron bits.

She could run away.

Without money, or a way to earn any, without protection. She knew the other Cinderellas would take her in at a moment's notice, and for as long as necessary. Meg had married a duke, and Persephone would be a marchioness one day. Tamsin didn't want to be a burden, even if they would never see it as such. She did not want them to tire of her as her family had. It would have to be a last resort.

Perhaps she could find some kind of work. Having a duke's daughter as a paid companion might be worth a salary, even if she was a novelty. Tamsin knew the kinds of smirks and sneers that would be shot her way with gleeful disdain if she were among her current acquaintances in such a capacity. She would just have to bear it.

It was better than marrying Lord Eaton.

She wasn't sure it was definitive enough. The power of a duke could close all of those doors to her. No one would hire her if they thought it would incur his displeasure. And her stepmother wouldn't hesitate to do it, to get her way. And as her father did not like a fuss, he would do whatever afforded him peace and quiet, no matter the personal cost to her. Hadn't he agreed with her stepmother and moved her out of the family home in order to "bolster the prospects" of her stepsisters? She really ought to have seen this coming.

Her other option was to still marry, only someone else entirely. And quickly.

Did she have the time to find someone amiable? Someone powerful enough to take on her father? In however few days or weeks that were still available to her? She wasn't sure, but it was worth a try. She'd been thinking about it already, truth be told. In a different capacity, of course. But at some point, the quiet echoing through her house had become too sharp, too heavy. The servants were not allowed to befriend her, and the ghosts were taking their sweet time showing themselves, despite the veritable hoard of cursed and magical objects crammed into her parlor. She wished she could relish the solitude, the way Priya did. It seemed to revitalize her, to center her. But lately, it had only made Tamsin feel more adrift.

And so, marriage. To a good man. Someone who would not disdain her interests or her friends. Someone kind. Surely that was an achievable goal. Within the year, certainly. But within the week?

Unlikely.

Perhaps she might still make this a triumph. Henry was back, after all, and he was the only man she had ever wanted to marry.

He was a viscount and would be an earl someday, which would be good enough for her father. And he had always been good enough for her, despite the poison his own father had seeded in his brain.

But since she'd stood with him in an empty house wearing only her stays and he hadn't been tempted, she had to admit her luck there might be more hope than reality.

Tears threatened again. And that would not do. She needed to be Lady Tamsin Bell, Cinderella.

With a vengeance.

Chapter Nine

V ENGEANCE WAS A fine thought, especially when Lord Eaton was suddenly at her side in the quiet square, utterly ruining what was left of her lemon ice.

Yet one more offense to lay at his door.

"Lady Tamsin, what a lovely coincidence." He wore a dark green cutaway coat, a blindingly white cravat, and that infernal smile.

She gave serious thought to leaping over the iron fence and taking to the streets at a dead run. It would certainly make a statement.

Instead, she kept her smile courteous. She had already antagonized him last night; she should probably get the lay of the land before she began her true assault. Perhaps he would be reasonable.

The bruise under his left eye did not bode particularly well.

"My lord, what on earth happened to your face?"

His lip curled before he forcibly relaxed it. "Nothing worth mentioning, I assure you. I have the matter well in hand."

She didn't care, beyond hoping whoever had punched him did so again. Soon.

"May I hope you have spoken to your father?" he asked.

She put her ice down. "I have."

"Excellent."

"I'm afraid there's been some misunderstanding."

He smiled indulgently. "I understand perfectly that a week is not very long to plan your wedding. But I imagine you have been daydreaming about it for years, and I have faith in your abilities. There is no one more fashionable."

She wondered what he would do if she vomited right on his perfectly shined boots.

"I'm sorry, my lord, but I've no intention of marrying." Of marrying *him* in particular.

"What's that to with anything?" he asked, quite sincerely, and as though she was one of her own odd curios behind glass. "It's already been decided between your father and I."

To be fair, it was not an unreasonable assumption. Many marriages were organized just so.

Not hers. Not to him. Not today.

Not ever.

For one, she was no longer a girl under her legal age of majority. She might not have many rights, hardly at all, it had to be said, but surely saying no was one of them.

It wasn't.

She wasn't naïve. She knew exactly how this glittering, opulent, and political world worked. Title and peerage and wealthy connections above all. This wasn't a fairy story, nor a play upon the stage.

But neither would she be a damsel in distress. He already thought himself a knight in shining armor.

Lord Eaton mistook her simmering silence, because of course he would. "It's natural for you to be nervous and excited."

She narrowed one eye. "You caused a lot of trouble for Meg recently," she said bluntly. "You nearly got her killed with your pettiness."

He waved that away. "How was I to know collectors and historians could be so relentless? Anyway, she landed herself a duke, didn't she? She should be thanking me."

"Thanking you?" she repeated softly.

She could not marry this man.

She simply could not.

Would not.

Eaton had been so cross that Dougal had punched him at the Pendleton ball—on Meg's behalf; well done, Dougal—that he had made the secrets of hidden historical artifacts that belonged to the previous duke of Thorncroft public knowledge. And he'd added a hefty reward for their discovery. Meg and Dougal had been overrun with collectors and antiquarians and treasure hunters. Some of whom had been aggressively insistent.

"I'm not marrying you."

He reached for her arm.

A cluster of plane tree seed balls that had wintered bounced off his shoulder. He started. "What the devil?"

Tamsin thought she caught a flash of red elbow patches among the branches and did not bother to hide her grin, not until Lord Eaton glanced at her. She looked back, mild as milk. "A squirrel, perhaps, my lord."

"Indeed." He straightened his coat, clearly reaching for his dignity. "As I was saying, I'm sure you'll love being married—"

Another seed hit him, this time on the side of the head, fuzzy and prickly.

Tamsin bit down hard on the inside of her cheek to keep from laughing. Or cheering. He was right put out.

"That was not a squirrel," he said, changing his grip on his walking stick so that it resembled a cudgel more than anything. "There he is, that little shite."

He swung for Jack. Luckily, Jack Nimble was as quick and agile as his name suggested. He swung into another tree.

Tamsin grabbed for Eaton's arm when he made to follow. "My lord, he's just a boy," she said.

"He needs to be taught some manners."

Not from you. It was a struggle not to say the words out loud.

Jack had no such qualms, and shouted them from the treetops. Literally.

Lord Eaton's face turned purple. Tamsin sighed. "Jack, you're not helping," she called out.

"You know that little—"

"Language, if you please. You are not the child in this situation, my lord."

"I won't tolerate this kind of interfering behavior from my wife."

"Good thing she won't ever be your wife, then, isn't it?"

Henry.

He crossed between the trees, handsome and serious as a scholar. The kind who knew secrets to make your toes curl. Especially with the intent gleam in his eye, the slight baring of his teeth.

Oh dear. She should probably do something about that. Other than admire it and the way it made her feel warmth in dark places, of course.

"Henry, how did you find me?"

He glanced at her briefly. "It's Gunter's on a fine, warm day— where else would you be?" His smile was just as brief before he turned his attention back to Eaton, who looked as though he might actually start hissing.

"You," Eaton said.

Henry raised an eyebrow. "That eye looks like rotted meat."

He wasn't wrong. Tamsin closed her eyes briefly. "Henry."

Eaton smiled.

Shite.

"Talbot."

"Eaton."

"I'll see you on Hampstead Heath," Eaton said. "Name your seconds."

Hampstead Heath was approximately a half-hour ride north of Hyde Park, the preferred spot for duelists everywhere.

"No," Tamsin said. "You can't."

"With pleasure," Henry said at the same time, because she might love him, but he was still a pain in the backside.

"Bollocks," Tamsin muttered. Loudly, she added, "Might I remind you both that dueling is illegal." As if that would matter. Honor, and whatever other ridiculous things duelists fought to defend, was at stake.

Not only that, but they had drawn a crowd.

Tamsin couldn't flirt or charm their way out of it. That was obvious. Never more so then when Eaton smiled his oily smile. "I might accept an apology," he offered. "With the obligatory whipping."

Tamsin closed her eye briefly. Demanding a return blow meant that Henry had struck the first blow. No doubt to Eaton's left eye. "Well done, you," she murmured to him, even as fear trampled through her.

Henry didn't look afraid. He didn't look bothered at all. "I believe I'm supposed to offer *you* a whip as a symbol of remorse," he said. "Had I any."

"I'll see you at dawn, then," Eaton said.

A gasp went through the small pocket of onlookers who were pretending not to onlook.

"Lady Tamsin, may I escort you home?" Lord Eaton asked pointedly, holding out his arm.

"My carriage waits just there," she replied.

He was not pleased.

He could bloody well get in line, because she wasn't pleased either. About any of it.

She waited until he was gone, and the others had wandered off to spread the news. "What the hell, Henry?"

"A moment," he said before reaching up into the tree and grabbing hold of Jack's ankle.

Jack tried to kick him. "Leave off, toff!"

"You'll have to reach the eagle's nest faster than that when there's a captain around, lad." Henry only passed one of his cards up into the branches. "If you see that other toff, or anyone dodgy, around Lady Tamsin again, you send word to me at this address. And notify the man near her house, likely with long black hair. Crow."

"Why should I?"

"Because we both want to keep her safe. And there's a guinea in it for you."

For that astronomical sum, Tamsin thought Jack might learn to fly. He grabbed for the card, and when Henry released him, he scampered off.

"Wait!" Tamsin shouted. She sighed, frustrated. "I wasn't finished with him." She turned on her heel, eyes narrowed.

"What man watching my house, pray tell?"

"Someone broke in through your window last night," Henry pointed out. "I'm not having it."

She didn't mention that a certain someone had broken in again and stolen Vasilisa. Not just yet.

"You're not seriously going to duel him, are you?"

"Jack? Of course not, he's just a boy."

"*Henry Talbot.*"

"Of course I am."

"You *know* his reputation."

He shrugged nonchalantly.

"If you kill him," she reminded him, "it still counts as murder, even if you're a viscount."

He shrugged again.

"You never used to be so infuriating."

He almost smiled.

She shook her head. "I can't believe you gave him a black eye! How did you even know my father's agreed to our betrothal? *I* didn't know about it until just an hour ago."

Henry turned his head. Cold fury marked his face, darker, deeper than any ocean. His voice was quiet and no less daunting for it. "I beg your pardon?"

"You didn't know?"

"I did not."

"What did you punch him for, then?"

"For being an arse."

When he started to stalk away, she darted to catch up. "Where are you going now?"

"To punch him again."

"No, you're bloody not," she informed him. "You're going to see me home."

"Am I now?"

She slipped her arm through his and clung like an obstinate barnacle. "You are."

They went down the walkway, passing servants risking life and limb to dash through the traffic, carrying trays of ices in glass cups for various customers waiting on benches. The sun was still bright; it was a perfect spring day. No one seemed to notice that Henry had just put himself in very great danger. Again.

A duel, of all things.

"You are a lot of work," she muttered.

"I was going to say the same of you," he returned fondly. It was that warm tone that weakened her knees as much as the sharp darkness he had acquired in the last year. The combination was compelling. Distracting.

He handed her up into the carriage, where a note been left on the seat. She recognized the seal, and Priya's handwriting inside. *Come and see me as soon as you can. I have information.*

Henry stayed on the pavement.

"Aren't you coming?" she asked.

"No, I have my second to notify."

"Henry. You can't be serious."

"It's too late for that, Tam," he said softly. "And just think, when I murder him, you won't have to marry him."

She wouldn't be able to marry Henry either, as he'd be hanged.

She didn't get a chance to tell him that. He'd already bowed and walked away. She watched him until he turned a corner and was out of sight. "To Lady Langdon's, please," she called up to the coachman.

"Yes, your ladyship."

There were many ways to win a duel.

You only had to be creative.

PRIYA'S REPUTATION FOR a preternatural ability to gather secrets and information was not unfounded. She'd heard about Tamsin's betrothal at approximately the same moment Tamsin was informed and had sent word as soon as she could. She didn't know about the rash of housebreakings the previous night, and she was quite put out by it.

She hadn't known about the duel yet either, of course. Tamsin had brought the news, along with a rant about male egos and antiquated rules of honor that should not apply, as Lord Eaton clearly had no honor to begin with.

They were in Priya's hothouse, tucked into a veritable jungle of orchids and lilies and lemon trees. It smelled green and fresh and loamy. Priya wore her usual work apron, and her glossy black hair was bound with tiny pearl pins in the shape of flowers. A tea tray had been brought out, and Tamsin accepted a cup and then promptly forgot to drink it as she paced between the leaves.

Her head was spinning. There was simply too much to sort through.

Her tea had not even cooled before Persephone marched into the hothouse, tossing her bonnet so that it landed in an orange tree. "Our friend, Henry," she announced, "and my husband, your idiot brother"—this aside to Priya—"have done an idiotic thing. Like idiots."

"I know," Tamsin said from where she had paced herself into a clutch of ferns. "I was there."

"Conall has offered himself as Henry's third," Persephone said.

"His *third?*" He would definitely not be talked out of this. That much was abundantly clear. "Is that even something people do?"

"Apparently, he already has a second. His former first lieutenant. Conall's already gone off to find a discreet doctor to attend." Persephone dropped into a chair. "They are trying to kill me." Her eyes were wide, panicked. "We have to stop them."

"Short of murdering Eaton ourselves, I'm not sure how to manage that," Tamsin said. They paused, considering.

It was a long pause.

Very long.

Tamsin made a face. "Best not."

"Spoilsport," Persephone muttered. "We could wrap his body in cloths and pretend he was a mummy. No one would know."

"Tempting."

"I've been trying to find dirt on him since the Pendleton ball," Priya said, thoroughly disgruntled. "I know he's hiding something, but I can't seem to ferret it out."

"You will," Tamsin said loyally.

"Not before this cursed duel."

"Then we will have to think of something else," she said. "We always do." Their eyes met. "We always do," she repeated.

"Exactly." Priya handed her a small cloth bag that smelled pungent. "You'll need this."

Tamsin nodded. "I bloody well will. The usual?"

"Yes, I put it together the moment I heard of your betrothal."

They all smiled at each other, gentle, honed weapons of chaos.

Persephone paused. "Wait, what betrothal?"

Tamsin finally dropped into a chair. "Ah, yes, that. Because today isn't dismal enough."

Persephone frowned. "Am I going to need a fresh pot of tea?"

"Whiskey."

"Bloody hell."

Priya pulled out the whiskey bottle she kept tucked away with her potting tools and wiped pollen off green glass goblets. "I also made sure this was full when I heard the news."

"What in the world has happened?" Persephone asked.

"My father," Tamsin said. "And Lord Eaton."

Persephone didn't need further elaboration. She physically recoiled. "Absolutely not."

"Apparently I am to be married this week."

"*This week?*"

Persephone took a sip of whiskey. Tamsin went for a considerably larger mouthful. It burned all the way down into her stomach. Priya refilled her glass immediately. She really did have the best of friends. If only Meg weren't in the country.

"Well?" Persephone asked. "What are we going to do about this?"

"We?"

She leveled a stare worthy of Cleopatra. "Tamsin Bell. I will put scorpions in your shoes if you imply that we are not with you, whatever your plans."

Tamsin smiled, and it finally did not feel like a grimace on her face. "I'm sorry."

"As you should be. We have several invitations for tonight. I wasn't going to accept, but I shall see if I can overhear anything of use."

Persephone's talent for eavesdropping was as honed as Priya's instinct for secrets and Meg's abilities to pick a pocket clean. Tamsin's only current gifts involved flirting. Depressing thought. She shoved it aside.

"Eavesdropping was easier when I wasn't a countess, to be sure, but I can still manage it. Conall makes it doubly difficult, I must say."

"Does it make him cross?"

"No. He's just too damned good-looking, and people won't stop gaping."

Tamsin laughed. "I see. Your problems *are* legendary."

"I suppose I could use it to my advantage. Let him be the misdirection." Persephone brightened. "That could work."

Tamsin hugged her. "I do love you, Percy." She touched Priya's hand across the table. "And you."

"And we love you back. Which is why you will not be marrying that toad Eaton."

"Agreed," Priya added.

"You know you can always come stay with Conall and me," Persephone offered. "We could hide you in a mummy's case, if we had to. I have a lovely, large specimen in the dining room. Not the same one I'd use for Eaton's corpse, of course."

"I appreciate that." She did. And best, Persephone would not bat an eyelash if Tamsin brought several skulls and a cursed tablet begging for the victim's eyeballs to turn to water.

"Meg would do the same. Not to mention the Duke of Pendleton."

"And I," Priya said. "You are always welcome here. I've already had a room made up."

"Thank you." It was humbling. And it made Tamsin feel a bit ashamed for still feeling lonely and strangely melancholy. The fluttering of dread and panic she laid squarely at Henry's feet. The rest might be ennui, but she had never had ennui and did not intend to start now. "I appreciate it, I truly do. But let's see what I can do to save myself first. Well, Henry tomorrow, then myself."

"Fair enough. What are our other options?"

"I could run away and become a spinster aunt to your children." She paused. The whiskey made her muscles feel a little looser, and some of the tension dissipated. "Ruination?"

Persephone, ruined before she turned twenty, paused as well. "I don't think you'd care for it," she said carefully.

"The sex?"

She rolled her eyes. "Not that."

"Good, because you remember Lord West and Mr. Copenhagen."

"Both very nice men," Persephone said.

Tamsin smirked. "You have no idea."

"Yes, we do." Priya grinned. "You wouldn't stop talking about them."

Tamsin grinned back. "They were worth talking about." Ladies, especially duke's daughters, were of course meant to come to the wedding bed as virgins. Which might be fine at eighteen, but to Tamsin's mind, ridiculous at twenty-eight, if it was not your choice. Discretion was the key. And since it could too easily be used as a weapon against her, why not use it on her own behalf?

"Are they worth marrying?" Persephone asked.

"Unfortunately not." Tamsin sighed. "West has since married, and Copenhagen moved to Italy to pursue art."

"Blast."

"Quite."

"We'll need a list, I think." Persephone pulled a small hand-sewn notebook from her reticule, along with a pencil. It made Tamsin feel better for some reason, that her friend was still more likely to carry pencils than perfume and pearl pins. Persephone followed her gaze. "I had these made for Egypt, so I could keep track of everything we saw. They are terribly useful." She pulled a face. "I can't draw as well as Meg, of course, but I can get by."

"Rembrandt didn't draw as well as Meg."

"True. Anyway, lists are more useful for me. And for you, tonight. Where shall we start? Lord Summers? He always dances with you."

Tamsin nodded slowly. "And Mr. Watson. They always save

me from the toe-steppers and the bores. And I save them from the ladies who are not above subterfuge to trap a husband." She winced. "I suppose I'm one of them now."

"Don't be ridiculous," Persephone said. "You're not scheming, for one. You're *planning*. And it's not as if you're forcing anyone to Gretna Green by the point of a musket. You will ask them politely, and they will be lucky to have you."

"I suppose."

"The real question is, is there anyone you fancy? If it has to be now, at least let the *who* be your decision."

Henry. Always Henry.

Could it be that simple? Could she turn this mess into something that might make her happy? Finally?

Priya rolled her eyes at the silence. "We all know how you feel about Henry. Stop being such a cabbage."

Trepidation wormed through Tamsin. She had stood alone with him, in her stays, in the middle of the night. And nothing. She had been in love with him for years, had turned down offers of marriage, had designed elaborate daydreams of his return. He would take her in his arms and declare his undying love.

But now the moment was here.

And the truth might hurt more than any duel.

"What if he says no?"

She wouldn't even have the daydreams then.

"He's not going to say no," Persephone scoffed. "Tamsin, what have you got to lose?"

Well, when it was put like that…

Something close to excitement kindled inside her.

"This is your chance," Persephone insisted. "Marry someone you actually love. You have to *try*. I've never known you not to *try*."

Persephone was right. If Tamsin was willing to ask Summers and Watson, whose given names she did not even know, then why not Henry?

Why turn cowardly now?

"Either way, try not to worry." Persephone patted her knee. "We took down a murdering traitor. We can handle Eaton." She said his name the same way she would have said the name of someone who had broken something ancient and priceless inside a barrow.

"My father…"

"Can be dealt with."

Tamsin had to smile. "That sounded ominous."

"He's just a man, Tam."

"And a duke."

"We are the Cinderellas. What's a duke to that?"

Chapter Ten

TAMSIN ATTENDED THE next ball wearing a stunning beaded silk dress and a smile sharper and brighter than the moon, weapons all. Diamonds glittered around her throat, in her hair, from her earlobes. She drank champagne, she danced, she teased. She was here to be noticed. Remembered.

So there would be no questioning her later.

It had to be tonight, and it had to be now. She had considered visiting Eaton at his house at dawn, but there were too many ways it could go wrong. And if her father heard about it, it would be too late anyway. If anyone at all suspected her, it would be too late.

It was already too late, in so many ways.

She straightened her shoulders. She absolutely would not give in to the wobbles. It was safest to carry this out in a crowded, boisterous house. She had a pocket full of mischief, and the very best of friends at her back.

Eaton didn't stand a chance.

It was surprisingly easy to move through the glittering mob on an errand of subterfuge, with a bright smile and a saucy wink. Women were accustomed to doing any number of things while wearing a polite, demure smile to hide the silent screaming. It was a skill she had long ago mastered, if not to hide anger, than at least to hide disappointment. Sorrow. All of which everyone here could choke on tonight.

Henry wasn't here. That made it easier. He saw her too clearly and would most definitely question her demeanor.

Eaton barely knew her, cared only for himself, her dowry, and the expected accolades. To that end, he had, of course, whispered their engagement into the ear of every notorious gossip. Tamsin received an equal number of glances filled with pity as with envy. She accepted the congratulations and pretended a shyness that only hid the disdain in her eyes from those who did not think to look for it. Violin music followed her about the ballroom.

Lord Eaton stopped her, impeccable in his blue coat and breeches. His hair was so artfully tousled that it only enhanced his general resemblance to a Greek statue. Too cold, too perfect, and too blank-eyed. She preferred Henry's new darkness, the scar through his eyebrow. She wasn't an idiot, after all.

"Lady Tamsin." Lord Eaton bowed. His bruised eye made her feel quite desperate to gloat. She curtsied instead, feeling the weight of the attention of at least half of the guests in attendance. "Have you met my sister? Lady Mirabelle Dunham?"

Tamsin curtsied again, recognizing her as Miss Stewart's friend from the Cabinet of Curiosities. It made sense now why she had looked so familiar.

Lady Mirabelle curtsied back, her smile both warm and curious. Her curls were the same buttery color as Eaton's, her eyes the same shade of blue. "Lady Tamsin, it's a pleasure to see you again. I've always wanted a sister."

Tamsin, who had two sisters who might dissuade Mirabelle of that notion, smiled. "Nothing's been settled yet, I'm afraid," she murmured.

Lord Eaton laughed too loudly. "This again? It's done, my dear. Best to accept it. Feigned coyness isn't you, after all."

Mirabelle turned a censorious glare in her brother's direction. "Philip, honestly." She smiled again at Tamsin. "Men."

Lord Eaton frowned. "What?"

"Do try some manners," Mirabelle whispered. "Romance, brother."

"Oh, it's that way, is it?" He winked at Tamsin, though it was closer to a leer, an invitation. She told herself not to gag. Not with so many people watching. Not yet. He pressed a kiss to the back of her glove. It would be so easy to punch him. Right in his perfect nose.

Alas.

A footman, bless him, passed by with a tray of champagne. She disentangled herself on the pretense of claiming a glass.

Eaton refused one. "Can't abide the stuff. Surely you've got some port laid away somewhere?"

Tamsin drifted away at the first opportunity. A glass of port would be the perfect camouflage. She followed the footman until he returned with the drink, but he did not once pause to leave it unattended. She floated around the gaming room, trying to get close to Eaton's glass, but to no avail. She couldn't even get near his plate at supper.

This was going to take something more direct.

More dangerous, too.

It would have been much more preferable had she been able to carry out her plan with the relative safety of the ball around her, but sometimes, a little devilry was called for. Surely saving the life of the man she loved was one of those occasions.

Saving her *own* life.

SHE SLEPT IN her gown that night so as not to have to wake her maid to help her dress. It was risky enough that the coachman would know she had come down to saddle a horse before dawn. He, at least, was easier to bribe.

Climbing into a saddle while wearing a ballgown was tricky.

Very, very tricky.

She let the skirts ride up to her knees and hoped her long cloak would cover her well enough. At least it was still dark, and the streets were empty. She had forgotten about the man Henry had set to watch her house. He stood across the street, only visible when he moved out of the shadows upon noticing her. He had long, straight black hair and the same kind of quiet wariness Henry had gained since the war. She waved at him. He looked briefly startled and then inclined his head politely.

"Mr. Crow, I presume?"

"Just Crow, my lady." He frowned at her. "You're not going off alone?"

She smiled. "Quite."

"I'm not sure Captain Talbot would approve."

"Well, someone has to save him from himself." She raised an eyebrow. "And he asked you to watch my house, did he not?"

He raised his eyebrow back, dry as toast. "I'm sure he'd prefer I watch over *you*, my lady."

"Well, I shan't be alone for long."

"I'm not sure that's a comfort."

She laughed. "Now you sound just like him. It's a bit damp out here—why don't you go around to the kitchen? Cook will be up soon, and you can have some breakfast."

"I don't think—"

"Pish," she interrupted him. "Watching my house and keeping it secure would be all that much easier from inside, I am sure. And why not do so with a cup of tea and a full belly?" She urged her horse into a walk. "Ta, Mr. Crow!"

LONDON'S UBIQUITOUS YELLOW smog was her only companion for several minutes. The gas lamps struggled to fight their way through the gloom. The echo of her horse's hooves on the cobblestones announced her like a church bell. A cat darted away, hissing.

Lord Eaton's house was not far from her own, closer to Grosvenor Square. As close you could get without being inside of it, actually. The door knocker was gilded and shined to a sunny glow, even in the dim light. Lamps burned upstairs. He was awake.

Of course he was awake—he was planning to kill Henry in less than an hour.

The coachman came down the lane from the mews, surprised to find a lady on the road. She handed him the reins. "I won't be but a moment," she assured him.

The butler was less surprised to find a lady on the doorstep at this ungodly hour.

"Lord Eaton is not at home," he intoned.

"Certainly he is." Tamsin brushed past him with a cheery smile. "He's about to head off for an illegal duel, and I am here to talk him out of it." She patted his arm. "It's quite all right, we are betrothed."

"Your ladyship?" He straightened. "I mean to say, he is still above stairs."

"Then I shall have some tea while I wait," she said. Finally, some good luck. "I assume his breakfast has been served in the breakfast room?"

"Yes, your ladyship?"

Poor fellow.

"Excellent, I am parched." She sailed away, and he scrambled to catch up and overtake her to at least preserve the semblance that he had chosen to guide her.

The breakfast room was quite pretty, pale blues and painted friezes. She'd have preferred hating it.

She sat down in front of the tea tray, ignoring the tantalizing aromas of toasted bread with cheese, rashers of bacon, and coddled eggs on the sideboard. She only had a moment. The poor butler was no doubt running up the servant stairs as fast as his polished shoes could take him.

She opened her reticule, added the dried herbs to a cup, and then covered it with sugar. She poured her own tea and set it on her left. She was drinking it demurely when Lord Eaton came through the door. He was a bit gray around the gills. That would help.

"Lady Tamsin, this is a surprise."

"Is it?"

"Bit risqué for you, isn't it?"

She shrugged one shoulder. She would not let him see an ounce of fear. He was going to try to use this moment to ruin her, that much she knew. She just had to ruin him first.

"Shall I pour?" she asked, leaning into the role of the lady of the house. If only for the briefest moment.

He smirked, utterly misunderstanding her. "By all means."

She filled his teacup as a footman rushed in, still half-asleep, to serve Eaton his breakfast. Tamsin shook her head when the same was offered to her.

"I have come, my lord, to ask you not to follow through with this duel."

He bit into toast cut into perfect points. "Too late for that now."

"It seems an odd form of courtship to attempt to murder one of my childhood friends," she pointed out.

"Such softness does you credit, I'm sure," he said more than a little patronizingly. The yolks of his eggs oozed out when he poked them with a fork. "But you cannot understand the nature of male honor. An insult must be met. I am of course sorry that you had to witness such a thing. But it will be over soon."

By that he meant Henry would be seriously injured. Or worse, dead.

More than likely dead, considering Eaton's history with duels. Nothing that could be proven, of course, but everyone knew of the four men he had already killed on Hampstead Heath. If not outright, then through the lingering pain of a festering wound.

She had tried.

Let it not be said that she had not at least attempted a different resolution.

Truth be told, she was vengeful enough to be more than a little pleased that she clearly had no alternative now.

Needs must.

"You look unwell," she said, all false concern. She pushed the doctored tea toward him. "My father swears by sweetened tea when his head is sore of a morning."

"I suppose if it's good enough for a duke, eh?"

She'd been counting on it. As well as his hangover.

He drank the hot tea in three gulps.

She smiled sweetly. "More?"

"No." He wiped his mouth and tossed his napkin aside. "And you should go."

She stood gracefully.

"Of course."

THOUGH THE SITUATION was less than ideal, something about the heath in the cold, glowing hours of dawn put Henry to mind of the same kind of morning at sea. The dewdrops gleamed; the mists rose and fell. There was a softness and a hard glitter, a silence and a chorus. It grounded him in a way he could not adequately explain. But enough to kill a man?

Yes, if it came to it.

For Tamsin.

For Persephone and Priya and Meg and the others.

He'd found Pierce at the Rose and Anchor and asked him to stand as his second. It probably wasn't done, to choose a man who was not from the peerage. But they'd stood shoulder to shoulder under cannon fire, and against the fickle, furious sea. Eaton was nothing to that.

Conall, who had not been invited, just showed up. He claimed himself Henry's third and would not be turned away, even when Persephone pointed out there was no such thing. She had been furious not to be his second. Henry didn't blame Conall; he was likely trying to save his wife from harm as much as him.

The doctor waited under the elm trees, his case in hand. The pistols were cleaned, loaded, ready. The sun glittered on the horizon. Eaton's second paced nervously through the tall grass.

Lord Eaton was nowhere to be seen.

And his second would have to fight in his place, should he not show up.

Henry didn't believe Eaton would back out of this duel, not for one moment. Something else was afoot.

"I'm sure he'll be here shortly," Eaton's second said. He was starting to sweat off the pomade in his hair.

"Better be, mate," Pierce said mildly, leaning against a tree trunk. He looked bored, which Henry knew to be untrue. The same way Conall's amused grin hid more clever calculations than most people could guess at. "Else I hope you know what to do with a pistol. Because this one's a Navy man."

The second drew up, offended. But not so offended that he could do much more than dab at the sweat on his forehead. Henry took that to mean that he was, in fact, not good with a pistol. Whether due to his obvious hangover or his skillset, Henry did not know. Did not much care. He had no intention of shooting a green-gilled, sweating bloke too stupid not to make friends with someone like Eaton. Shooting fish in a barrel was hardly a test of honor or proficiency.

The beat of horse hooves broke through the chill morning air. Dewdrops splintered and scattered. The second looked nearly nauseated with relief, then just nauseated as the rider turned out to be a messenger and not Eaton, after all.

"What the devil is going on now?" Conall murmured.

They had their answer soon enough.

Not from the messenger, who only bent down to hand the second a letter.

Not from the doctor, who seemed as confused as everyone else.

But from the thunder and tremble of three more horses, cantering into view, the sun rising in sharp spears of light behind them.

Henry recognized Tamsin from her silhouette alone. She slid out of the saddle, flanked by Persephone and Priya. They walked together, like a fashionable militia parade, in silver beads, green velvet, gold buttons.

Pierce watched them all like they were mad, but Priya most of all. Subtly. In the way only Pierce could. Meaning that he did not look her way once, but Henry knew damn well the lieutenant knew exactly where she was standing, what she was wearing, and right down to the color of her eyes. He pushed slowly off the tree.

"I've just felt the cold iron of Old Scratch himself enter my soul," Pierce muttered.

"Amen," Conall agreed, shooting his wife a look of both scolding and fondness.

Despite the circumstances, Henry couldn't quite fight a smile of his own.

"Well, they do know how to make an entrance."

Tamsin was only sorry she didn't have a sword, something suitably impressive, such as Excalibur. She felt better than she had since her conversation with her father, since Vasilisa had been taken. She felt like a Cinderella.

She lifted her chin when Henry stalked toward her, looking every inch a naval captain. He was unfairly handsome, his mouth stern, his eyes clever and clear.

"What's this, then?" he asked.

"Eaton's not coming."

"Yes, I gathered that." Behind him, the second's voice rose to a squeak as he babbled to the messenger. "What have you done, Tamsin?"

Henry's gaze was like a hand around her throat, stealing her breath. Oddly, it was not unwelcome. She wondered what that said about her. Giddiness threatened to froth and bubble through her. "I'm sure I don't know what you mean, captain," she returned archly.

Behind them, Conall went to his wife. "Percy, you said you'd wait for me at home."

Persephone stood on her tiptoes to kiss him. "Well, if you believed that, it's your own fault."

"She has a point, brother," Priya said.

The second interrupted, tugging at his cravat as if it was a noose. "News from Lord Eaton."

Henry did not look away from Tamsin. "And?"

"He's… not coming."

He snapped his head to the side, pinning the unfortunate man in place. "What?"

"He forfeits?" Conall asked, stunned.

"He's taken ill, I'm afraid."

"Convenient, that," Pierce said mildly.

"A doctor has been summoned," the second insisted, insulted. He finally noticed the women and started. He bowed jerkily, nervously. "Ladies."

"So you'll be fighting in his place, then," Pierce said flatly. "Bad luck for you, mate."

The second's throat rippled as if he was choking on air. "No… but… That is, Lord Eaton really has taken ill."

"That's not how duels work," Conall reminded him.

"He's *quite* ill. Cramps and tremors and"—the man winced at the presence of ladies—"other unfortunate symptoms."

Tamsin knew the exact moment that Henry realized what she had done.

She had slipped those same herbs into his father's drink more than once, silent revenge for the bruises Henry wore the way other boys wore waistcoats. Priya knew exactly which to mix together and how much went into a cup.

Tamsin smiled at the sweating second. "What a pity," she said. "Perhaps he just needs a purging." She fluttered her eyelashes innocently. "I suppose that means he reneges, then, and honor is satisfied."

"Er…"

"That does make sense," Persephone interjected.

"As much as any of this idiocy makes sense," Priya muttered.

"It's complicated," the second said.

"It's really not," Pierce said. "The rules are clear. Eaton didn't show, therefore as his second, the captain here, or the viscount if you lot prefer, gets to shoot at you."

The man gulped. It was reasonable to assume he was not a fair shot. Eaton would never have imagined he wasn't going to prevail. He would have looked for blind loyalty in a second and wouldn't even have considered the ramifications beyond that.

And now his second looked like he was going to vomit.

No doubt exactly like Eaton at this very moment.

Tamsin stepped back.

Henry sighed. "At ease. I'm not going to shoot you."

"You're not? Er, I mean, of course you're not."

Pierce snorted.

Conall just shook his head. "You need better friends."

This shocked the second more than anything. "Lord Eaton is an *earl*."

"And an ass."

Henry shrugged. "It hardly signifies. Word will be out by breakfast that he did not bother to attend his own challenge. In the meantime…" He raised an eyebrow at Tamsin. "Tamsin?"

She smirked. "Yes?"

"A word."

He backed her to the edge of a small grove of oak trees. She let him, because a thrill went through her at the way he stalked toward her. The way his eyes flared then narrowed, the clench of his jaw, the slash of his eyebrows lowering.

"Tell me you didn't go to Eaton's house alone before dawn."

"Of course I did."

He cursed. "Do you have any idea what could have happened to you?"

She narrowed her eyes, suddenly less thrilled. "Henry, I have been dealing with men like Eaton my entire life. I know *exactly* what could have happened."

"Then why put yourself in that danger?" He was trying not to shout.

She did not try. "To save your life, you ungrateful turnip!"

He shook his head. "Did you just call me a turnip?"

She flashed a grin, still angry, but mostly just fired up. "If you don't like it, pray, stop acting like one."

"Tam, I'm a better shot than you think I am."

She pinched the bridge of her nose to stave off the headache brewing. "Which only means to say they would have hanged you for murder when you shot Eaton," she pointed out. "Forgive me if I don't consider that much of a consolation prize. Or a testament to your skills. Or intelligence." She glowered. "See aforementioned turnip."

"I'm not fourteen anymore," he said quietly.

"Neither am I."

"And I'm not on the run anymore, either. You don't have to keep saving my life," he added.

"I won't have to when you stop insisting on putting it in danger!"

"I'm not yours to save, Tam."

"Of course you are," she snapped. The wind moved through the leaves at her back, tossing them around. She felt the same. She was the sunshine, the wind, the topsy-turvy trees.

"I'm not the Cinderellas' pet, though it's an honor, I'm sure." He stalked closer, stopping in front of her, just out of reach.

Always out of reach.

"That's not why." She wanted to call him something other than a turnip.

"Then why?"

The man was clever, skilled, broodingly handsome.

He was also stupid, apparently.

"Because I love you, you idiot!"

Chapter Eleven

T HE WORDS ECHOED around her.

She wouldn't take them back.

Not even when he stared at her that way, hopeful, stunned, shuttered.

She struggled to keep her voice light. "That can't come as a surprise, Henry."

He closed his eyes briefly, as if he was in pain. When he looked at her again, she could no longer read his expression—it was too calm, too *military*.

Either way, he didn't look particularly interested.

It was lowering.

"I can't marry you, Tamsin."

Not just lowering, heartbreaking.

He spoke gently, carefully. He didn't want to hurt her feelings. She'd hurt them enough already all by herself. She tried to keep her smile in place even as a part of her withered.

This wasn't how this was supposed to go. They were supposed to save each other. And he was supposed to *want* to.

She was as vain and flighty as Society accused and praised her of being. She'd thought there was more to his regard than there was. There was pain simmering, waiting to cut deep, but right now she felt oddly numb. Apart from her own body.

"I didn't mean a real betrothal, of course," she added, even though she *absolutely* had meant it. She just needed to undo this new brittleness, this odd tension between them.

She'd ruined everything.

"Just for a little while, to buy me some time," she continued, as if her entire life hadn't just burned to ashes in a single moment.

I can't marry you, Tamsin.

"You would cry off eventually." She tried to inject some levity into the conversation, which was suddenly heavy as a boulder in her lap. It might crush her if she let it. "We could tell everyone my collection of cursed poppets gave you indigestion."

His mouth twitched in a smile, but only for a moment. "Even then."

"It was silly to consider it," she hurried to add. "Never mind."

"It's not silly, it's just impossible."

She swallowed. "Do you have someone else in mind?" Why hadn't it occurred to her that he might already have a sweetheart? She would have to move to France. No, France wasn't far enough. Italy. Just for a month. Or two. A hundred. "A secret love?"

"No."

And just like that, she could breathe again.

Mostly.

"We should get back," Henry said. "People will start to talk if they find you were missing before dawn. And I guarantee Eaton will use it to his advantage now."

"He always would have." She wouldn't regret her actions. Better to burn everything down around her than be tied to the stake.

Let them talk. The gossip didn't scare her, not now, when Henry said he could not marry her. He'd never said he wouldn't have her, though, had he? Nor that he *wouldn't* marry her. Only that he *couldn't*.

Hope whispered.

Obviously, she was as flighty as everyone thought. Still.

There was time to sulk and then there was a time to act. And if she did not act immediately, it would be too late. The carriage was ready to barrel down the road, and it would drag her with it if she didn't find a way to break the wheels.

Soon.

Now.

Because there was one more option left to her that did not involve some kind of bodily accident or miracle.

Ruination.

It was quicker. And it was *far* more enjoyable than her other choices.

Tricky, complicated, and not without its own perils. But still, to be ruined would narrow her marriage options considerably. Her father would be furious. But she definitely wouldn't have to marry Eaton. Someone like him would never endanger his dignity with a scandalous wife.

But only if she ruined herself before he managed to ruin her first.

And she might, *just might*, get a night with Henry.

Finally.

Perhaps it was only the institution of marriage that he opposed. Not her, specifically?

She stood slowly, feeling more exposed than she had while standing in her shift and stays. She had already made herself desperately vulnerable. She may as well give her own happiness one more try. Before she ran out of time. He had gone to war; she could be brave in her own way.

"Ruination."

He sucked in a breath. "I beg your pardon?"

"And it will have to be *quite* thorough."

"You can't be serious."

"Of course I'm serious." Suddenly she was enjoying his discomfiture. She tossed her hair over her shoulder. She always left a few curls loose for this very reason. Flirtation, after all, was a battle, with moves and countermoves.

His eyes followed the gleam of gold, the shoulder bared by her ballgown. He swallowed, his throat muscles working as though it was difficult. And then his eyes narrowed. "Tamsin."

"Yes?"

"What are you saying? You're going to snatch up the first gentleman that crosses your path and suggest a public liaison?

Dear God, there will be a stampede."

"Of course not."

"Thank Christ for that, at least."

"Not just *any* gentleman," she continued. "*You.*"

How could she love a turnip so desperately? It was most unfair.

He did not speak for a full, long moment. Nor did he look away. Something in him went deadly still and deadly alert. It made her mouth dry, promised things to her body that she sincerely hoped he would follow through on, even though he looked as edgy as he did hungry. Even though he had already turned her down.

She made another attempt at levity. "You've already undressed me once this week, after all." *Please, say yes.*

His breath came out in a rush. "You are not asking me to ruin you," he said hoarsely. "You can't know what you're saying."

She tilted her head to the side. "Henry, I am nearly thirty years old. I know exactly what I'm saying. And what I want you to do to me."

Heat flared in his eyes. It was like being looked at by a pirate. There was an answering flutter in her belly, a tingle between her legs. She was surprised the air between them didn't catch fire.

It was encouraging. Very, very encouraging.

She stepped closer, until she could smell the salt sea and soap of him. As if he was already touching her. She poured every ounce of her considerable expertise with social graces into her smile, her voice, the brush of her fingertips over his lapels. "Have you never thought about it? Not even once?"

He was watching her as though she was dangerous. It made her feel powerful, giddy. Her stays were suddenly too tight, the silk of her dress too much.

"Well?" she pressed when he didn't answer. *Please, please, say yes.*

She was close enough now that she had to look up at him. She nearly let her breasts brush against his chest, nearly, but not quite.

"I've thought about it. About your mouth. Your hands on my

bare skin."

She had never been this wanton before, this forthright.

His jaw clenched, and then his fists. He was forcing himself not to reach for her. Happiness was a tiny flower in her chest that she could not fuss over, but she would protect it. Remember it.

"You don't have to marry me," she added. "If that's what you're still worried about."

The words were like thorns in her throat. She ignored the scrape and stab of it.

He finally swallowed, and the desire in his eyes banked, though it still smoldered. The rest of his expression turned carefully neutral. Disappointment was an unwelcome chill, even before he spoke. The charged energy between them remained, but it was controlled now. He was Viscount Stirling again.

"Tamsin, we can't."

She wouldn't let him see that his refusal shot straight to that little flower in her chest and tore at the petals. She lifted her chin, every inch the confident, irreverent duke's daughter. She even shrugged one shoulder nonchalantly, even though it was just another lie. He had every right to refuse her, and every right not to be chastised for it. "Pity," she said through the awful constriction in her throat. "I suppose I shall have to find someone else to kiss me."

His eyes narrowed. "I said I wouldn't ruin you," he murmured, closing in suddenly, forcing her back into the dark privacy of the trees. "I never said anything about not kissing you."

She'd never imagined he could be so intense.

And she'd imagined rather a lot, actually. She'd had years to build her daydreams, after all.

One moment she was standing at the edge of the grove, trying not to appear as dismal as she felt, and the next, the leaves had swallowed them up. Only his hands and the trunk behind her held her up. Her legs, certainly, had forgotten how. Every part of her that wasn't focused on where he touched her, and how, simply ceased to exist.

The warmth and steel of him blocked out the woods, the heath, all of London. He cradled her face, tilting it up toward him, digging his fingers into her hair. His knee was poised between her legs, teasing, sending sparks shooting through her. She waited for him to kiss her, his mouth a scant inch from hers. His eyes glittered; his mouth crooked into a faint smile.

She could grow quite obsessed with the crook of his mouth.

But still he waited.

Patiently, though the slight curl to his lip suggested he was using all of his reserves of willpower to stay where he was. It was delicious. Heady.

He hadn't spoken, but he was waiting for an answer. As if she hadn't said yes, screamed it at him inside her mind, for years now.

She lifted her chin: a dare, and a request. "Go on, then."

It was all he needed. Those invisible chains shattered, he captured her mouth with his, and it was hungry and desperate and thrilling. She kissed him back with all of the pent-up frustration and need that she had carried with her since he left for the war, all of those years ago. He sucked at her tongue, and she moaned into his mouth, and she wasn't even embarrassed about it. What were rules and polite flirtations and cool, dignified responses to this? Nothing. Absolutely nothing.

He pressed her harder against the tree, hands traveling over her, one along the curve of her waist, the other gripping the back of her neck. She was pinned, as if he was afraid that she might disappear. It amplified every curl of desire burning through her. She smoothed her palms under his coat, itching for the feel of his warm muscles. Itching for more, for everything.

When he finally tore his mouth from hers, she was panting. He trailed his lips along her jaw, nipping at her throat, her earlobe. Her hands curled into his waistcoat. He chuckled softly, darkly, and heat throbbed between her legs. Her thighs went soft. He slid his knee between them, pushing against her most intimate place.

She might actually turn into a candle, burning herself into nothing.

And she'd do so with a smile on her face.

She'd been kissed before: kissed in dark gardens, touched in secret rendezvous, caressed by candlelight. None of it compared to this single moment, dressed in far too many layers of hateful clothing, held against the sturdy roughness of an oak tree. He was hard against her hip, and she squirmed until he groaned. Until he panted her name, once, like it was ripped from him.

She wouldn't burn alone. That much she could promise herself. No matter what happened next.

Because he was already coming back to himself. She felt the shift, as if he was donning more layers, there the captain, and then the viscount. No longer simply Henry, the man, who threatened to consume her.

She tightened her hold, even as he tore his mouth from hers, catching his ragged breath. His hair fell over his forehead, tickling her. She was still perched on his thigh, and his hands were still in her hair, then dropping to her jaw.

He tilted her head back, his eyes blazing. She thought he might kiss her again—indeed, he lowered his mouth until it was so close that not even a breeze could come between them.

And then he stepped back.

The bastard stepped back, looking as cool as a ship's captain was expected to look. While she felt wonderfully disheveled and desperate. He only bowed, polite to the end.

And then he walked away.

Her only consolation was that he didn't just walk—rather, he backed away as if he'd encountered a lion in the perfectly manicured garden. Unless she was very much mistaken, his hand had trembled when he released her.

"Coward."

But she was almost smiling when she whispered it.

Chapter Twelve

THE GIDDINESS OF that surprise kiss, dark and delicious, was not enough to lift the dread in her stomach for long.

Henry was safe and alive, and that was as good an outcome as could be hoped for. But she'd still hoped for so much more. For everything, really.

And now reality was biting at her ankles, no matter how she tried to run. And through it all, she had to smile. That damned polite, daughter-of-a-duke smile. It had served her well for nearly thirty years, both as shield and weapon. But oh, today, it cut and sliced at her. It fit all wrong and offered no comfort.

And she knew neither Persephone nor Priya believed it for one moment. They kept sneaking concerned glances on the ride back to London, especially when Henry veered away from the group, declining Conall's invitation for breakfast, as did Pierce. Tamsin did not decline. Not only would she not have been able to get away with it, but she may as well be miserable with a cup of hot, sweet tea.

They were a merry party, despite her misery, stealing through the sleepy bustle of London. Servants and shopkeepers rushed down the sidewalk, battling carts and the occasional cow being led to a common green to provide fresh milk.

The Northwyck townhouse was situated in Berkeley Square, looking every inch a house fit for a noble lineage. It had the elegant columns that were all the rage, elaborate fanlight over the door, and carved pediment.

But inside, Persephone had already left her mark. There was a sarcophagus in the dining room, for one. Anubis, the jackal-headed god of the dead, currently held on to the calling cards of visitors, and someone's discarded crowned hat. He was rather dashing.

Gilded lotuses were painted along the ceiling, and several eyes of Horus watched them from unexpected places, like the floor tiles. The usual enormous bouquet of hothouse flowers one might expect were nowhere to be seen. Instead: glass cases filled with broken pieces of pottery, arrowheads, blue scarab beetles, gold beads dug out of the sands. Each with a neatly written note explaining their provenance.

The dining table was already set, and platters were sent up with a battalion of footmen. There was fresh bread, preserves, strawberries and cream, eggs with ham and trout, potatoes roasted with chives, and seven different kinds of cheeses. Tamsin drank three cups of tea, hoping they would steady her. And hoping no one would ask her questions if she was too busy eating and drinking.

As if that could stop her friends.

"Well?" Priya asked quietly.

Tamsin shook her head, trying to both smile and not cry. She was half successful.

Persephone set her fork down with a clatter. "*What?*"

Tamsin drank more tea.

"That doesn't make any sense at all," Persephone insisted softly.

Tamsin finally spoke. "He doesn't want me," she said.

"Well, that's just not true," Persephone scoffed. "He's obviously lying. But I don't know why. And I *always* know why."

"Then he must know his logic is not sound," Priya said. "And that you would only point it out to him."

"Bloody right I would." Persephone eyed Conall. "What do you know about this?"

"Nothing, love."

She eyed him for another moment, then sighed. "Well, that's

a shame."

"I cannot wait for him to see me," Tamsin said quietly. The words hurt worse than the time she'd tumbled from a horse and cracked her collarbone. All of the breath was stolen right out of her body, and yet she lived. "I have to find someone to marry within three days."

"Surely not?" Persephone asked. "Rumors of Eaton's dishonorable absence this morning are already making their way through London, if I know these two." She nodded to Conall and Priya, who exchanged smug looks. "Your father can't expect you to marry him now."

"I wish I could believe that," Tamsin said. "If I'm lucky, no, he won't." She didn't feel particularly lucky at the moment. "Even then, he'll find another candidate soon enough. He's on the hunt now, good and proper. My only hope is to be faster."

Her last bite of toasted bread stuck like glue in the back of her throat. It was dispiriting enough that Henry did not love her, but even as a friend, he would not marry her. She knew many marriages based on far shakier ground. She supposed she couldn't blame him for it. He deserved every happiness, despite her predicament.

She couldn't stop thinking about that kiss.

About how it finally felt to have Henry's strong arms around her, his mouth moving against her jaw line. Saints above, the man could kiss.

Part of her wished she'd never discovered that, so she couldn't miss it so keenly. The rest of her was just happy to have the memory of that searing heat to hold on to.

Priya touched her hand, her dark eyes fierce and kind. "You'll stay with me, as we discussed."

"Thank you. Only for a little while."

"For as long as you like," Priya insisted. "Tam, I'm a widow with a house large enough for ten people."

"The widow and the spinster."

Persephone grinned. "Sounds like a novel. The best kind, where the villains get soundly trounced and ladies get their happy ending, and damn everyone in their way."

KISSING HER WAS a mistake.

The best mistake of Henry's life.

One he could not repeat and would not regret for one single moment. Even if it made everything so much worse. To know what he was missing, what he craved and could not have.

Would not have.

The morning cold had put pink roses in her cheeks, but as the morning melted to sunshine and birds and apple blossoms, they turned to cherries. He'd never wanted a taste so bad. She had swallowed, as if she could read his thoughts. He'd nearly groaned out loud.

Kissing her was torture. Turning away from her had nearly done him in. But he'd survived betrayal, accusations of treason, vicious storms at sea on a boat taking on water, the food given to British naval officers, the alleys of St. Giles. He would survive this.

For her.

Logically, he knew that he could save Tamsin from Eaton by offering to marry her himself. All he had to do was say yes. It would take considerably less strength of will than saying no had taken. It still sat in his mouth, bitter and wrong.

But he couldn't say yes. Not like this. Not with his father's men at his heels, always ready to strike. It would be too easy for Tamsin to get caught in the crossfire.

But hell would freeze before he'd let Eaton marry her.

Murder was not out of the question.

He probably should feel bad about that. He did not. It *should* raise questions of honor and ethics and morality.

It did not. He would do anything for Tamsin.

A part of him sneered. If he could survive all of those hardships, then surely he had courage enough to marry her. To finally claim his happiness with both hands.

If only it were that simple. Even before he'd been assaulted by his father's footpads, he knew he was not good enough for her. But now he put her in danger just by walking by her house at night. If they had followed him to her house... He couldn't even think about it. She already had boys sneaking into her parlor.

Eaton sniffing at her heels. It was enough to deal with.

And the knowledge that he might have to drop everything and run was never far from his mind. He hadn't even unpacked his books. He always unpacked his books. But he couldn't run if he had roots set too deep, if he had a house that felt like home, demands, promises. If he had a wife. It wouldn't be fair. Not to mention that Tamsin would skin him alive if he went into hiding without her. She'd put herself in danger for him.

He couldn't stomach it. Would not countenance it.

And then, just to prove him right, he caught sight of a shadow in the trees before it dropped on him. Years on a ship, even before he was captain, had honed his ability to track movement in the distance, and to be aware of what was happening over his head with the sails and the rigging. Not to mention his bloody father's bloody men.

Who had invaded even Hyde Park, it seemed. He'd been walking for hours, trying to clear his head to little avail. Maybe a spot of violence might do the trick. His father's men were accustomed to a fight from him, but not like this. Not when his head was full of fear and anger and desperation for a woman within his reach that he could not allow himself to reach *for*. Not *a* woman, *the* woman.

His father's ox of a bully could suffer along with him. The bloodier, the better.

He'd never been much of a fighter as a child, much to his father's chagrin. He still preferred books and charting stars, He'd been on the receiving end of his fists too often to consider it a path he wished to follow.

But sometimes, it felt good to prove that he would not cower, would not back down. Was not the boy who hid in Persephone's cellar, or in the woods, or in his grandmother's attic. He no longer had to swallow his pride and his teeth. He did not have to watch his father burn his favorite books because he was afraid poetry would make his son soft.

And he did not have to let the fist currently whistling toward his head make contact. He blocked it with one savage move, and the surprised grunt offered him grim satisfaction. He pushed back, and the huge man stumbled. He might be made entirely of muscle, but he hadn't spent the last decade scrambling up a ship's mast or keeping his balance during a storm where the waves were tall enough to block out the sky.

"Fair warning," Henry said as another man came out from behind a tree. "I am not in the mood. If you continue, you'll be eating your teeth."

"Prove it, toff."

He settled into a grounded stance, knees slightly bent. It was easy to duck the first swing, a little more effort to duck the second. The third connected, and he staggered, cursing. He tasted blood. The ox grinned. Henry wiped his mouth and grinned back. The ox faltered. His friend roared, advancing. Someone ought to warn him about giving away his position like that.

Luckily, Henry was willing to oblige.

He burst into a run, throwing himself at a tall tree branch. He gripped it and then swung, planting his boots square into the other man's chest. He flew back, hit another tree, and then slumped, coughing and gagging for breath.

The ox looked angry and momentarily concerned for his own well-being. He was clearly smarter than he looked.

He charged, in for a penny, in a for a pound. He was strong enough that even a glancing blow sent Henry staggering, his ribs creaking. The pain in his side robbed him of his breath. But he was used to that: the bruising cold, needles of rain, the dank stink below deck. It didn't stop him, not for long. He retaliated, the first punch catching the ox in the jaw, the second in the nose. The third and fourth dropped him. The heel to the gut kept him there.

Henry stepped over their bodies and walked away, their groans following him. He joined the other aristocrats on parade on Rotten Row, tipping his hat courteously to those he crossed paths with. His knuckles stung, bruised and split. His side ached like the devil. His smile was perfectly polite.

No one mentioned the blood.

TAMSIN WENT TO Gunter's because she could not think of where else to go.

She couldn't stand the sympathy of her friends, dear as they were. It made her want to cry or scream, or both, and she was having a hard enough time not doing either to begin with. Her mind was cluttered with that kiss, the way Henry touched her, as if he was starving and she was everything.

I can't marry you, Tamsin.

Had she ruined their friendship? Was he even now packing to get on another great bloody ship?

I can't marry you, Tamsin.

The day had turned sunny and warm, the most perfect early summer weather, practically dripping with strawberries and lilac blossoms and ladies untying their bonnet ribbons.

It was insulting, really. The sky should be low and dull. Even the smog had taken a brief vacation.

Her mood was the only sour note as she stopped by the Cabinet of Curiosities before ordering her ices. The cloying air of the sweet shop tickled her nose, and she fled for the narrow, crooked stairs and the smell of dust and musty old things. It was a balm, even if Miss Stewart had no news for her. Vasilisa was still missing, and the other victims were not keen on sharing their own losses or their identities.

Tamsin ordered two ices, because some days just required two ices.

They were delivered to her on a stone bench across the street, under a plane tree in the square. At least Eaton was not there to ruin her sweets this time. She took another suspicious look around her, but no, she was safe enough for now. He was likely still sweating through the cramps and keeping close to the chamber pot. Served him right.

She did catch a glimpse of a red elbow patch, though. Jack stayed in the tree, but he lowered slightly, scowling at her. "You look sad."

"I suppose I am sad," she said.

He scowled harder. "Why? Is it that toff again?"

"It's complicated."

"Toff." He sounded world-weary. He dropped from the branch, wary but not running away. He snuck glances at her ice.

"Why are there two?"

"I have difficult decisions to make."

"And ices help?"

"Well, they don't hurt. Would you like one?" His angular jaw and bony wrists made her want to order three more, along with a cake and an entire roast.

"Don't need pity," he said.

She shrugged, knowing better than to push or react. "Have it your way, then. I'll just toss it out."

"You can't waste food!" He sounded as scandalized as an old Puritan caught at a dance around the Maypole. Naked.

She absolutely would not smile. "I'll tell you what—we'll trade for it."

"Trade?" His eyes narrowed suspiciously.

"You tell me what you did with that doll you stole from me." She raised a scolding eyebrow when he opened his mouth to protest. He shut it with a snap and a flush of red up his neck. "And you can have the rest of my ices. This one is quite nice." She took another bite. "It's burned toast."

He frowned. "That's not a flavor."

"It's like sticky sugar. The other one is elderflower."

He sat down on the edge of the bench, ready to run. His boots were too big and nearly worn through.

"I just need to know what you did with Vasilisa."

"Who's Vasilisa?"

"That's the name of the doll you stole. My mother made it for me," she pointed out gently. "I can't think it would fetch much of a price at market. It's just old."

He looked at her skeptically. "It's old enough, then."

Her mouth dropped open. "Oi, you little rat. Easy. I'm not an antique."

He flashed her a cocky grin. It faded when he added, "I didn't sell it."

Relief flooded through her. "Oh, I'm so glad to hear it."

He winced. "I gave it away."

"You *gave* it away." She'd have preferred if he'd at least gotten a meal from his criminal activities. "Why ever for?"

He hunched his shoulders. "I was paid to steal it, not to sell it."

"By whom?"

"I don't know exactly."

"You don't know." Vasilisa's disappearance was getting stranger by the second. "How can you not know?"

"Word gets around. There was a list, and your house was on it. I wanted to make sure no one like Victor got inside. He's not right, miss."

She was touched. Enraged, but also a little touched. "Thank you, Jack. Do you know why they wanted a doll?"

He shook his head. "We was only told to take something that seemed special, especially if it looked museum-like."

"And then?"

"And then we met a carriage and handed the item over. I never saw the man's face."

"But he was a man?"

"I think so."

"I don't suppose there were any markings on the carriage?"

He shook his head.

She sighed. "Well, honestly, Jack, even though I'm still a little peeved, you've given me far more information than anyone else. You could be a Bow Street Runner."

He puffed up his chest. "Yeah?"

"Absolutely." She pushed the fluted glass cups toward him on the bench. "Go on," she said. "A deal's a deal."

"Never made a deal with a lady before."

"We have the best things, everyone knows that." His eyes widened at the first mouthful. She smiled. "I told you burned toast was delightful."

"It's so cold!"

"Have you ever had an ice before?"

His eyes slid away from hers. "No."

Not a proper ice, then. Likely the melted remains nicked off a bench before the servers could reclaim the cups. "Well, try the elderflower, it's just as good."

He gobbled up a big bite. "It's like eating springtime." He

pressed his hand to his temple suddenly, eyes watering. "Why does it hurt?" He was stunned, offended. "Ow!"

She had to chuckle. "It's only because you ate too much, too fast," she assured him. "It'll pass quickly."

He stared at the ices with newfound respect, taking a smaller bite. "My brother has never had an ice."

"I didn't know you had a brother."

"He's only little."

"What's his name?"

"Why?"

She held up a hand placatingly. "I was only making conversation."

"Can I take these with me?"

She winked. "As long as you don't get caught."

"I don't get caught!" He was affronted.

"Good to know."

He had the cups inside his jacket before she could blink. He didn't take off right away, though. "Are you still sad?"

"Only a little. You've cheered me up, Jack." When he stood up, she added, "Wait, please. I want to let you know that I will be moving from my house shortly. But you can find me on Bolton Row. If you need anything, or your brother does. I hear the cook likes to make meat pies."

"Why would you move?"

"You mean, aside from needing to find a house with more secure windows?" she asked drily. He grinned. She shook her head. "The house doesn't belong to me."

"But it's *your* house."

"Not really. Nothing belongs to me."

Not her house, not Henry.

And wasn't that a kick in the teeth?

She was going to need a great many more ices to get through this.

Chapter Thirteen

N O ONE WAS going to marry her.

They all wanted her at their parties and at their picnics, but no one would stand up to Eaton, or her father the duke. Not for her and not for her dowry, which was now in question. Lord Summers was most apologetic, but he simply did not have the clout to procure a special license if the duke opposed him, and not the balls, frankly, to elope to Gretna Green. She couldn't blame him. You took those kinds of risks for someone you truly loved, not for someone you only esteemed. She couldn't ask someone to set his life on fire just to help her.

By midmorning the next day, the *ton* was like a beehive, all abuzz with news of her supposed indiscretions. No one was overly fussed with the fact that Henry was the second man of noble blood to punch Eaton right in the face in less than a year.

Or that he had shamed himself by not attending a duel of which he had been the challenger. That wasn't precisely true. They did care about it—it was shocking and salacious, after all.

Just not as shocking and salacious as Tamsin.

And Lord Eaton, as predicted, had decided that if he was going down in the eyes of the *ton*, he would take her with him. His ego was in tatters, his vanity scratched. He would know no greater offence. She probably could have pushed his mother into a pond, and he would not have reacted as deeply. She'd made a fool of him, and he would never forget that.

He still wanted her dowry, though, and the power of her family name. She admitted she'd miscalculated on that end. She'd hoped she wouldn't be worth the bother. She'd been wrong.

She had already lost track of the rumors, of what she had purportedly done, with whom, and where. She'd need to be a time traveler to have managed it all. And possibly an acrobat. He knew just what to insinuate and when to let the gossipmongers add their own spices.

But the one detail that stuck and was faithfully repeated was that she had visited him in the dark hours before dawn in order to seduce him. He hadn't been at the duel because she had been naked in his bedroom.

After which he'd taken ill.

That last part made her cross.

It hardly mattered that many did not even believe him. They still weren't above gossiping about it. It followed her through the ballrooms, like the susurration of the ocean constantly breaking against her ankles. It would take her down and drown her if she let it.

She was not going to let it.

Even if he insisted on being at every event she attended, fueling the gossip, watching her with that knowing smile. Like right now. It had started earlier in the day when she went to Hyde Park for a walk to clear her head. She had been searching for a little quiet, a little inspiration on how to mend the tatters of her life.

Instead: gossip.

Not that it wasn't expected, of course. But she usually wasn't the target. She knew how to flirt with the line of what was acceptable. She'd never wanted to be shunned or ostracized. These were her friends. And it was that knowledge that had her teetering on the edge of scandalous, without entirely being dragged under. No one turned away from her, or rescinded invitations. But they muttered behind their fans and raised their eyebrows in a way that had her gritting her teeth.

"Did you hear?"

"She's always been a little too wild, don't you think?"

"With the earl! And now they will marry."

It was like having her very own Greek chorus. And it was not enjoyable.

She ignored the first few comments, the arch looks. But it became very apparent that pretending obliviousness or refusing to deign their attention with a reaction would not be enough. Not this time. She had seen this played out before, and it was never pretty.

And damn Eaton to the devil if he thought she would shrink from the notoriety, right into his marriage bed. It was perfectly acceptable to trade a wedding for the patching up of her reputation. But like hell would she allow him the satisfaction.

By the time she reached the modiste, she knew she would have to make matters into her own hands. Again. And quickly. Luckily, her new gown was ready. It was stunning, slightly risqué, completely unique. Perfect.

Some weapons sparkled with beads, others with iron. She could be both.

She stopped to visit her father on her way home, hoping he would be appalled by the fervor. The butler took her to his study, where he was overseeing household accounts. There was no sign of Lady Chester, which would make matters somewhat easier.

"Tamsin." He barely glanced up from his ledgers. "Did we have an appointment?"

"No, Father."

"Didn't think so. Well, make it quick, I'm busy." He did look up then. "That color is very pretty on you."

"Thank you, Father."

"Well?"

She felt more awkward and nervous in this study full of golden candlesticks and fine leather books from her childhood than she had under the scrutiny of judgmental ladies at the park. Her father loomed large in all of her memories, vague but powerful, always proclaiming on the duty owed to the duchy by the Bell family. She had craved his approval so desperately. She still did in many ways, even having already given up on that. Her heartbeat didn't seem to remember that.

She swallowed. "Surely, you have heard the news of Lord Eaton?" she said.

He pursed his lips disapprovingly. "He's young yet, and duels are not uncommon with men of a certain temperament."

"He was going to fight *Henry*. That is, the Viscount Stirling."

"The viscount ought not to be punching his betters at the club."

His betters.

Tamsin's mouth dropped open. "Father, Lord Eaton did not show up for the duel. You must see how dishonorable that is." It was one of the many archaic and invisible rules that he lived by.

"It is not ideal," he agreed.

The constriction in her ribcage eased slightly. "Then might I assume the betrothal has been called off?"

"Whatever for? Don't be daft, girl."

And there it was again. The band of iron crushing her ribs together and stealing her breath. "But…"

"I hope he's learned his lesson, and the gossip will blow over, especially with a wedding to talk about instead. He just needs a woman's touch, I'm sure."

She wanted to scream.

"You turned down two dukes when you were younger," he continued. "An earl is perfectly acceptable under the circumstances. Don't be fussy, now."

Fussy.

Fussy.

Oh, she was going to start a fuss the likes of which he'd never seen.

Starting tonight.

Right now.

"Why, Lady Tamsin." Miss Walmsgate giggled as she made her way through the ballroom. "You *are* brave to attend this ball." Her friends also giggled, like a pack of jeweled hyenas.

Tamsin bit back a sigh and turned. She knew this game, however much she did not wish to play it. And she knew this society. If she showed weakness, it would be like chumming the waters.

They'd smell the blood on her and attack. She had to remain calm, cheerful, just a little bit mischievous. As if she was in on the joke.

"Whatever do you mean?" she asked, smiling her brightest smile. The one that rivaled the diamonds in her hair. Glittering and sharp, like armor. "Miss Wormgale, is it?" That last was petty, perhaps, but also satisfying.

Miss Walmsgate's giggle died. She was looking for borrowed fame, the kind that came of suddenly being able to say whatever horrid thing you liked to a duke's daughter, because everyone else had said it first. She expected to be remembered.

"Miss Walmsgate," she corrected Tamsin, sniffing. "Lord Eaton has told everyone what you did."

And there he was, just in earshot. He lifted his glass of wine in a toast. Everyone noticed.

Tamsin turned her back on him and held Miss Walmsgate's gaze. "Which is what, exactly?" Let her spell it out if she dared.

"Why, you..." She blushed. "You seduced him!"

"Did I? That doesn't sound like me."

"No need to be coy." A gentleman chuckled, overhearing the conversation, if you could call it that. "We already know you to be the brightest ornament of any Season."

"When you were a debutante, perhaps," Miss Walmsgate's friend said snidely. "But as a spinster?"

"You're marrying him, aren't you?" he asked over the titters. "Maybe you'll start a trend."

Was it possible to be bored of your own mistreatment?

"I'm certainly not marrying that cretin," Tamsin said.

The gentleman's eyes widened dramatically. "Of course you are. It's been announced."

"Consider, Lady Tamsin, that no one else will have you now!" Miss Walmsgate added. "He is very good to save you."

"He is not good at all," Tamsin said. "In fact, he was terrible." She lowered her voice, but not too much, and winked. "*Very* unskilled, alas. I would not recommend the experience."

Lord Eaton straightened, scowling. He'd heard *that* well enough. She wasn't sure what you'd call the color his ears were turning—puce? Maroon? It looked painful.

"I assure you," she continued, "I have much better taste." She paused, letting her mouth quirk slightly. "And much higher standards in…everything."

A shocked giggle, a gasp. Glances bounced back and forth between Tamsin's serene smile and Eaton's cold glower. She nearly blew him a kiss. Mostly to see if his head might explode. Petty or not, she felt better. She would not bow, and she would not break.

Which did not mean she could not amuse herself on the battlefield.

If he would not cease and desist, she would join the fray. And if no one chose to believe that she would not let him touch her with a ten-foot pole, then let him bear the brunt of the consequences of his own falsehood. His options were clear: he had lied, or else he was disappointing in bed.

"Lord Fulmerton," Priya said sharply, appearing suddenly at Tamsin's side. "I know what you do in Covent Garden every Wednesday at half past ten."

Lord Fulmerton recoiled. Then he fled. He turned on his heel and dashed between the dancers like a farmer at a fair chasing after a greased pig.

"I do love you, Priya." Tamsin grinned. "I didn't even see you arrive."

"I wasn't going to let you face this mob alone. And Persephone sent word that she could not make it."

Tamsin did not know a single captain or admiral with such loyal soldiers at their back.

Priya stood like a sword, elegant, still, and deadly. Her black hair was pinned with rubies, and she wore a stunning necklace of matching stones and gold drops from India. Her smile was as sharp as the rest of her. "Miss Walmsgate."

Miss Walmsgate, wisely, froze.

"Those are lovely paste pearls. What a pity you lost the originals on a game of whist at *that* party. You know the one I mean."

She blanched. "I…"

Priya blinked, acting confused. "Oh, I'm sorry, I thought we were sharing tales. I must have misunderstood the game."

"I've never had so much space around me at a ball in my entire life." Tamsin choked on a laugh as the crowd dispersed with a rather healthy amount of fear. "You really are diabolical."

Priya shrugged. She did not often speak of her first marriage, beyond that her husband, though much, much older, had been very kind. He'd helped her when the *ton* turned on her, most viciously. Tamsin had been in Venice that summer, but even Persephone and Meg did not know the whole tale. Suffice it to say that Priya did not suffer fools or cruelty.

"Shall we go?" Priya asked, sounding bored. "I am finding this event rather tiresome." She linked her arm through Tamsin's, well aware that everyone was straining to hear. "The entertainment has become dull."

They passed by Eaton, and Tamsin smiled at him, letting her gaze wander. "Quite flaccid, I agree."

She didn't burst into laughter until they were in the hall, and then they had to hold each other for a long moment. Tamsin dabbed at her watering eyes. "Oh, I am going to pay for that, I am sure of it."

"You're paying for it anyway," Priya said. "Might as well make it worth your while."

TAMSIN RETURNED TO a dark, quiet house.

The servants had gone to bed or else were sharing tea in the kitchen. A lamp had been left burning in the hall for her arrival. She floated through the drawing room, feeling a stark contrast to the overcrowded ballroom, to laughing herself to tears with Priya. She hadn't seen Henry, nor heard from him since their kiss in the oak grove.

She didn't know what to think of that.

Was it normal? It had only been two days, after all. He hardly visited her on a daily basis to begin with. But nothing *felt* normal.

She stood at the window and waved to Crow standing patiently across the street. She already knew he would not come inside, though she had asked him. It was silly for him to loiter in the dark when he could be comfortable in a chair in her parlor.

Not that she needed the protection. This was another of Henry's secrets.

She missed him already.

It was ridiculous. Laughable.

And yet true.

She let the curtain fall and wandered through the empty breakfast room, the music room. She was unmoored. And there was nothing to distract her in this empty house full of ghosts, but not the right kind.

Chapter Fourteen

THE NEXT MORNING, her stepmother paid her a visit.

Tamsin's fuss, though worth it, had not exactly improved matters.

Neither did her visit to her father. Lady Chester did not tolerate the notion that she might be undermined. She sailed up the walkway, and a footman scrambled to open the door before she could even reach it. She wore a hat with ostrich plumes tall enough to poke God himself in the eye. She pulled Carnation and Beryl in her wake, like two tugboats in matching pink bonnets that might have easily doubled as hot air balloons, should there be a shortage.

Tamsin rose from her chair. "Stepmother."

Lady Chester looked around the room, sighing at the collection of framed tarot cards, crystal balls, and strange little poppets with buttons for eyes. "Oh, honestly, you'll have to get rid of those ridiculous things when you marry. Clearly, you've been indulged too long."

Beryl smirked. Carnation just stared at her hands in their pink gloves. She always seemed so distant and woolly-headed, but Tamsin was beginning to see that she might simply be very adept at pretending not to be near her mother when she was on a rampage.

"Will you take tea?" Tamsin asked, because that was what you did when a duchess stood in your drawing room.

Lady Chester's spencer was trimmed with a truly astonishing number of gold beads. They caught the light when she waved her hand dismissively. "Certainly not."

"Then to what do I owe the honor of your visit?"

Carnation's mouth twitched in an almost-smile.

"I am having the house measured and redecorated," Lady Chester announced, signaling to the footman, *Tamsin's* footman, to admit the two men going round to the servant entrance. "Do let them in." She turned back to Tamsin. "Your taste is simply not au courant."

Tamsin frowned. "You're decorating my house?"

"Not your house, my dear. Your father's."

"But… I still live here."

"Not for long. You will quit this house by the end of the week."

Tamsin took an involuntary step back. "And move back home?"

"Of course not," Lady Chester snapped. "You'll be moving to the Eaton townhouse, you ninny. Your father has the special license, and you'll be wed by week's end."

Tamsin shook her head. "I won't."

Lady Chester smiled, but it was arctic. "Either way, you'll be leaving this house. You've been coddled entirely too long. I don't know what the duke could have been thinking, letting you take advantage of him."

"I wasn't." She wasn't. Was she? She already knew the answer. He would think so, because she was not acting the dutiful daughter. Because Lady Chester told him so. Because she thought Tamsin was standing between her daughters and advantageous marriages.

Lady Chester made the closest sound to a snort that a duchess might allow herself. "Don't take the gold candlesticks," she said. "They don't belong to you."

"Do take that, though." Beryl winced at the statue of a black dog, the kind said to roam the moors and eat unwary travelers. "It's positively hideous."

"It's unique. And two hundred years old."

She was briefly interested. "Is it expensive?"

"No."

She lost interest.

Lady Chester snapped her fingers. "Come along, girls. And let his be a lesson to you about pride and vanity when it is not warranted. About *gratitude*."

They left as abruptly as they had arrived.

Tamsin had known she would be moving soon, of course. She'd told Jack as much. Either as a wife or as a spinster in hiding, but it hadn't occurred to her that she might be cut off so abruptly and so soon. So summarily evicted from the family. Once again.

She was a fool to be even a little bit surprised.

Her father was not going to budge. None of the men of her acquaintance were willing to take him or Lord Eaton on. And she already knew every obstacle that would present itself should she try to hire herself out as a companion or, and she shuddered to think of it, a governess. She could not imagine lonelier work. All under the power of men like Lord Eaton.

Her options had whittled down in the space of a single day.

She summoned the footman, and he appeared, bowing. There were men behind him, already measuring and muttering about wainscoting and wallpaper. "Yes, my lady?"

"I'm going to need several trunks and baskets, and all of my softest shawls. Please inform Sarah." She would need to make sure all of her artifacts were well wrapped and packed. "And have the carriage brought round."

She would send her collection to Persephone immediately. She might not have control over her own life, or her own home. Or Vasilisa. But she had the best collection of occult items in England, and it was going to stay that way. She'd be damned if her stepmother's snooty decorators would throw out a single nail or piece of broken pottery from a witch's bottle.

They could take her hairpins and her slippers and her simpering china shepherdesses. But she'd stab them with a fish fork if they so much as looked at her Etruscan funerary death mask or the black mirror that belonged to John Dee and was rumored to act as a communication device for demons.

Chapter Fifteen

I T TOOK THE entire morning to pack up her collection. Longer than she'd thought and considerably less time than she might have imagined, considering what it meant to her. Poppets, curse tablets, witches' bottles, iron horseshoes, beads found in a barrow grave in the hand of a skeleton. They all had stories to tell, of where they had been, of how they had found their way here. They were companions, of a sort. Even if they had yet to produce a single ghost between them.

A ghost would have been preferable to her stepmother's men clomping about, clucking their tongues until she banished them from the drawing room. Let them rifle through her jewelry if they must. It wasn't their doing, and she couldn't fault them for their work. Only their manners.

After her luncheon, she'd filled the carriage with trunks and baskets and boxes and careful instructions for the delivery of said items. She only had her gowns and shoes and trinkets left to pack; everything else belonged to the duke.

She would wager good money on the fact that Lady Chester would count every piece of silver cutlery and every gold candlestick. Some of Tamsin's jewelry would be contested, especially if her stepsisters coveted any of it. But the bits she could claim for her own, she could also sell to help cover the added costs of her addition to Priya's household. It made her feel a bit better, a bit more independent.

She was walking through the house one last time, trying to figure out if she felt melancholy or anger or something else altogether, when Lady Mirabelle Dunham knocked at the front door.

Maybe quitting the house where everyone knew she lived wasn't such a bad thing.

She dredged up a welcoming, if wary, smile. "Lady Mirabelle."

"Lady Tamsin." Mirabelle curtsied. Her cheeks were pink as a cherub's. "You'll think me quite rude dropping by uninvited and outside of calling hours."

"Not at all. Do come in."

Mirabelle noticed the white sheets covering the furniture, and that odd quality to abandoned houses that was already apparent, even though Tamsin was standing right there in the foyer.

She wrinkled her nose. "I apologize for the mess," she said.

"I had heard you had a most unusual collection of artifacts." Mirabelle peered curiously at the ghostly chairs and cabinets. "Is that them?"

"No, I'm afraid not. They've already been packed away."

"Ah. A pity. Are you traveling?"

"Moving," she replied.

"Ah." Mirabelle paused delicately. She wore blue today and resembled one of the china shepherdesses. Her bonnet was trimmed with blond lace. "May I presume to hope you are preparing to move into my brother's house?"

Absolutely bloody not.

"I don't think that would be wise," Tamsin said instead. "I would offer you tea, but I honestly couldn't tell you if the cook is still in residence." Or if the cups had been packed. Once Tamsin started to bustle about, the household had fallen into a flurry of activity. She hoped her stepmother would keep them on. She had no idea who would live in the house now. Would it be sold? Kept for guests? For one of her stepmother's many cousins?

"I don't need tea, thank you. I'm sorry to be so blunt, Lady Tamsin, but I am here to discuss my brother. I am aware of his temper, but I want to assure you that he is a good man. Truly."

Tamsin's eyebrows rose, mostly because she wasn't sure how to respond.

Mirabelle smiled again, earnest, slightly pained. "But he *is* a lord, and you know how they are. They are entirely too accustomed to having their own way. It doesn't take much to get back into his good graces, though. A little flattery, a pretty smile. You'll have the hang of it in no time."

Tamsin did her best not to physically recoil. "Lady Mirabelle, I appreciate your honesty. But allow me to tell you that I am not keen on living my life coddling a man's temper."

"Who is? But what are our options?"

True.

And yet...

"Though they are few, I will cling to my ability to choose a man who does not need petting." Especially when that man would have complete control of her life, her body, her dowry. In the eyes of both the law and Society.

Marriage was dangerous business.

Mirabelle looked at her pityingly. "That is the wish of a girl fresh out of the schoolroom. Not a woman getting older and in possession of a somewhat... tarnished reputation."

Tamsin exhaled. "Tarnished by your brother's lies."

"Forgive me, but did you not visit him, unchaperoned, at dawn?"

A headache threatened to stab her in the back of the eyeballs. "I went there to convince him not to try to murder a dear friend. Not to seduce him."

Mirabelle took her hand earnestly. "Have you considered, my dear, that your friend tried to murder your future husband?"

The laugh escaped Tamsin before she could stop it. She tried to soften it because Mirabelle was not her brother. And she did seem genuinely concerned.

"If you apologized, I am sure he would accept it."

"I am afraid that I am not the least bit sorry. But I do thank you for your concern." It couldn't be easy being Eaton's sister. Tamsin imagined Mirabelle had had a great many uncomfortable conversations with the women in his life, from chambermaid to noblewoman.

"Consider, then, that the matter has already been decided by both your father and my brother. Please don't antagonize him needlessly. I know he thinks highly of you. You have all of the accomplishments and polish he admires."

She very much doubted that was still true.

He might, however, still think highly of her dowry and her connections.

"I'm afraid there's really nothing else to say." If she was not going to marry Henry, she would at least marry someone she could respect.

"Forgive me. It was kindly meant," Mirabelle said, distraught.

"There's nothing to forgive," Tamsin assured her. "But you must excuse me. I am late for an engagement."

She had not planned on descending on Priya so soon, but she suddenly could not abide staying in this house for a moment longer.

PRIYA, BEING A fine friend and one of the cleverest women of Tamsin's acquaintance, was waiting in the greenhouse with several bottles of wine and a small mountain of food.

"You are a saint," Tamsin said, dropping heavily into a chair. The familiar scents of warm air, green plants, and dark earth were comforting.

"Have some wine."

"I haven't had supper yet."

"Psh."

Since the day felt like it had been approximately a month long, Tamsin did not argue. She sipped at white wine and nibbled on slices of cheese and apples. "I'm s—"

"Ah." Priya cut her off, pointing a trowel at her. There were leaves stuck in her dark hair. "Don't you dare."

"I was just going to—"

"Apologize. You were going to apologize."

"For invading your house."

"There will be no apologizing. Drink more wine."

Tamsin had to smile. Some of the tension dissolved from her

shoulders. She hadn't realized how stiff she had become, muscles slowly turning to stone over the course of a few days.

"I have a gift for you," Priya said. She passed Tamsin a piece of foolscap. "The names of three other collectors who were robbed the same night you were."

Tamsin beamed. "Priya. You should be in charge of the government."

Priya scoffed. "I'm too good for them."

"True." Tamsin scanned the names. "Miss Montague, Lord Chevril, and Sir Wormwood."

"Do you know them?"

"Only in passing, from auctions and exhibits and the like."

"Do they collect oddities like you do?"

She nodded slowly. "Yes, but all varied. There's no pattern that's immediately obvious. Miss Montague prefers items with a provenance of torture. Sir Wormwood is infatuated with love spells." She drummed her fingers on the table. "I'll sort it out."

"I know you will."

"I suppose it could just be a very clever robbery ring looking for things that might fetch a good price."

"But?"

"It just doesn't feel like that."

"I'll keep digging as well."

"Thank you. I—"

"You'll shut it, Tamsin Bell."

Tamsin blinked.

"You were about to apologize again."

"I wasn't," she grumbled. She absolutely was. "Maybe it's a good thing I'm here for companionship. You've gone a bit feral."

Priya laughed. "Only a bit? I'll try harder."

Tamsin grinned. "I have every faith in you." She sobered a little. "Still. My father might not take kindly to your helping me."

Priya snorted. "I am not afraid of people, Tamsin. They are afraid of *me*."

"Even dukes? He's a powerful man."

"*Especially* powerful men."

"Of course," Tamsin returned with a laugh. "Duly noted."

"Your father doesn't have shocking secrets, but I guarantee it would take me all of ten minutes to find something useful on your stepmother." Priya paused thoughtfully. "I may start a folder on her. I can't think why I haven't done so before."

"Remind me never to make you mad."

"It's best not to—" She broke off with what could only be described as a growl of frustration. "Speaking of making me mad." She stood at one of the windows, hands on her hips.

Pierce stood in the back garden, leaning against a tree, his boots lost in a patch of garden. He was calm, focused, like a pulled bowstring. He wore a dark gray jacket and cap.

"Mr. Gallagher," Priya shouted through the open window. Tamsin could count on one hand the number of times she had ever heard Priya raise her voice. "Those roses do not benefit from your hulking shadow. They need sunlight at this time of the day. Move!"

He raised his eyebrow, waited a long moment, which put Priya in danger of vibrating into another plane of existence, and then calmly stepped to the side, saving the roses.

She narrowed her eyes at him. "I am not bringing you tea," she added fiercely, though he had not asked.

When she turned back, Tamsin was grinning.

"What?" Priya muttered.

"At least Henry was considerate enough to send us handsome bodyguards."

"He's not handsome." Her cheeks were flushed. Very flushed. Interesting.

"I see." Tamsin tucked her tongue into her cheek.

"Just hand me that wine."

Tamsin filled her glass right to the top, very gauche. And sometimes necessary.

"Why is Henry cluttering my back garden with Irishmen, anyway?" Priya asked, struggling not to glance out the window again.

"I assumed you'd know by now," Tamsin said.

"I don't. It's very annoying." Priya drank a considerable amount of her wine and then ate a piece of cheese carved into the shape of a rose. She chewed it like it was the head of her enemy.

"I didn't know you were a cannibal," Tamsin said.

Priya frowned slowly. "What?"

Tamsin peered into her empty wine glass. "Nothing. Never mind."

"Didn't he say anything to you about it?"

"Who?"

"Henry. How much wine have you had?"

"More than you. Catch up."

"Right." She drank obediently. "About Henry? He hasn't told you why there's a handsome Irishman outside?"

"Handsome, is he?" Priya hissed.

Tamsin laughed. "No, the rotter. Although, to be fair, we were accosted by Eaton at the same time, and then there was the duel." And the kiss. The non-proposal. "I haven't seen him since Hampstead Heath."

"Neither has Persephone."

"Well, that can't be good." A kernel of concern dropped in her belly. What if he'd left London? England altogether? "But it must be related to the charges of treason, mustn't it? Could it be Lord Fairweather? Henry was stabbed by footpads. They might have been hired by Fairweather." The wine was starting to make her head fuzzy, but that seemed a logical enough conclusion.

"That man can't do anything to anyone anymore. He's been banished from England."

"They should have hanged him."

"They still could."

"Good."

"And you wonder why I live in constant terror of the fairer sex," Conall said drily, ducking under a fern that had no business being as tall as it was. Even the plants were terrified to anger Priya.

"Conall!" Priya smiled at him. "Did you see the handsome man in the back garden?"

"I did."

"I won't bring him tea. I don't care how blue his eyes are."

Tamsin giggled.

He shook his head at them fondly. "Are you two drunk?"

"Of course not," Tamsin informed him loftily. "When ladies drink, they are inebriated. Which we aren't. Because we're *ladies*."

"Your logic is as terrifying as the rest of you," he pointed out. "And just as drunk."

"You're very pretty." She patted his arm.

"I know."

Priya rolled her eyes so hard she made herself dizzy. "Not you too!" She wobbled accusingly at Tamsin. "His great, big, swelled head is already the size of Edinburgh." She lowered her voice. "And he's married to Percy."

Tamsin rolled her eyes right back and then thought better of it. "Ouch. I don't want to *marry* him." She laughed. "Be serious. He's not Henry." Her eyebrows lowered. "The ass."

Conall kissed the top of her head. "He'll come around."

"Before Friday?" she grumbled. "Because that's when my father's decided I'm to marry Eaton."

"You're not marrying Eaton."

"Told you so," Priya interrupted smugly. She ate more cheddar shaped like a rose. "I like cheese."

"Me too!" Tamsin said.

"You could marry cheese!"

"I could!"

"Where's Percy?"

"She can't marry cheese; she's already married Conall. He's very pretty."

"Blech. But she should be drinking with us!"

"The mind boggles," Conall said. "But she will be sorry to have missed out on the afternoon's entertainment."

Priya propped her chin on her hand, her eyes half-closed. "Why are you here, then?"

"I'm just checking in on my baby sister."

"Liar."

Priya snorted so loudly that Tamsin jumped in her chair. "I'm awake!"

"As amusing as you both are, I'm going to take my leave." He tugged his sister's hair gently, then Tamsin's. "Don't marry cheese."

"No promises," she mumbled in response.

Conall laughed loudly. Priya shot him a sidelong glance. "Shh."

"I'm going to send some footmen in here to see you to your chambers. And have your cook have a headache remedy at the ready."

Priya's eyes were completely closed now. "You're a good big brother."

Tamsin was sure she hadn't dozed off, but Conall was suddenly gone.

"Did you notice that he never said why he was here?" Priya mumbled. "He thinks he's so sneaky, but he's not. *I'm* the sneaky one."

"The sneakiest."

Seeing as the footmen were too scared to poke the fine ladies sleeping so soundly in the greenhouse, they covered them with blankets and left them there.

In the garden, leaning against his tree, Pierce smiled.

Chapter Sixteen

"YOU LOOK TERRIBLE."

As a greeting, it was not Persephone's politest.

Her truest, perhaps. If Henry looked half as bad as he felt, then most definitely.

She hugged him. And then she pinched him. Hard.

"Percy, ow, damn it," he said. She'd been pinching him since they were in leading strings. Usually when he deserved it.

"Serves you right. Where have you been?" She sniffed the air. "Never mind."

"I bathed," he grumbled, running a hand through his damp hair, though he took her meaning well enough. He'd kissed Tamsin, then visited his grandmother for tea before disappearing into the Rose and Anchor, and had not left again until a few hours ago.

He was still wishing the sun would go out. Just for a little while. His head ached like the devil, but if he mentioned it, Persephone would only tell him he deserved it.

Instead, he looked around hopefully. "Have you got any tea?"

She narrowed her left eye at him. Whatever she saw in his face, beyond the fact that he hadn't bothered to shave, made her sigh. "Yes, I have tea. And muffins. You need to eat."

She wasn't wrong.

She led him further into the building. The façade was unassuming, but only for the moment, if he knew Persephone at all.

The interior had already been enhanced with every kind of embellishment. The main room boasted murals of the pyramids of Giza, queens wearing triangular wigs and black kohl around their eyes, not to mention giant palm trees in one corner, green silk leaves waving gently. A truly enormous replica of the Sphinx dominated the center of the room, with the head of a man wearing a headpiece and the body of a lion. It was a deep golden brown that brought to mind hot sun and desert dunes.

Persephone patted a giant paw with deep affection, as though it were a real cat. "The legs are a guess, of course. The sands have covered most of this poor fellow's body since the time of Marcus Aurelius. Did you know he was the last person to truly excavate around the sphinx?" she asked. "We spoke to a fascinating man, Mr. Caviglia, while were there. He hopes to begin his own excavations soon. Think of what he might discover!"

She showed him the other rooms: ancient Rome in honor of the Duke of Pendleton's obsession, but also Mesopotamia, Greece, and a collection Henry had helped her dig out of the Celtic barrow graves around their village when they were young. And by "help," he meant that he did exactly as she ordered or else he suffered lectures on the sanctity of history, as well as more vicious pinching.

It would be unlike any museum London had ever seen. It would be perfectly Persephone.

"Do you think it would be too much to have the area scented with Cleopatra's perfume? Or something near enough, anyway. Rose and frankincense and a little cardamon?"

"No."

"Told you so!" Conall called out from the floor above. "Everything would go much faster if we just started from the assumption that I am right."

Persephone made a rude gesture, but she was smiling.

"I saw that," he added immediately.

"You did not."

"Didn't have to," he returned smugly. His laugh sounded through the floorboards.

Henry smiled. "You're good together."

"I know," she said cheerfully. She wrinkled her nose. "Still, the other antiquarians might not take me seriously if I douse the place with perfume. Even if it's historically accurate."

"Sod them all," Conall shouted.

She smiled. Henry nudged her. "You finally got your museum," he said, genuinely pleased for her. "You may as well make it your own. You've only been dreaming about this since you were eight years old."

She beamed, all pride and stunned joy in her striped muslin dress. "I think we should call it the Northwyck Museum."

"The Persephone Museum," Conall interjected, still just a floating voice. Clearly it was a conversation they'd had several times already. "Otherwise, everyone will think I had something to do with it."

"You did," Persephone protested to the ceiling.

"I bought a house. You're doing the work. You're the expert."

Henry watched his childhood best friend melt a little and grinned. "I like the Persephone Museum," Henry agreed. He caught the look she sent him. "But the Northwyck Museum has a ring to it as well."

"Coward," Conall muttered. Loudly.

"I prefer to think of it as prudence."

"For that, you'll have extra sugar in your tea."

The tea was hot and strong and went a long way to making him feel human again. Persephone sipped from her own cup, looking at him over the rim. "You're being an idiot."

"Men drink to excess sometimes, Percy."

She skewered him with a glare. "Not just an idiot, but an imbecile."

He sighed.

"I know perfectly well that you love Tamsin."

He choked on a bite of pastry.

"I can see it on your face," she insisted. "Under your Captain Face."

"My what?" he asked, mostly to buy himself time to come up with a plausible story. Of course he loved Tamsin. She was bright and beautiful, strong and fearless. He fairly ached to sink into her, to taste her on his tongue, to hear the sounds she made when he dragged his mouth along her spine. Persephone might have saved his sanity, but Tamsin had saved his soul. She was a thread of light that had wrapped around him, which he had followed out of the war.

"Your Captain Face," Persephone continued, thankfully unaware of the train of his thoughts. Some things you did not share with your sister, even if she wasn't really your sister.

She knew too much already, clearly.

"It's your new face, the one that's all broody and stern. I'm sure it's very commanding and manly, but it makes me want to pinch you."

"You know," he said drily, "there are men who are afraid of me."

She raised an eyebrow. "I am not a man."

He raised both back in response. "Clearly."

"Thank God for that," Conall shouted. "No offense to you, Talbot, but you're not pretty enough for me."

"None taken," Henry replied. The sound of his own raised voice reverberated slightly inside his skull. He knew the men Conall had taken up with back in their school days, and Conall was quite right: Henry was not pretty enough.

"Stop eavesdropping!" Persephone called back.

"You first."

"Like that's going to happen," Henry put in. They grinned at each other. There was something comforting to the bickering, the cheerful pokes. They brought to mind long summers running through the fields of Little Barrow, wishing on falling stars, stealing fancy iced cakes from his grandmother's tea tray while she was entertaining. "I've missed you," he said to Persephone.

"It's your own fault," she replied. "Stop leaving and you can stop missing me." She hugged him. "I always miss you when you're gone."

"I'm no longer in the Navy."

"But you're still thinking of running."

He leaned against the wall. "Did you become a mind reader when I was away?"

Not that she would have to. She had helped him run away countless times. She knew his tells. One of the many reasons he would never play cards with her. She saw too much.

"Henry, do you not care for Tamsin?"

"Of course I do!"

"Then I don't understand. When I ruined myself to get off the Marriage Market, you wrote to tell me you would have married me. I believe you called me a pea-brain."

"You *were* a pea-brain. Anything could have happened to you."

"And to you, dolt. You were at *war*." She handed him a plate of macarons. "But you were more than willing to save me, then why not Tamsin? Who actually needs saving, and rather urgently?"

He sighed, putting down the macarons. They were like glue in his mouth. "I'm not safe."

She paused for a beat. "What does *that* mean?"

"Percy, can you let it be?"

"Absolutely not." He smiled briefly. She rushed forward to take his hands. "Are you in danger?"

He didn't want to worry her. The last time she had tried to save him, she was nearly killed by the man who had framed him. But he knew her well enough that she wouldn't stop, and he wasn't sure if that was safe either.

"Possibly."

"But Fairweather is gone."

"Yes, but someone is following me."

"Who?" she demanded, affronted. "Conall!"

"I heard, love."

Henry sighed again. "I'm safe enough, Percy," he said. "But I won't bring Tamsin into a possibly perilous situation. Not until I know more."

"I see." She tilted her head. "Are we sure those footpads weren't sent by Eaton? Because neither Conall nor Priya could find anything out of the ordinary. But we already know Eaton hates you."

"Could be," he said. His father was exceedingly good at covering his tracks. More, no one would think he would be mad enough to send men after his own son. Even if they knew him. "I can't take that chance. Not with Tamsin."

"Tamsin is already in danger from Eaton," Persephone pointed out.

"And if it's something else? Someone else?"

"Then we'll figure that out too. Tamsin needs help *now*. You're trying to keep her safe tomorrow, but she needs the chance to *have* a tomorrow."

Put like that, it turned his blood to ice. "She's too stubborn to marry Eaton."

"Of course she is. But he is not a good man, and her father is a careless ass. There are too many ways this could go terribly wrong for her."

She was right.

"And you love her."

Right again.

He scrubbed a hand over his face. "Of course I love her."

"Ha!" she crowed triumphantly. "Conall, you owe me two pounds."

"I never took that sucker's bet, love."

Henry shook his head. "Percy, what if I can't protect her?"

"You can protect her from *this*, today. Tomorrow, you can protect each other." She gave him a helpful, fond little shove. "Go after her, idiot. You know exactly where she'll be."

"The woman has a busier social calendar than the bloody queen."

"Why do you think that is?"

"Pardon?"

"Have you asked her why she likes ghosts so much? And parties?"

"What does one have to do with the other?"

"I guess you'll just have to ask her."

"If I can find her."

"She is worried and upset and has too many thoughts to think. You know exactly where she is."

They said it in unison: "Gunter's."

TAMSIN WOKE UP with a sore head to match her sore heart.

And a vague recollection that she had decided to marry cheese.

She wasn't sure if that was proof that she should drink wine less often or *more* often, honestly.

They had woken near midnight, snuck down to the kitchen for bread and strawberries, and then wobbled to bed. Tamsin had been put in the Violet room, decorated with all shades of light green and purple, violets painted on every available surface. Priya's house had a definite theme, with the Rose parlor, the Orchid breakfast room, the Lilac bedroom, the Ivy bedroom, and the dining room dripping with every kind of flower. It was comfortable and cheerful and very likely to have dirt on the floor.

Tamsin put on a green walking dress, aided by Priya's lady's maid. Juniper was thrilled to be pinning the hair of a duke's daughter, especially seeing as Priya used her lady's maid mostly for gossip from other household servants and not for fashions. Juniper was starved for the opportunity to use her artist's eye. She paired the green dress with a deep mauve spencer with military buttons, and the effect was quite striking.

It was lovely for Tamsin to be able to let down her guard a bit. It was strange to stand about half-naked every morning with a woman you knew reported back to your stepmother. It was refreshing to talk about headache powders and polished boots and not have to second-guess every word.

The sun was still entirely too bright and meddlesome, but all in all, she felt better. Sometimes being kicked out of your family, and then your house, was a chance to lance a kind of discomfort you had become too accustomed to.

She spent the day directing the trunks of the rest of her belongings, which Priya had sent her carriage and two footmen to fetch. She helped Juniper unpack her dresses and her jewelry, most of which her stepmother had already confiscated. She fully expected to see them next around Beryl's throat. She had nothing rosy enough to satisfy Lady Chester's determination to dress Carnation only in pinks.

She did not eat even when a supper tray was brought up to

her room. She drank enough tea to rival the Thames. But she had no appetite, and neither did Priya, who only left her chambers once, and that was to tell the butler to sell all of the wine remaining in the cellar.

Despite the state of her head and the state of her life, Tamsin couldn't stop thinking about Henry.

Even her flirtatious affair with cheese was not enough to change her heart. She missed him, and she was terrified she had ruined things forever between them. She could resign herself to not having him for a husband, but she simply could not imagine not having him in her life at all. She had misread the entire situation, but surely, he would be able to forgive her.

She had been so certain that she could make him love her. That he simply needed time after his trials. But sometimes you simply did not get the thing you wanted, the thing you were certain was meant to happen.

And you had to find a way to carry on.

Starting with three ices from Gunter's.

She arrived as the sun set behind the white mansions of Mayfair, turning them all shades or rose and gold. Lamplighters went from post to post, and carriages began to pour through the streets on their way to the theatre or various parties. It felt strange not to be among them, but the idea of twirling in a waltz was more than she could bear. More than her reputation could weather at the moment. She'd cast up her accounts, and they'd have it that she was with child by morning.

She only intended to eat the lemon of the three ices—it seemed safest for her stomach and the dryness of her mouth. At some point last night, she had apparently decided that marrying cheese was the same as eating the approximate weight of a husband in said cheese. She might need all three ices to quench her thirst. For now, she set the extra dishes on the edge of her bench. Parmesan and orange. She had every hope that Jack and his brother would love them.

And she knew perfectly well that he was watching her even now, as she went over the list of the other robbery victims once more. She didn't know where he was, but she'd caught that telltale red of his elbow patch when she first sat down. He wouldn't be far.

She let the cool lemon soothe her dry throat and considered the list. Even sober, she could not find the thing that linked them. It had to be something about the items stolen, perhaps. Though why anyone would bother hiring a pickpocket to steal a child's doll was beyond her. She would write a note to the others and see if they were willing to talk to her, to tell her what they had lost. They had a better chance of solving this mystery together.

For now, she would walk a little and clear her head of the last of the cobwebs. She stood slowly, giving Jack ample time to realize the moment to claim his ices had come. The trees did not shiver around her; the branches did not creak. He was playing it close to the vest. But if she hoped to be able to feed him something other than frozen sweets, she had to play it just as calmly, just as patiently.

She wandered away, forcing herself not to look back to see where he had been hiding. By the time she reached the pavement, she allowed herself a peek. The ices were gone. She smiled.

And then a hand shot out of the carriage beside her and hauled her inside.

Chapter Seventeen

H ENRY COULD NOT get there fast enough.

He ran because he knew full well the traffic would be too congested. His brain skittered like a pebble on ice, trying to find purchase. He could save her from a bad marriage now, but how to save her as the days went by? How to keep Tamsin safe if his father knew how much she meant to him?

Everything.

She meant everything.

But would she believe him now? That he loved her and had always loved her? He would prove it to her every day. That, at least, was a task he knew he was perfectly suited for. Better than being a captain or a viscount.

If he could just find her.

He broke into a run, shocking several elderly men. A sense of urgency pressed on him, not unlike that moment between the loading of the cannons and the firing of them, when an enemy ship loomed too close. He hoped it was simple anticipation, simple impatience now that he could let himself want her.

But it didn't feel simple.

He'd been to Berkeley Square a hundred times, possibly a thousand. It didn't look any different—the well-appointed carriages, footmen lighting torches, ladies carrying the trains of their complicated ballgowns as they were helped into carriages. Gentlemen stopped to bow, servants weaving between them.

Gunter's had been crowded, as the day had been too sunny and perfect for it not to be. But now it was lit with painted glass lamps, and the crowds were thinning.

Henry launched over the iron railing to the square across the street because it was faster than walking round to the gate. He stalked through the trees, looking for familiar honey curls, for a group of admirers, for a skinny lad with red patches on his elbows.

With the last, he was successful.

Jack's eyes were wide as teacups, and he clutched two glasses of ices in his hands.

"So you've been talking to Tamsin," Henry said. "Where is sh—"

"I was coming to see you, sir, as you said!" Jack burst out. That was when Henry noticed the excitement over sweets was actually agitation, fear.

His own sense of dread intensified.

The mantle of a captain slammed over him. He stilled. "Tell me," he demanded. "Slowly."

Jack took a deep breath. His explanation was not measured, but at least it was understandable. "She was just here! She was walking away, and someone grabbed her!"

Ice coated every single breath in Henry's lungs.

"Who? What did they look like? One man or many?"

"I didn't see them." Jack seemed equally ready to rage or weep. Henry knew exactly how he felt. "But I think there was only one?"

"What did the carriage look like?"

He took another fortifying breath and squinted, trying to remember. "Black, plain, but with fine windows. No crest, though."

"And the coachman?"

"He didn't even blink an eye, that tosser. His coat was green."

"Which direction did they go? Which road?"

"That way!" Jack pointed north. "I threw one of my ices at the door," he added.

Something to track, then, something better than a hired hack in the beehive of hired hacks that was London.

"Good lad," Henry said. He was already moving. "Don't worry."

"You'll get her back?"

"I'll get her back."

The promise of cannon fire was in his voice.

TAMSIN REFUSED TO betray an ounce of the fear she was feeling.

Not one flicker.

Lord Eaton sat across from her, expression both triumphant and irritated. He was dressed as though he was expected at court, instead of stealing girls off the bloody street. She hoped, most fervently, that his cravat choked him.

"You're a lot of bother," he drawled. "You'd better endeavor to be worth all of this effort."

"I assure you, I am not worth it." Her arm already ached from where he had grabbed her.

"You'd better hope you are."

His leg was stretched out, blocking any access to the door. The space was confined, thick with cologne and stuffy with summer. She wasn't sure how to escape.

So, she screamed.

Loudly.

Very, very loudly. It was more of a screech, really. Something worthy of a banshee.

For all of the good it did her.

The carriage did not slow down. The coachman, who *must* have heard her, blithely ignored her. None of the people they sped past on the street noticed. At least not beyond a glance at the hackney barreling by too fast. There were people everywhere, servant girls with baskets of fruit, flower sellers, girls with empty baskets after a day of selling bunches of violets or watercress, men carrying heavy boxes from the butcher or the candlemaker, dogs barking, street sweepers.

And not one of them was able to help her.

Her shout did, however, annoy her captor. Eaton grabbed her by the spencer and shook her hard enough to snap her teeth together. He tossed her back onto the squabs. Her bonnet tumbled off her head, partially crushed.

"You've played the shrew long enough," he snapped. "I don't have the patience for any more of your spoiled antics."

Apparently, he hadn't cared for her addition to his gossip at the ball.

She shoved down the panic and poured the regal chill of ducal children everywhere into her voice. She knew it was the only thing he might respond to now. "*My* spoiled antics?" she asked. "Lord Eaton, surely you've heard the idiom about the pot and the kettle."

"You forced my hand."

"So, on top of it all, this is now my fault? I can't *imagine* why I won't marry you."

His lip lifted off his perfect white teeth. "You will marry me. Today. It's done."

"No."

"I've got a special license that says otherwise."

"I have the ability to speak, which also says otherwise."

"For now." He shrugged one shoulder. "You're fond of gossip and word games, Lady Tamsin. But they won't save you now."

"If you wish people to gossip favorably about you, you might try acting less like a villain in a gothic novel."

"Histrionics," he dismissed her. But there was a flash of ire in his eyes and enough venom to give her pause.

She wasn't going to talk her way out of this. Or charm her way free. Not with him, not now. He was not the first fortune hunter or earl to force an heiress to the altar. No one much cared, so long as the heiress in question eventually received the protection of marriage. As if marrying the man who would do you ill was any sort of protection at all.

She wanted to scream again. No one would know where she was. Priya might not even realize something was amiss until the evening.

"You may as well get comfortable," Eaton advised. "Do you want to look disheveled for your own wedding?"

"Oh yes, because *that* would be the scandal." Her jaw was

beginning to ache from his shaking of her. A throb of pain replied from her temple.

While she could hope that the clergyman Lord Eaton was dragging her to would balk at a forced marriage, the truth was, he could easily be bought off. Or he might believe Eaton's likely excuses of the natural nerves of a bride. He might call her unhinged. She might even appear so, because if she was forced to the altar, she had every intention of biting the bridegroom.

Once again, she wished she had Persephone's ability to predict people by watching them closely, or Priya's knowledge of their worst secrets. Meg could have stolen his special license right out of his pocket without his noticing.

Tamsin could flirt. And throw a cricket ball.

Hardly a terrifying arsenal.

Still. Something was better than nothing.

She smiled at Eaton, sweetly, coyly. The haughty confidence etched in his every movement intensified. He smirked.

"That's better," he said.

Right before she kicked him in the balls.

HENRY FOUND THE first unoccupied hackney and leapt up into the seat. The driver cursed, raising his fist.

"Five pounds if you let me drive," Henry snapped.

The driver lowered his arm. "I'm not leaving me perch."

"Fine, move over." Henry took a coin out of his pocket. "The rest when we get back."

The driver bit the coin, smiled a smile missing several teeth, and slid over, relinquishing the reins. "Aye."

Henry berated himself the entire time he pushed through the blasted evening traffic, ignoring the shouts and curses of pedestrians and drivers alike. He ought to have had Crow watch Tamsin, not just her house at night. He'd assumed she'd be perfectly safe surrounded by the *ton*.

He really was an idiot.

"Look for a coachman wearing a green coat," he ordered the driver, who only nodded, which made Henry assume he was wearing what Persephone had called his Captain Face. Fury and fear pierced him like a thousand icy iron nails. Anything could have happened to Tamsin. Anyone could have snatched her. And she could be headed anywhere.

He forced himself to breathe, control the horses even as he pushed them, to track the surrounding carriages as he would have tracked stormy waves or grumbling sailors. He glanced at each window, looking for the telltale smear of a melted ice.

"Green coat!" The coachman pointed.

And a dirty window.

Henry brought up his borrowed hackney parallel to it, despite the danger and the hurried corrections from oncoming carts and carriages. The smog vibrated with curses. He shoved the reins at the driver. "Keep us steady."

"You're daft as the devil."

"Just do it."

He didn't wait for a confirmation, only stood on the box seat, finding his center of gravity. It was no different than scaling a mast in a storm or keeping to your feet under a surprise swell.

Mostly. It was dangerous and foolhardy to the extreme.

And entirely necessary.

The green-coated coachman glanced over. "What are you—"

Too late.

Henry leapt.

The wheels wobbled on the uneven road. The carriages swung as the horses galloped too fast. He was in the air, falling or flying. Only the landing would tell.

Green Coat swerved his carriage just enough to widen the space between them to an unpredictable width. Henry didn't land on the roof, as he'd planned, but at least his hands did. He held on, body flung out like a ribbon in a high wind. His bones threatened to snap. He only grunted and pulled himself up, dogged and determined.

He didn't pause to catch his breath. There was no time: the horses could rebel at any moment, a deep rut could appear in the road, a wheel could snap. He yanked at the coachman's sleeve hard enough to send him reeling. Then he slid into his place, catching the reins before they snapped loose. He slowed the horses, breath by breath. And then he leapt down, ignoring the gaping passersby.

"You're right mad," the hackney's driver shouted down, but he was grinning. "And you owe me five pounds."

"You'll get your money as soon as you get us back to Mayfair."

Henry ripped the door open, something very like panic strangling his throat.

Tamsin merely looked up at him, sitting in her pretty striped dress, with an earl sprawled unconscious at her feet.

"Took you long enough, Captain Talbot."

Chapter Eighteen

I T WAS BOTH shocking to see Henry and somehow also completely expected.

When someone had broken into her house, he was there to help, even when he wasn't even supposed to be in England.

When she had to speak to her father, he'd been there to offer his arm.

When she needed to escape a very public waltz with Eaton, Henry had appeared once again.

She very much wanted to throw herself into his arms, to kiss that darkly handsome face.

She didn't.

It took a considerable amount of self-control and a reminder that he would not want it, so she didn't. She stepped down out of the carriage, as if she was alighting to attend some ball.

Well, that was the plan, anyway.

Instead, he hauled her out, his eyes slightly crazed. "Are you hurt?" he demanded. "Did he hurt you?"

She shook her head. She would have answered him with actual words, but he was skating his hands over her shoulders, down her waist. They were going to have to establish some rules. If she wasn't allowed to kiss him, then he wasn't allowed to run his hands over her body. However much she wanted him to. However much she wanted to lean into the touch.

She nearly moaned.

That would not do.

"Tamsin, *did he hurt you?*"

"No," she finally said. "I'm fine."

He glared at the heap of fine silk that was Lord Eaton.

Tamsin knew for a fact that if Henry had his way, Eaton would not wake. Ever. "You can't murder him." Tamsin pointed, stepping more fully in front of him.

"Are you sure about that?"

She huffed a sigh. "I seem to spend an inordinate amount of time telling you just that, actually." He was so close. She could feel the warmth of him, see the grain of his rough beard, the simmering in his brown eyes. "How did you even find me?"

"Your little pickpocket helped."

"Jack? Is he all right?"

"He's fine."

"Oh, good, he's—" She broke off when the green-coated coachman stepped down from his perch, scowling. "You!" She pointed an accusatory finger at him, just like a vengeful witch in a storybook. He had the intelligence to look briefly uncomfortable. "Tell me, do you always ignore the screams of women shoved unwillingly into your coach?"

Henry stilled. "You screamed?"

"Fat lot of good it did me, but yes."

Henry moved quicker than the snap of a sail during a hurricane. The coachman did not see him coming. He only knew the sudden grip of Henry's fist around the back of his collar and then his face colliding with the side of the carriage. There was a crack, a spurt of blood. He slid to the ground.

"Well," Tamsin said, twitching her skirts away from the blood. "I can't say you didn't deserve that."

She might have been the one who was abducted, but Henry was the one who looked dazed. Seething with violence.

For her.

She absolutely should not find that thrilling in some deep, secret part of herself. Clearly the events of the day and her impeding marriage to cheese had addled her wits.

"If you won't let me kill him," he said, his jaw clenching,

"then let's move away from here."

She nodded, but first turned to make sure the door was wide open.

"What's that for?" Henry asked.

"It looks like rain," she said. "I want him to be very, very uncomfortable. And if he drowns, well, that's hardly our fault."

He smiled, quickly, like a candlewick catching a draft. "So you're not opposed to his murder, after all?"

"No, I'm opposed to yours," she pointed out. "For a Navy man, you're not very stealthy."

"Stealth is not easy to come by when you're wielding cannons and a first-rate, three-decker ship."

"Well, you're back in London now, so you must remember to murder with stealth."

He shook his head. "Only you could make me smile at a time like this."

She shrugged as they made their way around to the hackney he had commandeered. He kept her tucked in close, raking the area for threats. It made her melt a little. Which was not helpful.

No melting.

Friendship.

Friends didn't make each other melt.

"How did you manage to knock him out?"

"I pretended his head was a cricket ball and I was the bat. After I kicked him in the bollocks."

He barked a laugh. She preened, just a little. She decided she was owed a moment of smugness. Eaton had been taken entirely by surprise. And Henry's laugh had become all too rare.

"Imagine what I could do if I wasn't hungover," she muttered.

"You too?" he asked drily. He scrubbed a hand over his face, weary underneath the predatory alertness. There was something else to his expression, something she couldn't understand.

"'Ello, miss." The hackney driver tipped his cap.

She smiled at him. "Hello. Thank you for the daring rescue."

He blushed. "'Tweren't nothing."

"He's right," Henry grumbled. "All he did was make five

pounds."

"Shrewd as well as heroic, then."

The coachman blushed harder, right to his ears.

"All right." Henry nudged her around toward the doors. "Enough of you. You don't know if he's got a weak heart."

She grinned, swinging her bonnet from its ribbons.

He narrowed in on the crushed brim. "What happened to your bonnet?"

"A casualty of war, I'm afraid."

"He did touch you." His tone was steady, his words even. It was more threatening than a yell or a punch.

She touched his elbow. "I'm perfectly well, I promise. He was taking me somewhere to be married."

"That much I gathered."

"I said no."

"That much I also gathered."

She fought a wince. "I'm not sure that I'm going to able to stop him next time."

"There's not going to be a next time," Henry said. "I promise you that."

"He's not going to give up my dowry. And he has my father's blessing. And no one's brave enough to take them on and marry me, at least not without a guaranteed dowry. Which we both know my father will withhold if he feels himself to be embarrassed in any way."

"Tamsin."

She shook her head. "Please, don't." She smiled, and if it was a little resigned, a little sad, she couldn't entirely help it. "Don't fret, Henry. You made yourself quite clear as to your position on marriage to me. I didn't mean to put you in an awkward position. And I'm not going to embarrass you by begging."

His arm came out to block her as she made her way toward the hackney steps. His hand crossed her body to grip her waist. And then he bent his head, just enough that his mouth nearly brushed her ear. His voice was a dark growl, soft but deep. "What if I want you to beg?"

She stilled, swallowing. Heat sparked through her. "I don't

understand."

"What if I want you to beg me not to stop?"

Her breath stuttered. Desire threatened to weaken her knees. "What are you saying, Henry?"

"Get in the carriage, Tamsin."

THE MAN HAD lost his mind.

And this was coming from a woman who collected skulls and had recently been engaged to *cheese*.

There was no other explanation for the rough whisper in her ear, for the way he looked at her even now, from the other side of the carriage. His knees were between hers, sprawled apart to create just enough tension against her own as to send delicious shivers into her core.

"I don't understand," she said again. "You don't want me."

"Of course I bloody well want you," he growled.

"You don't want to marry me."

"I want you happy and safe," he said. "Preferably both of those things, in my bed."

She wasn't sure what to say. She was half afraid she was imagining this, hearing him all wrong.

"You needn't look so surprised," he said gruffly.

"You said no."

"I was wrong."

She leaned forward. "Henry, I've had a trying day. Please speak plainly."

He leaned forward as well. He was close enough to kiss. "I'm not going to let Eaton harass and harangue you. I'll marry you, Tam."

"To save me."

He inclined his head.

It wasn't exactly a declaration of love, but perhaps that might come later. Love changed, after all, grew deeper, sent roots into unexpected soil. It might be bittersweet, but she could it make it work for both of them. She had to believe that.

"But what about you?" She wanted to say yes so desperately. Why was her traitorous mouth still moving? "What if you regret it? What if you… want to marry someone else one day?"

"I won't regret it." He sounded very sure. That was something, at least.

"You'd do that for me?" she asked softly. "Truly?"

"Yes."

If she hadn't fallen in love with him all of those years ago, she would have fallen in love with him right then and there.

"And to think, I almost married cheese."

"What?"

"Never mind."

He took her hands. "We could make a proper go at it, I think," he said, seriously. "We get along, we always have. And there's heat between us," he added, voice turning hoarse.

She swallowed. "Yes."

"Friendship and heat. Few are so lucky in our circles in regards to marriage."

"I suppose that's true. And we'll figure it out." They always figured it out. She let a tendril of hope and want take hold inside her ribcage. "And you're not fussed over my collections."

"I can do without that shrunken head, but yes." He ghosted her a smile. "But you can't traipse about alone anymore. For my own sanity, if I'm not with you, you'll take Crow or Mr. Gallagher or a great, big, strapping footman—preferably with muscles the size of my head."

She chuckled. "I don't think you have to worry about Eaton after we marry." How strange to say it out loud.

"Promise me."

She nodded. "Fine. I promise." It might help also with her theft problem and the suspiciously timed auction. She decided not to mention it right then. It would keep. He was concerned enough as it was.

"Before we get out of this carriage and ambush the rector…"

"Yes?"

"I have a condition."

Chapter Nineteen

THE CONDITION WOULD take some getting used to.

Some consideration.

Definitely a longer conversation.

But she would worry about it later. They were already on the rector's doorstep.

"I've heard this house is haunted," Henry whispered in her ear. "Perhaps you'll have a ghost as an attendant."

"You do know how to flatter a girl."

"I know it's not St. George's, or the archbishop, but Sandringham here can get it done for us," he said. "Do you mind?"

Tamsin shook her head. "That's fine."

The butler was not convinced. It was nearly midnight, after all. "The rector does not receive at this hour," he said, looking down his nose. He was quite tall, and it was quite effective.

"He'll see me," Henry said, stepping inside. "Viscount Stirling. And the daughter of the Duke of Chester."

The butler's eyes widened, but he quickly regained his composure.

"Stop terrifying my servants," the rector said mildly, coming down an impressive staircase of carved mahogany. He was younger than Tamsin would have expected, and he did not look particularly surprised.

Henry inclined his head briskly. "A word, Sandringham."

Mr. Sandringham sighed. "Very well." He turned to the butler. "Have Mrs. Harris bring up a tea tray and apologize to her on behalf of the viscount." He extended his arm to Tamsin, all courtesy. "My lady."

She twinkled at him. "Hello."

He blinked. "Hello."

Henry rolled his eyes, striding past them. "He's a man of the cloth, Tam. Have some pity on him."

She kept smiling at the rector. "You're very kind to see us."

"Not at all."

The parlor was tidy, with dove-gray wallpaper and an abundance of chairs and silver candlesticks.

Henry wasted no time with explanations or flattery. "We need you to marry us. Tonight. Now."

"That's not precisely how the church does things."

Henry's glance was deeply, deeply sardonic. "We both know that's not true."

Tamsin nudged him with her elbow, stepping between them. "We'd be very grateful for your help, Mr. Sandringham."

"Well."

Henry groaned. "I don't know why I bother. You should just do all of the talking."

"Yes, we know that already," she murmured. She winked at the rector. He blushed, chuckled. "I know it's all very untoward, but you're the only one that can help us."

"Also, your debt will be cleared," Henry added drily.

Mr. Sandringham paused for a beat. "Really?"

"A debt?" Tamsin asked. Henry rarely gambled, and he probably wouldn't fleece a rector.

"The viscount here saved my cousin's life last year," Mr. Sandringham explained.

"When he was Captain Talbot?"

"Exactly."

Tamsin beamed at Henry proudly. "Did you really?"

He shifted uncomfortably. He looked like he might be blushing. The urge to tease him was nearly as irresistible as the urge to kiss him.

"But it's as if you'd really hold such a debt against a person," she said.

Henry lifted an eyebrow at her. Tamsin sent him back a quick grimace, suddenly remembering that they needed this debt.

"Erm, that is, yes, much debt. Honor. Manliness."

Henry shook his head, smiling. "Very smoothly done."

"Thank you, I thought so."

Since the rector was smiling as well, she wasn't overly concerned.

"Might I ask why the sudden urgency to be married on a Thursday night in my front parlor?" he asked.

Tamsin bit her lip. "Um."

"Are you… in a delicate condition?"

"No."

"Watch it, Sandringham," Henry said mildly.

"It's a fair question," Tamsin pointed out. "But no, that's not the issue. The issue is that I was just abducted by a fortune hunter."

The rector frowned. "Shall I call a magistrate?"

"It was an earl."

"Ah."

"Exactly," Tamsin said. "It's getting a bit tiresome, I don't mind telling you. This is a neat solution, and there are worse fates than marrying one of your oldest friends, wouldn't you say?"

"That's a very measured and rational approach, my dear," he said. "But what of your father? Surely the duke can intervene."

"Do you know my father, Mr. Sandringham?"

Her father had been married to Lady Chester by the Archbishop of Canterbury, naturally, but as Mr. Sandringham was the rector of St. George's—Mayfair's parish church—they surely would have met. "I have had that honor, yes." She met his gaze steadily. It took him a moment. "Ah."

She nodded. "I am long past my age of majority, if that is a concern."

"And I don't give a damn for her dowry," Henry added.

"I should not like to have the duke as an enemy."

She laughed. "And you shan't. My father would very much like to see me married."

"I see."

"Your cousin was, what, eighteen years old when old Boney tried to kill him?" Henry asked idly.

The rector sighed. "Yes, all right. Point made, my lord. You still need a special license," he pointed out.

"Blast," Tamsin said. "I'd forgotten that bit."

"We have a special license," Henry said, not an ounce of emotion in his voice. He pulled a folded piece of parchment from a pocket inside his coat.

She stared at him. "You have a special license?"

"I do."

"These need to have both your names on it," Mr. Sandringham reminded them. "And an oath made to the archbishop."

"It's been done."

Tamsin ought to probably blink at some point. "How long have you had that?" she demanded.

Henry shifted slightly, the way he had as a boy when he was shy and being singled out. "A few days."

"*A few days?*" That was romantic, wasn't it? Or was it maddening? Honestly, she couldn't tell.

"I didn't want to worry you," he mumbled. "I'd hoped you wouldn't need it."

Less romantic.

As Tamsin's whirling mind whirled a little harder, Mrs. Harris arrived with the tea cart and a bright smile, displaying the very good timing of a very good housekeeper. Her lace cap was slightly crooked, but she did not otherwise look as though it were midnight and not noon. "I hear we have a wedding," she said. "How romantic."

That was up to more debate than Tamsin would have assumed, considering the circumstances.

Tamsin smiled back at her. "Mrs. Harris, is there somewhere I might put myself to rights?" She might not need an elaborate ceremony in St. George's with several hundred guests from the aristocracy, or a new gown, or even friends as her witnesses instead of a butler and housekeeper she had never met before—but she'd be damned if she was going to say her vows with limp hair and travel smudges on her face.

"Oh my dear, of course!" Mrs. Harris bustled Tamsin straight out of the library and into a small retiring room. "I'll bring hot water straightaway."

Tamsin stared at herself in her looking glass. She was not a fresh-faced debutante. She looked exactly like what she was: a woman tentatively reaching for happiness with pins falling out of her hair and buttons missing from her spencer from being seized off the street. She shrugged off her spencer, adjusted the bodice of her gown, and pulled her hair into a passable twist that would have horrified Juniper with its simplicity.

At least the last of the smudges under her eyes from overindulging were hardly noticeable by lamplight. She was used to being in public fashionably dressed and with shining hair. Perhaps a little lip rouge. But none of that seemed to matter to Henry.

He was still willing to marry her, without the glittering crowd who wanted her for their parties, and without her dowry.

With a special license in his pocket.

He'd turned her down with a special license in his pocket.

For someone she knew and liked so well, he certainly was rather inscrutable. But an inscrutable groom she loved versus a fortune hunter with a disregard for everyone?

No contest.

The situation might not be ideal, but absolutely no bloody contest.

She marched back into the parlor, less like a blushing bride and more like a woman with a reticule full of weapons. She could be both.

"I'm ready," she announced.

"Wait." Henry frowned at the rector. "Haven't you any flowers in this place?" He marched back out to the foyer and returned with two glass vases stuffed with lilacs. He fussed with them on the table and then fussed with the grate, coaxing the coals back into flames. He lit every candle he could find and arranged them just so. "There. It's not the cathedral, but this is still a bloody wedding, after all."

Tamsin wanted to kiss his face.

Every part of him.

The rector smiled indulgently. Mrs. Harris pressed a hand to her chest. "Such a romantic gentleman," she said, sighing. "I do so adore a love match."

Tamsin and Henry exchanged a quick glance but did not disabuse her of the notion.

Because despite it all, Tamsin was beginning to feel loved.

"Are we ready?" Mr. Sandringham asked. "As touching as I'm sure this is, I have a brandy and warm bed waiting for me."

"Just one more moment," Henry said, glancing at the clock. "If you please."

Tamsin frowned at him. "Why?"

"One more moment." She was about to push him for more details when he thrust a cup into her hand. "Have some tea."

"I've had tea."

"Have more."

"Henry, what's this about?"

"Yes," Mr. Sandringham said. "I was under the impression that time was of the essence."

"It is."

A knock sounded at the door.

Mr. Sandringham threw his hands up. "Now what?"

Now what, indeed.

Priya, Persephone, and Conall hurried into the parlor, each smiling and smug down to the core.

Happiness sparkled inside Tamsin. She beamed at Henry. "How did you manage this?"

"I sent word when you went off with Mrs. Harris."

"Henry, thank you," she said softly.

"We needed rings, didn't we?" he asked. He lowered his voice. "And you know as well as I do that Persephone would have murdered me if I did this without her."

There was that.

Priya and Conall were lugging pots of orchids and roses from Priya's greenhouse. Persephone darted forward, beaming. "I'm so happy for you!" she said. She nudged Henry. "And very glad to see you're not an idiot.

"Thank you," he returned drily.

"Meg and I had a wager."

"Meg's not even in London."

"I wrote to her. She owes me a pound."

"Lovely."

As Tamsin listened to them, her eyes stung. She had never been warmer, safer. Happier.

Henry, on the other hand, looked alarmed. "Are you crying? What's wrong?"

"Nothing."

"I knew this wasn't good enough." He narrowed his eyes accusingly at the small parlor, the lack of ornamentation.

She shook her head. "It's absolutely perfect."

He studied for a moment before Mr. Sandringham cleared his throat. "If you please?"

Persephone shoved rings into their hands. "I brought these back from Egypt. It's all I had," she added apologetically. "But did you know the ancient Egyptians may have been the first to wear wedding rings?"

Tamsin's ring was made of blue faience, carved with delicate lotus blossoms. Henry's ring was gold, with a simple lapis lazuli cartouche. There were hieroglyphs scratched into it, but they had faded.

"We still can't translate those," Persephone said, following Tamsin's gaze. "But yours was pulled from the grave of a queen or a priestess. They were going to toss it away!" She wrinkled her nose. "You don't mind, do you? I have others, but they aren't as interesting."

"She would only mind if the lady in question was *not* horribly murdered or cursed in some way and on a ghostly quest for revenge," Henry said.

He wasn't wrong.

Persephone nodded. "That's what I thought too."

"But we can get you something else," Henry offered.

Tamsin shook her head. "I love them."

"Something in a poison ring, maybe?"

She paused, considering. "Well…"

He grinned. Her future husband knew her well.

Husband.

"Best we get started," he murmured. "Before Sandringham falls asleep on the settee."

The rector straightened when they approached. "Are you sure?" he asked Tamsin, even as Henry scowled. "This is very rushed, and I would not be doing my duty if I didn't confirm."

He had decorated the parlor, sent notice to her friends, all to make her comfortable. Happy.

She smiled, bright as the May Queen.

"I'm sure."

Chapter Twenty

THE CEREMONY WAS simple and quick and just right.

And in a few moments, she was married.

They were married.

Priya and Persephone tossed flower petals. Conall shook Henry's hand. Mrs. Harris wept. And Mr. Sandringham waved his hand. "Yes, yes. Congratulations. Now get out, the lot of you."

Mrs. Harris poured more tea, ignoring him. Tiny iced cakes were eaten. There was teasing, toasts, and hot glances. It was better than any wedding breakfast Tamsin had ever attended. And she'd been to one where the couple entered through a procession of swans carved from ice. She'd seen brides arrive on white horses laden with red roses, diamonds gifted to all of the guests, and, once, an actual river made of champagne.

But this was what she wanted. A stolen, happy moment with her friends in someone's cozy parlor. Laughter, stories, flowers. And Henry.

Always Henry.

And then her father arrived.

His knock was loud, arrogant. Logical or not, she would have known it anywhere.

Mr. Sandringham, oblivious, just shook his head and sighed. "Did you invite all of Mayfair?"

Tamsin held her breath.

"Tamsin Bell!"

Definitely her father.

Henry's hand slipped into hers. "It's done now. Nothing he can do about it."

Which wasn't precisely true, as they had not yet consummated the marriage, but Tamsin nodded.

The rector winced. "I had to send word," he said. "I did not think he would come at this hour."

Tamsin couldn't entirely blame him. People didn't, as a rule, antagonize dukes.

Except for Henry.

And Priya.

And Persephone.

And Conall, who didn't move from his lean against the wall, or alter his sardonic smile, but she knew he could. Would.

Her father thundered into the parlor, wearing a very fine embroidered waistcoat and a diamond cravat pin the size of a quail's egg. He peered down his nose at Tamsin. "Now what have you done, girl?"

"Married," she returned, trying not to feel all of eight years old. She was an adult, for God's sake. "Just as you wanted."

"What about Eaton?"

"He gropes ladies," Priya interrupted. "All of them."

The duke stared at her. "Pardon?"

"You heard me."

He clearly didn't know what to say to her, so he rounded on Henry instead. "What's your angle, boy? Her dowry?"

"If you think Lady Tamsin needs an incentive that is not Lady Tamsin herself then you do not know your own daughter," Henry said. "Your Grace."

"A shoddy, hasty marriage in the dead of night? What are you doing?"

"Making sure my wife—your daughter—is happy and cared for, which is something we both know you never much bothered to do."

The duke blinked so hard that Tamsin wondered if he was having some sort of fit.

"Good night, Your Grace," Henry added. He extended his arm to Tamsin, and she took it, as polite as a procession into supper at Buckingham House. He tightened his hand over hers, as though he was afraid her father might try to physically take her from him.

"Father, please be happy for me."

His face softened. "Do you truly want this?"

"I do."

"Well, I suppose he'll be an earl one day."

"And he's already a war hero," Persephone reminded him helpfully.

The duke shook his head. Tamsin relaxed. He wouldn't fight her. She knew that, logically. He did not have sustained fighting in his nature. But now that she had Henry for her own, she was feeling quite feral about protecting their marriage, whatever it might look like.

"Very well, very well," her father said at last. The rector visibly relaxed, enough so that the butler reached out to steady him when he swayed. "Can't say I like that it wasn't done at St. George's."

"It might have been if Eaton hadn't tried to abduct me earlier today."

"What now?" He harrumphed. "Just a bout of high spirits, I'm sure." He didn't sound entirely sure, which was a step in the right direction. When every single person in the room stared at him, he relented. "Well, done is done. We needn't worry about him anymore, I suppose."

He turned back, pausing in the doorway. "Oh, and Tamsin, your stepmother would prefer you not visit the Bruton Street house, if you insist on leaving it in shambles."

"Shambles?" She hadn't left the house in shambles.

"Open windows, knickknacks on the floor." He clicked his tongue disapprovingly. "It's childish, especially for a married woman and a viscountess."

Henry met her gaze.

She hadn't been back to house since yesterday.

If someone had broken in again, she knew it wasn't Jack. Was it the unknown man who had hired him? It had to be. If so, he was growing bolder.

And she was growing angrier.

Chapter Twenty-One

THEY RETIRED TO Priya's townhouse, and Priya disappeared almost immediately, vanishing into the shadows. When Tamsin led Henry to her bedroom, feeling both shy and eager, they found it filled with flowers.

The Cinderella Society never left a woman behind.

She smiled at the lilacs and the violets and the fat white peonies, at the beeswax candles on every surface.

"They don't miss a thing, do they?" Henry asked.

"They really don't," she agreed fondly.

She lit the candles and then stopped, not knowing what else to do.

She knew what she *wanted* to do.

She *wanted* to leap on the poor man and bite into him like an apple.

But one probably ought to show some decorum and not go around biting people. Handsome men. Her husband. She'd only embarrass him. It wasn't his fault that she had dreamt of this very moment for years now.

And clearly, he had *not*.

He swallowed, clearly uncomfortable. "Tamsin, you know we don't have to…"

"Oh." She fiddled with the edge of her sleeve. "Do you not want to?" When he only stared at her, she looked away, grimacing. "Of course you don't. You've done enough, and you didn't really want to marry me in the first pl—"

She broke off when he closed the distance between them like it was an affront. She had to tilt her head up to meet his gaze, which threatened to devour her, even as it searched gently, patiently for something. "Is that really what you think?" he asked softly.

"You've been running from Society, from London, your whole life." *Running from me.*

"And now I've married its queen."

She bit the inside of her cheek. "I'm sorry."

He grasped her chin firmly, forcing their gazes to meet again. "I'm not," he said darkly. "Do you hear me, Tam? I'm not sorry. I might not be able to give you what you need, but I can keep you safe."

"What about the rest?" She motioned vaguely to the bed, embarrassed but determined to know where they stood.

"The rest?" he repeated, stepping closer, eating up the few inches left between their bodies. "It would be my very great pleasure to explore the rest with you." He trailed his fingers up her jaw and tightened them in her hair with just enough delicious force to make her catch her breath. "But I don't want you to feel pressured."

"I don't," she assured him. Was that her voice? All breathless and needy? She swayed toward him. "I thought *you* might feel forced." It was the last step to making their marriage legal, after all.

He shook his head. "Let's make a pact," he said. "Whatever else happens, it will not follow us into this bedroom. Here we are simply Tamsin and Henry. Together."

She'd never wanted anything more. And she wanted to believe him with every breath and bone in her body. How was she supposed to keep her expectations low and logical when he insisted on being so considerate? So devastatingly kind and forthright.

She nodded, because she could not find the words. And then there were no words. They were entirely unnecessary. They would only get in the way, only complicate already complicated matters. For tonight, at least, let bare skin and shared breaths be enough. There were many ways to love a person, after all.

Tonight, she chose this way. This man.

And he chose her.

"I should call for Juniper," she said.

"You won't need a lady's maid," Henry said, his voice low and rough in her ear. "Or have you forgotten that we've done this part before? I certainly haven't forgotten." He smiled against her, and she knew it was wicked just by the feel of it. "I suppose I shall have to remind you."

He spun her around suddenly until her back was pressed to his chest. His body was warm and hard against hers, promising all sorts of things that made heat and wetness gather between her legs. His fingers were agile and quick as he dealt with the fastenings of her dress. It fell in a puddle around her feet.

A Cheval mirror stood before her, and he smiled at her reflection, she in silk stockings and stays, he fully dressed. The juxtaposition ran through her like a shiver. There was something feral in his smile, like the wolf catching Little Red Riding Hood in the woods. Like a starving man offered a feast of frosted cakes. He nipped at the side her neck as if he could not help himself. It shot need and want to her core. Her breasts tingled.

"Do you care for these stays?" he asked.

"No?"

"Oh, I was hoping you'd say that." That wolfish grin again, and suddenly there was a dagger in his hand. "It's taking entirely too long to undo."

Her mouth went dry with want. He flicked his wrist, and the dagger cut through the laces with ease. Her stays gaped, and he pulled the pieces apart, freeing her. He tossed it to the floor and pulled her chemise over her head before it had landed. She stood naked except for her stockings and their little blue satin bows. The rasp of his coat against her bare back was unbearably intimate.

"Just look at you," he murmured appreciatively.

She was accustomed to being watched, but not like this. Not with this kind of intensity and hunger, not as if she was too bright, like the sun. "I don't want to look at myself," she said. "I want to look at you."

He smoothed his palm down her spine, clasping her bottom briefly. He moved around her hip, over her thighs, and then dipped into the heat of her.

She swayed backward against him. *"Henry."*

His chuckle rasped and sent more sparks over her neck, up her thighs. She wanted more, so much more. She also wanted his infernal clothing consigned to the devil. She opened her mouth to tell him exactly that, but his fingers slid into her, invaded her, seemed to control her very breaths. It wasn't a soft exploration—it was a claiming. The force of the sensations shooting through her made her moan, made her stretch up on her toes, even though she wanted more. Her head fell back against his shoulder.

"That's it," he murmured. "That's my beautiful girl."

He brushed his palm against her bud, and she gasped. He pressed, circling it until her knees weakened and she wasn't sure she could stand on her own for much longer. He plunged his fingers inside her again, retreated, advanced again and again. Her gasps filled the room as his teeth scraped under her ear. His hand moved mercilessly, the other pinning her against him, holding her up until the pleasure sharpened, stole her ability to think or worry, to focus on anything but the wave building inside of her. It swept up her thighs, narrowed to her core, and then shot through her like fireworks.

She was limp against him for a long moment, waiting for her heart to calm. She cracked one eye open. "You're still fully clothed."

"I am."

"I don't care for it," she said. He touched her again, and she squirmed. "You're trying to distract me."

His other hand traveled up to her breast, circling her nipple until it puckered. "And if I am?"

She reached behind her, stroking firmly over the hardness of him.

He groaned, stilling. "Tamsin."

She squeezed gently then pulled at his waistband. "Captain

Talbot."

He growled, tugging her around to face him. She pushed at his coat and pulled his shirt up, frantic. He yanked at the buttons of his placard until he could finally shove off his pants, leaving them tangled with her discarded dress. His member sprang up, hot silk over steel, and when she closed her eager fingers around it, he groaned again. She teased him, soft strokes, followed by pressure under the tip, up and down.

"You started it," she said, loving the way he reacted to her, pushing into her hand, muscles of his hard thighs tensing to keep him still.

"Shall I finish it?"

"Can you?" She moved her attentions lower, cradling his balls, squeezing.

And then the back of her knees hit the bed and she fell back against it, his strong body closing over hers. She ran her fingertips over the planes of his back, the tautness of his backside. His chest blocked out the candlelight, leaving just enough to gleam over his skin, hair, the smooth scars that laced him. One day she would ask about the ones she did not know about; she would kiss each and every one.

But not tonight—tonight she had lost the ability to move or form coherent thought. His weight was delicious on top of her as he moved to lick at one breast. He sucked it into his mouth, rolling his tongue over the nipple, pulling until she writhed, panting. His hardness nudged her gently. He ran the tip of his shaft through her folds, and her thighs fell open.

She clutched at him, urging him on. "*Now*, Henry."

He pushed a little, but not much. He was just inside her entrance, and her intimate muscles quivered. "Now?" he whispered hoarsely, teasing them both. He increased the pressure on her bud. "Are you sure?"

She widened her knees and pushed up, and he slid into her wet, hot slickness. She tightened around him, a small pain, the burn and stretch of her body accommodating his invasion, and then only pleasure. Searing, all-encompassing pleasure. He made a sound that made her feel like a goddess. She shifted again, imploring him to move. He eased back slowly, so slowly, and then pushed into her, just as slowly. His chest gleamed above her as he moved.

"Damn your military discipline."

He laughed, and when the line of his strong shoulder finally dropped close enough to reach, she bit gently, using her teeth until he groaned out a curse.

And then there was no more teasing. No games or thought or worries.

There was only the two of them in the flickering gold light, feral for each other. The pace Henry set was steady and deep, his muscles straining, his mouth on her throat. She met every thrust until another orgasm began to uncurl inside of her. He didn't stop or alter the rhythm until her little moans turned to gasps and her entire body became a ballroom, all whirling colors and soft lights and glittering air.

He followed within moments. She wrapped her legs around him as he came, groaning. He dropped his forehead to hers, catching his breath. She kissed him softly. "Husband."

He kissed her back. "Wife."

Chapter Twenty-Two

A N HOUR LATER, Tamsin opened one eye. "Where are you going?" she asked him the moment he touched the door.

He'd been so quiet, pulling on his clothes, his boots. He could walk belowdecks between swaying hammocks filled with vigilant sailors and not wake a single one. His wife, it seemed, was better trained than any sailor.

Well, she *was* a Cinderella.

His wife.

A warm thrill shot through him at the word resonating inside his head. Followed by the usual, expected dread.

This was one joy his father would not touch.

Although he did not really expect Father to trouble the daughter of a duke—in fact, he'd be thrilled with his daughter-in-law—he still wouldn't be able to resist testing Henry further.

Testing.

What a word for the things his father did.

Henry would protect Tamsin at any cost. He would find a way to put an end to this madness once and for all. He wanted to share a house with his wife, to eat coddled eggs across from each other in the morning, to sit in front of the fire at night and hear her stories of the various events she'd flitted between. To be free to kiss her at any time of day or night. To stand at her side proudly. There were trials ahead.

But sweet rewards as well.

"Henry?" Tamsin said when he stayed lost too long in his inner landscape. She was warm and mussed, and the only thing he wanted was to crawl into that bed with her, to devastate each other again and wake up, limbs tangled, satiated and rested.

But Henry did not sleep well.

And though he might feel better than he had in years and Tamsin might be a balm to every chafe in his soul, he knew he still would not sleep. He would either lie awake listening for threats until every muscle screamed, or he would wake sweating and shaking from nightmares. He didn't want to disturb her. It would hardly be a pleasant memory of one's wedding night.

And they were *more* than pleasant thus far.

"I'm just going for a walk."

"Now?" She sat up. The sheet wrapped around her, slipped off her shoulder, showing tempting, soft skin. She frowned.

"I don't sleep much," he explained. "And not well."

"So you walk, when you're not reading. I remember those towers of books you used to make in the library."

"Exactly."

"I'll come with you," she declared.

"Tam, it's the middle of the night."

She shrugged. "I like the night."

Of course she did. His cheerful, witty, slightly macabre wife. "Hoping for ghosts, are you?"

"Always."

"I'll see what I can do," he said. "Remember what we talked about?"

"Yes. Your condition, which I think is excessive, I might point out." She stood up. Her bare toes poked out from under the sheet she now wore like a queen wore a coronation gown. Lord, she was a vision. "And your *condition* starts tomorrow, at the ball of your choosing. I've been invited to four."

"Four?"

"I am very sought after. Like a table decoration."

He frowned. He'd heard her say similar before, and he did not like it. He hated the way she seemed resigned to it, like it was something she'd had to make her peace with. "You're not a decoration, Tam."

"And you're not changing the subject, Henry. I'll have my wedding night, thank you very much."

He smirked. "You had your wedding night."

"I mean to have all of it, *Captain Talbot*." The way she said it never failed to stir him, make him hard. "If you're walking, then I'm walking."

He narrowed one eye at her in a vaguely autocratic fashion. "It might not be safe," he reminded her.

She snorted. "I'm not afraid of you."

His worry was not a match for her smile, or his own answering grin. "I know you're not afraid of me. Who wants that?"

"Then it's settled."

"Apparently," he said fondly. "If not fear, a little healthy trepidation would not go amiss."

"You'd hate it."

"True."

One night. He would have one easy, happy night that his father could not taint. It was late enough as to be almost early. They'd be safe enough. The streets would be mostly deserted, which would make sneaking up on them nearly impossible. And honestly, he wanted to show her the only London he could stomach: London at night. If there was anyone else who could see the beauty in the eerie fog, the echoing clop of hooves, the shadows that seemed to move of their own accord, it was Tamsin Bell.

Tamsin Talbot, Viscountess Stirling.

"Help me dress," she demanded.

"Where's the fun in that?"

As it turned out, while he vastly preferred undressing her, there was some joy in the opposite as well. Not to mention a kind of nostalgia, bringing to mind helping her in her bedroom earlier in the week.

Had that really only been a week ago?

He helped her shimmy into a new set of stays, unable to resist kissing the top of her spine, the smooth line of her shoulder, and then the curve of her bottom when he reached for the laces. She shivered, and he smiled against her skin. "I suppose we don't have to walk at all."

She turned to look down at him, imperiously, happily. God, he could eat her up. "I was promised a tour of dark London, where the ghosts lurk."

"That you were."

He watched her pull up her stockings and tie them with little blue ribbons and wanted to be nowhere else in the entire world. His mouth went dry. He itched to touch her again.

Too soon, she was done with her task, and he helped her lace up a walking dress. She braided her hair, and he'd never seen her look so carefree, so comfortable. He couldn't remember the last time he'd seen her when she wasn't trussed up for some ball or promenade under public scrutiny. She glittered, and he loved that about her. But he loved this quiet glow even more, like a secret shared between them.

They snuck downstairs like naughty children, avoiding creaking stairs and banging doors. Tamsin was laughing when they finally made it out to the front step, and he couldn't resist bending down to kiss her, to share that laugh, even as it turned into a breathy little gasp that made him hot all over.

He could have stood right there and kissed her all night.

Only the knowledge that they were likely safe from his father's men at this time and in this place, outside his usual haunt, had him pulling back. He'd happily lose himself in her when it was safe, when he didn't have to monitor that shadow, that scuff of a boot in the distance.

They walked in comfortable silence, and this was yet another version of Tamsin that he adored. Most knew her as a charming, chattering magpie. Society thought she was a bonbon, a placid pond. He knew she was the whole damn ocean. One he'd happily drown in.

He pulled his attention back to the fog and the very few lights burning in upstairs windows of the houses they passed.

Apparently, a wedding night turned one into a poet. But poetry would not keep her safe.

He turned them away from the road leading deeper into

Mayfair, which would be cluttered with carriages carrying the *ton* home, or onward to darker delights. Instead, he chose a quieter neighborhood that eventually led to a row of shops and the deep, ever-present smudge of the park.

A sign creaked above their heads, over a curved door set with iron nails.

"Story has it a witch lived here once," he murmured. "She left spells under the threshold to protect herself, and when they came to carry out her body after a strange fever took her, two watchmen died on the very spot."

Tamsin eyed the threshold stone. "Has anyone dug underneath?" she asked. "Witch bottles were quite popular in our grandparents' time and before that."

"Not even one shiver." He shook his head with mock disappointment. "Just ghoulish curiosity." He bent his head, letting his mouth skim her ear. "That's what I like about you, Tam."

Her breath caught.

"I like teasing you, too," he murmured.

"I've noticed."

"I can't help it. I love all of the noises you make."

She blushed and squirmed, ever so slightly. It made him feel like a king. He nipped at her earlobe, dragged his lips along her throat. Her hands slipped under his coat, skimming his chest. When he finally kissed her, she met him eagerly, lips parted. Little bites, long strokes of their tongues, ragged pulls of their breaths. He wanted it all. Her little moan had him pushing her against the column, kissing her harder, deeper, licking down into her cleavage, using his teeth to tease at her soft, heated flesh.

And then a cat leapt off a nearby windowsill, knocking over several empty crates. The clatter was loud, sudden. Intrusive.

Explosive.

His blood froze in his veins even as the rest of him leapt into action. He shoved Tamsin behind him in the doorway, pulse roaring in his ears, hands perfectly steady and suddenly filled with knives. It took a moment to realize it was just a cat, another to assess the street, the other shadowy doorways and nooks. He looked up as well, used to checking the sky, and he checked the rooftops the same way for danger.

Tamsin touched his back gently. "Henry."

He lowered his knives.

"Henry, it was just a cat," she said softly. His pulse quieted. "We're perfectly safe."

He should be the one giving assurances, not her.

Damn it.

When he turned to her, he was a viscount again, knives put away, intimate knowledge on how to incapacitate a man shielded behind good manners. Memories ruthlessly shoved down deep in his gut. They had no place here. They would not touch Tamsin.

"I apologize," he said, somewhat stiffly.

She looked at him for one silent moment, seemed to make a decision, and then rolled her eyes. She rolled her eyes at his weapons and the lurking danger. She was indomitable. "I was promised a walk," she reminded him cheerfully. "And ghosts." She tugged him back onto the sidewalk. "I only ever see this London from my carriage window at night, and I'm usually too tired to really notice it. It's rather nice."

"It has its advantages."

She slid him a sidelong glance, the kind that promised trouble. A faint whisper of dread moved through him.

He returned the glance. "What is it?"

She sighed. "I don't want to ruin the evening, but I suppose I should mention that Vasilisa is missing."

He frowned down at her. "Your doll? You said Jack hadn't taken anything."

She nodded. "He came back after we'd left for the May Ball."

"That little rotter. I'll get it back for you." They'd have a little chat, he and the boy, about stealing from ladies' parlors.

"It's already gone."

"Who did he sell it to and why?" he demanded.

"He doesn't know. Someone put word out that collections were to be rifled, and when he heard one of them was mine, he took the job to shield me. Partly."

"A strange sort of chivalry, but fine."

"Three others were stolen from that night, but that's all I

know. Not what was taken. Not yet, anyway."

"Give me their names."

"I've already sent word. We're to meet the day after tomorrow."

"With me."

She shook her head. "Not if you want your condition to stand."

He swore. She was right. He hated it, but she was right. He was starting to fight battles on two different fronts, and that did not put him in the best position. "You'll take Crow," he said. "And possibly an army."

"They aren't the problem," she reminded him. "Miss Montague, Lord Chevril, and Sir Wormwood are hardly evil masterminds."

"Hmph." He kept her tucked against his side, just because he liked it. The fog scattered, just enough to show the yellow lamplight, the yellow moon. "Still, your childhood doll makes for an odd target."

"Jack was told, as I imagine they all were, to steal whatever looked to be the most valuable, or cherished."

"Not the most expensive?"

"Apparently not."

"I *don't* like that." He was already sorting out what he could do about it. "Why didn't you tell me sooner?"

"We've been a little busy," she pointed out drily.

Point taken. But he didn't have to like it.

A strange sort of comfort, but at least his father wouldn't have focused on Tamsin before now and certainly wouldn't have involved other collectors. He wasn't behind this.

There was something else at work here. Some*one* else.

That was decidedly less comforting.

"Henry?"

"Yes?"

"Did you just growl?"

He raised an eyebrow. "I'm quite sure that viscounts don't growl."

The rest of the walk was peaceful, uneventful. He could

afford to notice the way Tamsin held his arm, her curiosity about everything around them, the smell of vanilla that seemed to follow, fighting even the wet, not-entirely-pleasant smells of London.

By the time they returned to Priya's house, it was still dark, but carts had begun to roll down the streets and servants were stirring in attics and basements. Henry walked Tamsin to the front door for the last time in what might be weeks. Months. There was no telling.

He'd be back tonight, of course, but he'd have to sneak in through an open window, or else scale the back wall to her balcony. He kissed her as if none of this was complicated. As if this was an ordinary marriage and an ordinary wedding night.

He tipped her chin up with his hand. "Don't forget your promise."

She snorted. "I'm not obeying you."

He laughed—he couldn't help it. "I wasn't talking about the wedding vows."

"Well, good."

"You'll be careful."

She rose on her tiptoes to kiss him lightly. "I'll be careful if you will."

"That wasn't the agreement."

She shrugged one shoulder and grinned. "I'm sure the Navy taught you not to fight a losing battle."

He groaned. "You have everyone fooled into thinking you're a little songbird, don't you?"

She looked mildly smug. "I'm sure I don't know what you mean."

He leaned down as though he was going to kiss her, let the moment stretch until her lips parted slightly on a breath, and then whispered in her ear, "You don't have me fooled, little crow."

She wrinkled her nose adorably. "Crow? Shouldn't I be a swan or a hawk? Something more dignified?"

"An omen of death who collects shiny things? I stand by it."

She chuckled. "I suppose that's fair enough." She turned her head slightly, bringing her mouth closer to his, tempting him beyond measure.

"Good night, Tamsin."

"Good night, Captain Talbot."

After the door shut quietly and securely behind her, Henry counted to ten. "Eight…nine…"

Pierce appeared at his side.

"Right on cue," Henry said.

"What have you gone and done now?"

"I've married her."

Pierce's eyebrows rose. "Felicitations." They watched the door shut behind Tamsin. "What are you doing out here, then? And why is she not at your very fancy ancestral house? Or at least your posh townhouse?"

"It's still not safe."

"Your father?"

Henry nodded curtly. "My father."

Chapter Twenty-Three

T AMSIN'S FIRST SOCIAL event as a married lady ended in an argument with her new husband.

A coldly whispered argument that raised more than a few eyebrows.

When they arrived, and were announced, her new title rippled through the sea of silk dresses and starched cravats. "Viscount Stirling and Viscountess Stirling."

Heads turned instantly. Conversations died, started up again in furious exclamations. No one had known the viscount was on the Marriage Market, and no one had expected that Lady Tamsin Bell, of all people, would surprise everyone with a secret wedding.

She floated through the room in her most elegant gown, a deep amethyst embellished with silver beads. Her elbow-length gloves were soft, pale yellow, almost the exact shade of her hair. She'd dressed to conquer, and this, at least, was one battle where she had some experience. Henry knew how to defeat footpads and pirates, but she knew how to defeat Society.

She had no illusions. They had hardly rushed to support her in the last week. But they could be led. And tonight, she would lead them.

"Lady Stirling!" The host of the ball bowed over her hand, appearing in front of them so suddenly that she nearly tripped over him. "That you would choose *our* soiree to debut as a viscountess! We are honored."

Of course he was. He was also one of the biggest gossips of the *ton* and would feast and dine on this story for ages. Anything that happened tonight would be trotted out at dinner parties and over brandies at the club for weeks. Months, if it was a boring summer.

Tamsin smiled. "Not at all, my lord."

Henry just inclined his head, looking stiff and displeased.

"A secret ceremony," someone else said, tittering. "How very chic of you."

"I want to elope too," a debutante murmured.

"Absolutely not," her father snapped. "You will be married in front of God and St. George's, preferably to a duke."

She rolled her eyes. Tamsin winked at her.

As they moved through the guests, the same conversation greeted them, like flotsam to the shore. Congratulations, proclamations that they had suspected all along, invitations to tea. Henry said little, growing more and more dour. Glances began to travel between the guests, back and forth between Tamsin's smile and Henry's very un-groom-like dourness.

Music frothed around them and the candles flickered as dozens of couples began to line up in pairs on the dance floor. Diamonds sparkled, from hairpins to waistcoat buttons. Their hosts bustled up to them, beaming. "Lord Stirling, Lady Stirling, would you do us the honor of leading the first dance?"

It might not mean much in the real world, or on the deck of a ship, but to the *ton*, this was a great distinction. Especially leading the dancing in place of the hosts.

Tamsin curtsied. "Thank you, my lord."

Henry didn't move. The cold severity in his face should have made him less attractive. It was most unfair that it did not. "I don't think so."

Her smile wavered. "My lord?"

"I'm not going to encourage this farce," he said.

There was a gasp behind her. A hiss of whispers. She swallowed. "It's only one dance."

He stared down his nose at her. "I rescued you, didn't I? I did my part as your childhood friend," he said coldly. "Let it be enough."

They had everyone's attention. Even the musicians had paused, sensing the energy swirling in the corner of the room. She'd expected to feel like it was a lark. She had not expected the twinge of hurt. She felt her cheeks go pale. "Henry, please."

Henry's military stance or expression did not falter. If anything, he stood straighter. Arrogance dripped off him like icicles. "You are my viscountess," he said. "And I will treat you with all of the dignity the title demands. And we were friends once, but let us not pretend this is more than it is. I had plans that did not involve rescuing you from Eaton's clutches. I had a love of my own."

Every nagging fear slid through her, like sea serpents in a glassy green ocean. She was transparent, filled with trepidation, all sinuous flashing scales and sharp teeth.

"Find someone else to flit about with you," he tossed over his shoulder. "I'm for my club. These events are tiresome."

Everyone knew what he was saying. As the reigning queen of social events, he found Tamsin tiresome.

And there was no denying the parallels of the May Ball, when he'd saved her with one of these dances. Her throat was tight and itchy. Her pretty and polite smile, the one the gossip magazines wrote about, froze into a grimace.

"Lady Stirling." Lord Mackenzie offered his arm. "Please grace me with this dance."

Lord Mackenzie was beautiful and sought after. He always had a compliment and witty word at the ready, all softened with a Scottish burr. And a smirk. A charming rake, if she'd ever seen one.

"Tamsin," he murmured. "Dance with me before they sense a true weakness."

She flowed into the movements, the music and the familiar pattern leading her when her brain would not.

"I'm not sure I like your new husband," Lord Mackenzie said. "I've never known Talbot to be cruel. He's not his father."

"Do you know him well?"

"We were at Eton together."

She nodded, keeping her chin high, her steps graceful. They danced the next dance together, then drank champagne and nibbled on tiny salmon and leek tarts in the shape of fish. Everyone watched her carefully, but she was used to being watched. She smiled; she laughed; she and Lord Mackenzie played off each other with bon mot after bon mot.

For one excruciating hour.

After which she made her escape with a minimum of further fuss. Society knew that her love match was no different than most of their marriages arranged for convenience or duty to a title. Lady Stirling was respected by her husband, but he would not dote on her. He had no particular feeling for her, certainly nothing to make the poets weep.

She, on the other hand, might very well weep.

Instead, as she left the party for a deserted hallway, someone pulled her through one of the open doors and into a parlor festooned with ribbons and a parade of white porcelain poodles, from the miniature to one the size of a pony. "Gah!" she said.

It took a moment to focus on the man who pressed her against the door.

Gone was the impassive, cold expression, the precise military bearing. Henry was just Henry again.

"I'm sorry, Tam. I'm so damned sorry." He touched his forehead to hers. "I hated everything about that."

She relished the nearness off him, the warmth of his arms on either side of her. It melted some of the unease that had prickled through her. "I agreed to it."

"Did Mackenzie find you?"

"You sent him?"

"You didn't think I'd really abandon you on the battlefield, did you?" He shook his head. "I never want to do that again."

"I still don't think we had to in the first place."

"There are those who would hurt you if they knew I cared about you."

She leaned back slightly to meet his stormy, dark eyes. "So, you do care?" she teased.

He groaned. "You know I do."

"Hmm. You might have to prove it."

"God, I was hoping you'd say that."

In one motion, he reached behind her to turn the key in the lock and also took her mouth like a man starving, adrift with only salt and rum. She kissed him back with every ounce of passion, with the same deep need. To chase the pleasure, to cleanse themselves of the necessary falsehoods they'd paraded through the ballroom.

She slipped her hands under his waistcoat, desperate to feel his warmth, his hard stomach. Any part of him she could reach. She noticed in some distant part of her brain that she wasn't embarrassed to be on fire for him. It was the most natural thing in the world.

His fingers found her, tracing between her legs, teasing, gliding softly, and then he slid them inside her, and the sudden sweet stroke had her thighs trembling. It sparked through her, like embers catching. She clutched at his arm and squirmed against his hand, trying to catch her breath. Her dress confined her, pulled taut against his sleeve.

"Fuck this," he said savagely, suddenly, whirling her away from the door and pushing her down onto a table. Poodles rattled alarmingly. Henry didn't notice, didn't care, only pulled her dress up, baring her ankles, her knees, her thighs, the hot place between her legs where her pulse suddenly throbbed. He bent his head and licked a stripe up her, parting her folds, grazing her nub. He licked her again, sucking gently, then harder. Her thigh muscles quivered. "You're mine," he growled against her.

"Yes," she gasped.

"Say it, Tamsin." He pulled back slightly, and she nearly whimpered. "Say it."

"I'm yours."

He licked and sucked at her, feasting on her body as though nothing could give him greater pleasure. As though guests weren't waltzing and whispering just outside the door, as though nothing in their world was wrong.

No, not that nothing was wrong, but that nothing was as

important as this moment. That making her come was the only thing that mattered.

He moved his fingers inside her again, stretching her slightly even as he found a rhythm with his tongue that made her gasp. She writhed as the pressure built inside, waves that gathered and gathered, until they crashed inside her. Sensation carried her away from herself, spun her around, running up her legs, through her core.

Afterward, she lay there wondering where her bones had gone to.

Henry lifted his head, grinning.

"I can feel your smugness from here," she muttered.

Still grinning, he helped her sit up, pulling her skirts down. When he twitched them into place like a proper lady's maid, she stared at him.

"We are not finished."

"We'll be caught if we linger."

She reached for his hips. "I don't care."

She brushed a hand over his hardness, and he groaned. She was just undoing the first button of his placard when the door rattled. She jumped.

Someone on the other side giggled.

"This one's locked. Try the next one," she said.

Henry kissed her, hard, quick. "I'll see you soon, wife."

And then he slipped out the open window and disappeared into the shadows.

She leaned out of the opening, sated and also thoroughly disgruntled that their sport had been cut short. "Viscount, you come back here."

His chuckle floated back to her. "That's Captain Talbot to you, little crow."

She grinned into the darkness.

When Tamsin stepped out of the bedroom the next morning, Priya and Persephone were both there waiting.

They hadn't even the patience to wait in the breakfast room with tea and toast. They stood in the hallway, all but vibrating with impatience. Priya wore green, Persephone dark blue, and they both looked very nice. Tamsin was reasonably certain that if she mentioned it, they would murder her on the spot.

"Well?" Priya asked.

"What happened?" Persephone blurted out.

"What do you mean?" Tamsin brushed past them. "Is there tea?"

They chased her down the stairs. "The gossip columns of several of the morning papers insist that although you were presented for the first time as the Viscountess Stirling, Henry was, and I quote, 'disdainful and coldly dutiful towards you,'" Persephone said, sitting down as Priya poured the tea. "Which is utter hogwash."

"He was all of those things," Tamsin said.

Persephone narrowed her eyes. "Now what are you two up to?" she asked. "Honestly, your courtship is exhausting, and this is coming from someone who was nearly murdered during hers. More than once."

Tamsin drizzled honey onto a muffin, not the least bit offended. Persephone was right. Except that Tamsin was in on it now, and that made all of the difference. She might not fully understand Henry's reasons or the catalyst behind his current plan, but she would. She'd get it out of him. Soon.

In the meantime, what they did, they did together.

"Honestly, I'm still not sure what's happening," Tamsin said. "But we're fine. We did quarrel, publicly, but it was on purpose."

"On purpose?"

"Yes. He does not want certain people to know we care about each other. We are to act like he has reluctantly done me a service."

Priya sat back. The sideboard behind her barely had space for food; it was too crowded with pots of roses and orchids. "Henry wants to control what people think about you two."

"Yes."

"He wants them to think he doesn't love you."

She went back to her muffin. "Yes." He might not love her. He hadn't said that he did.

"He wants them to know you matter as his viscountess, but not that you personally matter to him. Why?"

"He is in full protective mode but not very forthcoming as to the actual details," Tamsin replied drily.

Persephone sighed. "Ass," she said fondly. She popped her chin on her hands. "As far as romantic honeymoons go, it's severely lacking."

"So you'll remain here, then, I assume?" Priya asked.

"Do you mind?"

"Of course not." She stirred honey into her tea, tapping the spoon with a snap. "I do mind that I don't know what secret he's hiding, or his motive."

Persephone grinned at Tamsin. "Uh oh."

Priya pointed her spoon at Tamsin. "I'm going to do some investigating." It was a warning and a promise.

"I would expect nothing less," Tamsin assured her.

"Well, if that's settled, pass me the strawberry custards."

"I've been called to Norfolk, to assist on a dig," Persephone said. "Can I trust you and Henry to sort yourselves out on your own?"

"Everything is fine, Percy."

"Hmph."

"Asked for you directly, didn't they?" Tamsin asked, knowing it would distract her. "To help in their barrow."

Persephone smiled smugly. "About time, too. I think it might be a hoard of gold." Her eyes gleamed.

Priya shook her head. "Are you sure you're not a dragon?"

BREAKFAST WENT LONG, as it always did when plans needed to be planned and plots needed to be plotted. Tamsin did not know where Henry was or what he was doing. She wouldn't see him until much later. It was probably ridiculous to miss him.

She took herself off to visit the Cabinet of Curiosities, trailing a footman and Crow. It wouldn't hurt to see if Miss Stewart had any new information on the thefts. There was time before she was set to meet the other targets in a secluded corner of the park. It would not do to give it away that they knew each other and suspected some sort of larger nefarious purpose to the thefts. Because that simply didn't make sense. Not even days later.

The sweet shop was busy, and she amused herself buying candy for Jack until the bustle quieted. If he could steal from her, she could sneak food into his pockets when he wasn't looking. Proper food would be tricky, so she'd start with lemon drops and chocolate nonpareils and nougat.

Mr. Stewart finally nodded her through, and she darted up the stairs.

And crashed headlong into Mirabelle.

"I'm so sorry," she said as they righted themselves.

She might not know how she felt about some aspects of her marriage, but she knew exactly how she felt about this.

Awkward.

Horribly, horribly awkward.

She did what she always did when she was stuck in an uncomfortable situation: she smiled. "I really am terribly sorry."

"As am I," Mirabelle said. "I wasn't paying attention."

"Is Miss Stewart here?"

"She's already left for Scotland."

"Ah." Botheration.

A small, heavy silence descended between them. How did one say: *Your brother is a tosspot and I'm not sorry I jilted him?*

"This is rather awkward," she said instead.

Mirabelle's shoulders relaxed instantly. "It is, isn't it?" She wrinkled her pert nose. "Never mind my brother, Lady Tamsin. Oh, I suppose it's Lady Stirling now."

"It is, yes." And thank God for that.

"It's lucky you've come, actually."

"It is?" Tamsin latched on to the change in topic with no small amount of relief. She picked her way through chests and trunks and unopened boxes. "This is a lot of new things all at once. Did you need help sorting them?"

"No need," Mirabelle assured her.

Pity. Tamsin could have used the distraction. And the odds and sods she could see poking out of piles were intriguing. "Is that an 'Obby 'Oss mask? From Padstow?" She'd yet to see the procession of the dancing horse, but it was at the top of her list.

Mirabelle laughed. "Miss Stewart did warn me about collectors." She pulled a sheet over the item in question. "These are for the Midnight Market. I've been told peeking is strictly forbidden." She smiled gently to soften it. "Even to friends."

"Did you say a Midnight Market?" Excitement curled through Tamsin.

Mirabelle shook her head. "Every invitation I have handed out has garnered that same look. I don't mind telling you I was a little taken aback at first. I'm not used to collectors or strange relics like these. I'm only helping Miss Stewart as a friend."

She handed Tamsin a folded piece of parchment. Tamsin took it with near reverence. No wonder Mirabelle was uneasy with this kind of obsession. She most definitely wasn't alone. But Tamsin knew this carefully plain paper, the lack of seal, the tiny symbol in the righthand corner. She cracked the seal. It was like unwrapping a present.

You are cordially invited to a private auction. Three days hence, midnight.

The Midnight Market was always held at night, disguises optional but often chosen. And only on the rare occasion an estate sale held items of interest to eccentric collectors like herself, or the Cabinet needed to clear some space. A collection of cursed items, folkloric history, haunted artifacts.

And possibly Vasilisa.

Because the timing seemed far too coincidental.

"Will you attend?" Mirabelle asked.

Tamsin beamed. "Napoleon himself could not stop me."

TAMSIN SPENT THE next two hours walking from one end of Rotten Row to the other. It was not unusual to see her promenading and greeting friends, and so it was nothing out of the ordinary for her to stop to talk to Miss Montague when she first arrived. Or that sometime in the middle of the afternoon she wandered into the wooded areas and met with Sir Wormwood. Or even that Lord Chevril stopped her to tip his hat and congratulate her on her recent nuptials. That he also wanted to talk about the Midnight Market was no one else's business. They didn't notice.

And afterward, Tamsin had to accept three invitations to tea, two for an art exhibit, four for suppers, and six for balls. Someone wanted to know her opinion on yellow ribbons, on the fashionability of masquerade balls and whether it was passe for a lady to cut her hair short like Lady Caroline Lamb.

No one would remember Miss Montague, Sir Wormwood, or Lord Chevril, were they even noticed in the first place.

Sometimes having a reputation for being a social butterfly was useful.

That all of them had received the same invitation to the market made her all the more convinced that it was connected somehow.

Crow shook his head when she sought him out for her return walk. "Do you know all of the London aristocrats?"

"Feels like it sometimes."

"They seem quite desperate for your attention."

"For today." She shrugged one shoulder. She knew better than anyone that the attention and the accolades were fleeting. But they'd been a comfort, nonetheless. She wasn't sure she liked that about herself sometimes.

"I think you sell yourself short."

She looked at him, surprised.

He didn't elaborate, only motioned to a carriage waiting at the end of the row. "Your carriage awaits," Crow said.

She frowned. "I didn't bring a carriage."

"And yet."

She trusted Crow, of course, but the truth was she'd been abducted in a similar nondescript carriage not two days ago. She unlatched the door and poked her head in curiously, but cautiously. "Henry!"

Her husband waited on the seat with a crooked smile. He put a finger to his lips. "Shh."

She glanced around, but no one had heard her. Crow bowed and walked away, whistling. She climbed inside the carriage, smiling. "What are you doing here?"

"I'm sure it's only proper a husband should escort his wife."

The horses moved slowly, pulling them toward the exit of the park. It would take some time to get through the traffic, and Tamsin was never so glad for it as she was now. She hoped every carriage between here and home lost a wheel. If she only had stolen moments with Henry, she would make them last. She'd make them count.

"And what have you been up to?" Henry asked.

She brandished the invitation at him excitedly. "All of the targets received one of these."

He skimmed it. "The Midnight Market?"

"It's my favorite," she said. "You never know when it might happen or what treasures you might find."

"Tell me you don't go to these alone?" She waved that away. He groaned. "Tamsin."

"What? It's not as if—" She broke off suddenly as the carriage veered slightly, changing the shadows inside when a spear of sunlight snuck through the swinging curtains. "Henry, why is your face bruised?"

"It's nothing."

She leaned forward. "If I suddenly showed up with a bruised face, would you say it was nothing?"

Something lethal passed over his face. "No."

"Well, then?"

He pulled her up from her seat and settled her so that she straddled him. Her skirts rode up to her thighs. There was nothing between them but his breeches. He hardened against her. Flutters went through her lower belly.

"Henry, I know what you're doing," she scolded, but her voice was all wrong, breathy and wanting. "We have to talk."

"Is it urgent?" he asked, pushing her skirts further up her thighs. "Really urgent?"

"You're bruised."

"I'm fine."

His fingers brushed her quim, gently, teasingly. And then he was stroking and passing over her bud, fingertips slick with her need. He moved his teeth over her collarbone and sucked at the spot where her shoulder met her neck. She gripped his coat, trying to hold on.

"Do you really want to talk right now?" he whispered in her ear, tauntingly, nipping at her lobe.

She arched into his touch, squirming to get closer. "N-no."

"Thank God for that."

She fumbled for the buttons of his placard and then the buttons behind those ones, cursing the person who invented buttons to the devil and back. He laughed hoarsely, shifting her weight just slightly so she could free him. He sprang hard and smooth into her hand, and she stroked him once, twice.

The carriage continued to pull them through London's busy streets as he slid into her. She gasped, feeling the sudden stretch and the slight burn that turned into something so much sweeter. He yanked her dress down, pulling her breasts from their stays so he could suckle at them. She curled her fingers through his thick, dark hair, moaning.

The carriage dipped and jerked over the uneven road, intensifying every thrust of him inside her. She rolled her hips back and forth, and he groaned.

It was frantic and honest and it consumed every nerve ending she had. The pressure built everywhere, even in her hair, the tips of her toes. It was swift and sudden and would not be controlled. Henry touched her like she was fragile, special, but also like he might die if he could not fill his hands and his mouth with her body.

She couldn't help herself. "I love you, Henry."

His eyes flared and he captured her mouth again, desperately, even as he thrust deeper inside of her, pushing her into her climax before she could say it again, before she could wonder if he would say it back. He was ruthless, mastering her body like a ship, steering her this way and that, right into the waves.

When she found her pleasure, he followed soon after, and they gasped and cried out together mere moments before the carriage rolled to a halt.

She was flushed and breathless when a footman opened the door, but at least she was fully dressed. Henry was pressed back into the shadows, face hidden.

"Be back here two hours past midnight," she murmured.

"Or?"

"Or I shall go on an adventure without you."

He visibly shuddered.

Chapter Twenty-Four

"WHAT ARE YOU wearing?"

She was trying to kill him.

There was no other explanation as to why she was perched on a branch of a tree outside her window, wearing breeches. Tight breeches. Made of soft leather. Her thighs were strong and utterly distracting.

When she hopped down to the ground and spun on her heel, he wondered if he had already died and no one had informed him. It was heaven to see her trim bottom encased so tightly in that leather and absolute hell not to be able to peel it off her immediately.

"Do you like it?" she asked.

"No."

She tilted her head, grinning. "Do you love it?"

"Yes, damn it."

She laughed. "I was going to draw on a smart little beard, but it seemed a lot of bother. Would you still like me if I had a beard?"

"Yes." He noticed, of course, that she had said "like" and not "love." She was trying to keep things light and comfortable, the way she always did. He hated that he was suddenly someone she had to perform for, hated with a deep passion that he had not returned her declaration of love.

Because of course he bloody well loved her.

More each and every day.

But if he told her that, there would be no stopping her. She'd find out about his father and put herself in danger. She still might. And though their ruse was working so far, would it work as well if they were mooning over each other? His father had to think him indifferent, and therefore Society had to as well. It was the only thing the Earl of Culpepper listened to.

And so here he was, words clogging his throat, his heart aching and the rest of him desperately hard, all because of a pair of leather breeches.

She tilted her head. "Well done, you," she said, oblivious to the battle being waged inside his head. Daily. "There was no hesitation at all. I almost wished I'd gone ahead with the beard. I'm sure I'd be very dashing."

"Tamsin, I would like you were you to grow fins." Truth. Half-truth. *Like* was such an insipid word, and suddenly he hated it.

"Fins? That seems painful. Let's stick to breeches for the time being."

"Where did you even get those? They don't fit." They were too tight. They fit perfectly.

He wanted to remove them with his teeth.

"Priya has an attic filled with disguises," Tamsin said. "Do you know, I don't think she is entirely on the up and up."

He snorted. "As if any of you are."

She shrugged, still grinning. She smoothed her hands down the tops of her thighs, and his breath may have strangled in his throat. "I could start a fashion."

"God help us." He lifted an eyebrow. "In the meantime, where are we off to? I thought the Midnight Market was in three days. And I wasn't aware it required pants."

"We're going to the Cabinet of Curiosities, where I believe the collection for this market is being stored."

"And?"

"And what?"

"What aren't you telling me? For starters, why now?"

"I don't want to be disturbed."

He scrubbed a hand over his face. "It's closed and locked up tight, isn't it?"

"Yes, I imagine it is."

"And why can't you visit during the daylight hours like a normal person?"

"I tried that, but Miss Stewart is away and Lady Mirabelle is in charge."

"As in Eaton's sister?"

"Yes, so you can see why she wouldn't let me have a peek." She crossed her arms, vexed. "It strains credulity that my stolen doll isn't there."

"I don't like that Eaton is involved, even peripherally."

"Neither do I. He's not a real collector; he just likes to make trouble."

"Why not wait until the market to be sure?"

She was incensed. Her cheeks flushed, and her lips moved into what was dangerously close to a pout. He nearly groaned out loud again.

"I won't risk someone else getting it, though I can't imagine why they'd bother. More to the point, I won't give a penny to this blasted thief! Buy back my own property! It's extortion."

"I see your point." He did, of course. And he could never cage her, would never want to change her. She was impulsive, brave, determined. He was only grateful that she had included him in her foolhardy plan this time.

"I could go by myself, I suppose," she muttered.

She started to walk away, and he darted closer, wrapping his arm around her until they were pressed together. "You're pouting, Lady Stirling."

"I am annoyed, Lord Stirling."

He kissed the tip of her nose. And then he drew back under the very real threat she might bite his off in retaliation. He bowed. "Lead the way, wife."

HE KNEW EXACTLY how charming he could be.

It was infuriating.

Even more infuriating when it made her hot in every place

he'd ever kissed.

That was a lot of places.

Even with the bruise on his cheekbone he had yet to explain, the scar through his eyebrow, the calm distance he kept around him like a shield, the man fair smoldered.

It was deeply unfair.

She had the very unladylike urge to lick him.

Later. Definitely later.

For now, this would have to do. A late-night scrape that may or may not land them in considerable trouble.

"I like these late-night walks," she said, trying to put a little extra swagger in her stride. The fog was thick, cloaking them from view. A hackney rolled past them, and the sound of hooves echoed, but Tamsin could barely make out the shape in the gloom. Perfect.

"Aren't you missing some sort of event?" Henry asked.

"There'll be others." She shrugged. "There always are." Voices drifted toward them, drifted away. "Are you going to tell me who keeps attacking you?"

He glanced at her out of the corner of his eye. "And what would you do with this information?"

"What?"

"What would you do?"

"Does that matter?" She stopped walking for a moment. "Henry."

He shook his head. "I will tell you," he promised. "But not now. Not yet."

"Why not?" Frustration laced her question.

"Because I haven't solved the problem yet."

She poked him in the arm. Hard. "That's why you talk to people about things."

"Don't push, Tam. Please."

She narrowed one eye. "Oh, I will *absolutely* push, captain," she replied. "Just not right this second as we have arrived."

He looked across the street. "Stewart's Sweet Shop?"

"Yes."

"I thought for sure we were breaking into Gunter's for lemon ices."

"I haven't ruled it out." She was still irritated, but there was a job to do. The mystery of the theft was complex and befuddling.

Much like her husband. But only one of those problems was likely to be solved tonight.

"How did you plan to get in?" he asked.

"There's a side door," she explained. "It doesn't look very sturdy."

They crossed the street, Henry noting the line of the roof, counting windows, staring hard at the roof. She followed to the side door in an alley that smelled like sugar and rot. Empty crates were piled against the wall of the shop. It was decidedly less picturesque than out front.

"Are there living quarters above?" he asked.

"I don't know. I don't think so," she replied. "The second floor is where the Cabinet operates from, but I don't know about the third floor."

He nodded once thoughtfully, and then started to scale the wall like he was strolling through Hyde Park. He used a crate to help him reach a windowsill, then swung to another, hanging from his fingertips.

"Henry!" she whispered. "What on earth? You'll fall and crack your head open."

He chuckled. "Unlikely. I did this for years on a ship tilting to and fro. This building has much better manners and isn't actively trying to pitch me off to my own death."

He pulled himself up as if gravity was merely a suggestion. The muscles in his arms strained and his thighs pushed against the material of his pants.

All in all, it was a lovely view.

A stirring view.

Or would have been, if she hadn't been holding her breath, praying he wouldn't plummet to the ground.

When he had opened a window left unlocked because only lunatics climbed up buildings, she allowed herself to enjoy the further view of his backside as he slipped into in one of the upper rooms. She waited in the alley, listening intently for the shout of an insulted person being awoken from sleep by an intruder. She heard singing from one street over, two cats fighting in the green, but no alarm being raised.

No Henry, either.

She jiggled the door handle, but it was still locked. She stepped back, looking for the light of a candle being lit, but the building remained dark and quiet. "Henry?" she whispered.

Nothing.

Something was wrong.

She eyed the crates, the spacing of the windows. There was no way she could follow him up that way. She was going to have to find a way to break down the door, as had been her original plan. She'd left an iron crow in among the debris earlier in the afternoon for just such a purpose.

She dug it out; the metal bar was heavy and cold. "Apologies, Mr. Stewart," she murmured. She'd make sure to send money in the morning for the damage she was about to do.

Wanted to do.

Struggled to do.

Forcing the door open had sounded simple in her mind. But the door did not oblige. Rotten door.

She couldn't get the end wedged in enough to create the necessary leverage. There was no window to break. She lifted the iron crow like a cricket bat. She would just have to bash at it until it gave in.

She was swinging back for her first assault when the door swung abruptly open.

The iron crow whistled through the air. She fought to stop the momentum. Henry dodged backward, saving his skull by mere inches. "Jesus, Tamsin."

She lowered the bar sheepishly. "I thought you were in trouble."

"And you decided cracking my head open would improve matters?"

She wrinkled her nose. "Sorry. You've very good at ducking."

"I've had practice." He stepped aside. "Come inside. Quickly."

The corridor was plain, no lamps lit, the crunch of broken candy underfoot. Steps led down to the kitchens, another opening toward the shop. Tamsin led Henry up the narrow, creaking stairs. She winced with every step. Henry was a quiet, steady shadow at her back. She went through into the main space for the Cabinet of Curiosities, moving carefully to avoid toppling the maze of assorted bric-a-brac. It would have been a good precaution.

Had there been anything to avoid disturbing.

The room was empty.

She froze, her mouth dropping open. "Burning bollocks of a donkey."

Henry choked at the litany of curses. "You'd make a sailor proud."

She made a full circle of the room. "This place was full just a few hours ago," she said, incensed. "Trunks and boxes and absolute chaos."

There were only the usual items kept in a locked, glass-fronted cabinet: painted cards, crystal balls, beads taken from barrow graves. A shrunken head.

No Vasilisa.

She swore again.

"They moved everything."

Chapter Twenty-Five

TAMSIN WAS IN the foyer waiting for the carriage to be brought around to take her to a later supper party. She had chosen a blue tulle over white silk, with a wide beaded ribbon under her bust. Juniper had wound a matching ribbon into a bandeau to hold her hair back. She looked the part of a viscountess, even if her entire attention was on the empty Cabinet of Curiosities.

She'd thought herself so clever. She should have realized that the collection would be moved to a more secure location after the rash of thefts. It was the logical thing to do.

She did not have to like it.

Priya was puttering in her greenhouse, and Tamsin had yet to see Henry. It was too early in the evening for him to risk a visit.

Which was why the knock on the front door took her by surprise.

A footman rushed to answer it, Tamsin peering over his shoulder. Pierce stood, rain dripping off his cap, holding a bedraggled Jack by the back of his collar. "I believe this belongs to you?"

"Leave off," Jack spat, struggling.

"Thank you, Mr. Gallagher," she said. "Jack is welcome inside. Come in out of the rain, both of you." She caught sight of a familiar figure crossing the walkway, keeping to the shadows of the many, many hedges and plants gracing the front of Priya's house. She would know that quiet, confident gait anywhere. "That will be all," she added hastily to the footman.

He shut the door and bowed, leaving her to her dripping guests.

She led them quickly to the Fern parlor, as it had a French door leading out to the side gardens. She unlocked it, and Henry slipped inside, rain dripping from the brim of his hat. He nodded to Pierce.

Tamsin turned to Jack. "What's wrong?" She knew without a doubt that he would not have sought her out, not at this time and not at this house, if it wasn't very serious. He was frantic and miserable and wet to the core. "I'll get you a towel and some dry clothes." Priya would undoubtedly have something that fit him in her attic of disguises.

"No!" he burst out. He was on the verge of tears, holding them back with a determination that belied his twelve years.

"Are you hurt, lad?" Henry asked quietly.

"No, it's my brother," Jack blurted out. "He needs help. You said you'd help me," he added to Tamsin. "I'm sorry I stole from you, but—" He gulped.

"Of course we'll help you," Tamsin said calmly. "You've a captain here at your disposal, and his first lieutenant. And me." She went to the tea cart, which had been brought up while she waited. The tea was still warm, and she poured a cup, adding extra sugar and a healthy dollop of cream. "Have some tea to warm up and tell us what's happened."

She pressed it into his hands, and he took it because even pickpockets did not know how to refuse a lady dripping sapphires, with that steel in her eye. He gulped it down. "Simon is a chimney sweep," he said. "He's not a fingers, like me."

"Even if he were," she said gently, "we would help him. How old is he?"

"Eight. He's scrawny enough to fit in the chimney, but he got stuck last week. He gets scared in small, dark places."

She swallowed back concern and worry and fury at sending children into such tight, dangerous places. Pierce looked just as furious. Henry wore his captain's mask: confident and calm. But she saw the clenching of his jaw.

"Where is he now?" he asked.

"He was cleaning some toff's chimney today, and one of the older boys dared him to crawl into a corner cabinet, and they locked him in." Jack gulped again. "He'll be too scared to call for help, and even if he does, they'll think he was stealing."

He was very likely right.

"Which house?" Tamsin asked.

"A big one off Berkeley Square. It has a blue door. I can't get him out myself; they're having some party and they have big dogs in the yard." He held up his arm, showing the rips in his sleeve and his red patch. "They aren't very nice."

Tamsin sucked in a breath.

"Were you bitten?" Henry asked.

Jack shook his head.

Tamsin exhaled. "That sounds like the Braithewaite house. Lord Braithewaite is still convinced the French will breach the Thames. He's had those dogs for a few years now."

"What do I do?" Jack wailed, suddenly very much a young boy.

"You don't have to do anything at all," she said. "I happen to have an invitation to that party."

"Is that where you were headed?" Henry asked.

"No, but it's where we are going now." She turned to Jack. "The captain and I are going to attend. And we shall make a fuss."

Jack's eyes widened. "A fuss?"

"Something very dramatic, indeed. And while everyone's attention is on me, Henry will get him out."

"I can help," Pierce said quietly.

Henry shook his head. "I'd rather you be here. Just in case."

They exchanged a meaningful look that Tamsin was very much going to come back to later.

In great detail.

"What if it doesn't work?" Jack whispered.

Tamsin met his eyes directly and replied, very seriously, "Then I shall set fire to the ballroom and cause a proper commotion."

"Gor." His fear retreated slightly under awe. "You'd do that?"

Henry flashed a very quick grin to bolster him. "That's the least of what she'd do. You've got yourself a Cinderella, my boy. You could take London itself if you had a mind to it."

"Tamsin," Priya said from the end of the hallway.

"Yes?"

"The Braithewaite dogs are very fond of beef with brown sauce."

"Do I want to know how you know that?"

"It's a thrilling tale, if I do say so myself. If you add a drop of laudanum to it, it will make them very sleepy but won't harm them."

Jack frowned, poking at the holes in his coat. "They tried to bite me."

"It's not their fault they are owned by a man with mashed turnips for brains."

"Two Cinderellas." Henry nudged Jack. "You could take all of England now."

THE BRAITHEWAITE HOUSE was lit up like Vauxhall Gardens. Torches lined the drive, which was clogged with carriages running out to crowd the street on both sides. Candles burned at every window. Lamps hung from tree branches. It made for a spectacular effect, though not one that was particularly conducive to sneaking about.

As rain began to tap on the roof, Tamsin adjusted a hairpin and pinched her cheeks to make them pink. Jack looked at her as if he was seeing her properly for the first time that night. The light glinted off her necklace.

"You look very pretty, miss."

"Charmer," Henry murmured.

"Thank you, Jack," Tamsin replied. "Sometimes that's the only weapon I'm allowed, so when I must use it, it must be sharp."

"You look sharp as a knife, then."

"Now that *is* a compliment."

"You know what to do?" Henry asked him. He nodded.

"Good lad. If there's trouble, you sit tight and wait for me. And remember, if anyone sees you, you were sent with a message for Lord Stirling."

"I can do it."

"I know." Henry looked to Tamsin. "And you, Lady Stirling?"

She tossed a ringlet behind her shoulder. "Are you asking me if I can hold the attention of a ballroom of bored aristocrats?"

The corner of his mouth twitched. "I beg your pardon."

"As you should."

The sudden flare of heat in his dark eyes sent flutters through her. She could well picture him on his knees, begging for her touch.

And she knew perfectly well he was picturing her on her own knees, begging for him.

She was glad Jack had already slipped outside and was scratching the horses' necks for comfort. The carriage was suddenly too close and too warm. Henry's low laugh made her thighs clench together.

"Ready?" he whispered in her ear.

She turned her head and nipped at his lower lip, flicking her tongue over it to torture them both. His sharp intake of breath sent a throb of arousal arrowing between her legs. "Are you?"

"Minx."

"Captain."

"You may not know this, but after my time at sea, I have become very proficient with knots, Lady Stirling."

She swallowed, images flashing. "I look forward to proof of that, Lord Stirling."

He froze briefly as he came down the carriage steps behind her. There was a faint groan. "You're killing me."

She laughed throatily. She'd had no idea she could make a sound like that, so full of need and promise and curiosity. He stopped her with a firm hand, fingers digging softly into the nape of her neck. He tilted her head back slightly, a command.

"You want proof, Lady Stirling?" His words were soft, barely audible, but she felt them everywhere. "I can make you come with a short piece of rope and my mouth."

She swallowed, breath catching.

He smiled into her hair. "I too look forward to proving myself," he added before stepping away. "Be careful."

"You too," she said.

"Watch for me."

As if she had done anything else for the last ten years.

She forced herself to walk toward the house, which was spilling over with light and music. She did not look back to make sure Henry and Jack had not been spotted, however much she wanted to. She suddenly had a modicum of sympathy for Lot, incapable of resisting one glance over his shoulder. The glance that had turned his rescued wife to salt.

She was stronger than Lot.

She had to remind herself of that three separate times between the carriage and the front door, and then once more on the way to join the crush of guests already halfway soused and eager to dance until dawn.

The ballroom was hideous. Hundreds of mirrors, too many roses, too much gold. It was a cacophony of excess. There were three opera singers, an acrobatic dancer dangling from silk ropes from the ceiling, musicians hidden behind gauzy lengths of beaded drapes. She stopped to murmur a request to them before moving on.

The entire affair was painfully overdone and exceptionally distracting.

Perfect for their needs.

Tamsin circled the room, greeting friends and acquaintances, making sure she was seen. Somewhere, Henry and Jack had hopefully already fed the dogs. Henry would soon be inside the house, unlatching the window of the library and then presenting himself to be seen and gawked at. He'd hate every second of it, and still he hadn't hesitated—he'd gladly do so to help a little boy locked in a cupboard.

She made another round before spotting Lord Mackenzie leaning against the wall in the languid, seductive pose of rakehells everywhere. He fairly smoldered.

"Lord Mackenzie, just the man I was hoping to see."

"Lass, you aren't the first woman to say that to me, but you are the most beautiful."

When she responded with a flirting, smoldering smile of her own, his faltered. He looked flustered. And mildly terrified.

"What are you doing?" he asked under his breath.

"I thought you were a notorious rake, my lord," she teased. "I shouldn't have to explain."

"Do you know how one becomes notorious?"

"No, but I feel certain you can explain it to me."

"By staying alive, Lady Stirling," he said drily. "I very much would like not to have my bollocks shot off by your husband."

She smiled, just as seductively. Heads turned; whispers kindled.

"Stop it," he fairly begged.

"Oh, I do like you." She giggled.

"Don't."

"Am I correct in assuming that you owe my husband a debt of some sort?"

"Aye." He nodded. "My little brother was on the ship with Henry and that traitorous pile of worms Fairweather."

"I figured as much." It was becoming a pattern, she'd noticed. Henry, for all that the Cinderellas had saved him, had been very busy saving everyone else even while under siege. "Then let me assure you that he will be not only be overjoyed to find you flirting outrageously with his wife, but he is counting on it."

There was a beat of silence, a lift of an eyebrow. "My dear lady," he said, suddenly all charm and charisma. "Why didn't you say so?"

His demeanor changed, flashing quick as a lightning beetle. He didn't just walk, he prowled toward her.

Despite herself, she felt a blush staining her cheekbones. "Well, you are good at that, aren't you?"

He grinned, before remembering to lace his smile with dark promise, with suggestions too disreputable for a stuffy ballroom. She trailed her gloved fingers up his arms, leaning closer and chuckling warmly. The first notes of a waltz floated through the crowd.

"Perfect." Tamsin smiled. "Just as I asked."

"You are terrifying, you know that?"

"Why does everyone keep saying that?" She let him lead her to the dance floor. "Besides, you ought to meet Priya."

"There are more of you?"

She winked. "So many more." Everyone else saw a sultry wink, a devastatingly handsome lord gathering her far closer to his body than propriety generally allowed. Especially as he was not her husband.

Even she had never flirted so outrageously in her life. She wondered that no one noticed that or questioned her sudden brazenness.

Lord Mackenzie bent his head to whisper in her ear. She knew that his expression must be inappositely hungry by the swell of reaction around them. He looked every inch the rake, but all he said to her was: "I assume this is for a good cause?"

"The very best."

"Good, because here comes your husband."

She forced herself not to look again. They needed a longer distraction, a proper build of tension. She curled her fingertips into Lord Mackenzie's thick hair, right at his nape, above his collar.

His hand traveled lower along her spine. "How much of a bother are you looking to make, my lady?"

"*Quite* the bother."

His hand moved lower still, respectable, but barely. "I hope I don't get my nose broken for this."

"I won't punch you," she promised.

"I wasn't only worried about you."

She knew the exact moment when Henry began to stalk through the crowd toward them. Guests all but leapt out of his way, dancers whirled to let him pass, necks craned. She let herself glance in his direction, then away, bored. She whispered to Lord Mackenzie. He laughed, and it was a low, caressing sound not often heard on a ballroom dance floor.

"Lady Stirling." Henry's greeting cracked like a whip.

Lord Mackenzie twirled her once, for effect.

Muscles twitched along Henry's jaw. "Lady Stirling, I am speaking to you."

She rolled her eyes. "Finally, you decide to talk, and of course, it's only to interrupt my fun."

He lifted his chin, staring down his nose at her, stern as a king. As they were playing, she decided she could absolutely indulge in the little thrill it gave her. She pushed back, just enough to see the answering hot thrill in his own gaze. Barely there, not noticeable to anyone else. Just her. And just for her.

"You will cease this behavior," he demanded. "It isn't fitting to the title of viscountess."

"You won't even look at me," she returned, in the kind of whisper that couldn't help but be heard. She added a pout. "But he will."

"Don't be dull, old chap," Lord Mackenzie put in.

"That's my wife."

He shrugged. "If a beautiful woman needs attention, who I am to deny her?"

"Go home, Tamsin," Henry ground out.

"No," she said.

"This is not the way to get my attention."

"Enough," a woman interrupted, even as the rest of the guests edged closer, thrilled with the theatrics.

"Well, you're right about that," Henry snapped, turning on his heel and stalking away.

Tamsin glanced at the clock surreptitiously before glancing at the woman who had joined them. Henry would need at least five minutes, more if possible.

And then her eyes widened.

Her avenging angel?

Carnation.

Carnation, in her candy-pink dress with matching jewels in her hair, along with a single magenta ostrich plume that pointed an accusatory finger at whoever stood behind her.

"Carnation?" Tamsin said, no longer pretending to act surprised and actually being surprised. "What are you doing?"

"I can tell something is afoot," Carnation replied in hushed undertones. "Am I helping or hindering?"

Truly stunned, Tamsin could only say, "Helping."

"Then forgive me, my lord," she murmured to Lord Mackenzie.

Right before she slapped him.

Hard.

Loudly.

Carnation, who had never looked more like a strawberry ice than she did at that very moment, slapping London's most infamous, handsome-as-the-devil rake.

Honestly, Tamsin would have cheered if she'd had the presence of mind. As it was, she couldn't help the grin. "Oh, well done, Carnation."

"Stop grinning, you lunatic," Lord Mackenzie muttered as he straightened. He made a show of touching his cheek, eyes narrowed. The red splotch was not feigned.

Carnation did not balk or falter in any way under his scrutiny. She tilted her chin up in silent challenge. "You should have a care in how you treat a lady."

"Apparently." His Scottish burr deepened as he considered her.

The others were so engrossed in the little play they were providing that Tamsin couldn't have moved back a single inch without treading on someone's toe. Even the footmen were watching, riveted, trays of drinks forgotten.

"A few more minutes," she breathed.

"Are you sure?" Lord Mackenzie asked.

"My reputation can take it," she assured him.

"I'm not sure mine can."

Carnation crossed her arms dramatically. Tamsin had the distinct impression that her stepsister was enjoying herself immensely.

"What do you have to say for yourself?" she demanded.

Lord Mackenzie was flummoxed. "Pardon?"

"You heard me."

"I am not accustomed to explaining myself to women I have not been properly introduced to."

"Lady Carnation, may I present Lord Mackenzie," Tamsin interjected cheekily. "Lord Mackenzie, this is my stepsister, Carnation Bell."

He touched his cheek. "Delighted, I'm sure."

"The pleasure is all yours."

Tamsin had never seen this version of her stepsister, and she was fairly certain the pleasure was actually all hers. She glanced at the clock. "I should go."

"Do you need us to continue?" Carnation asked. It was difficult to whisper when so much attention was being turned their way. She lifted her fan to cover her mouth.

"If you could," Tamsin said, "I would be grateful."

Lord Mackenzie made a showy, dramatic bow. "I insist on dancing with the woman brave enough to slap me." He winked. "In public, anyway."

More shocked gasps. No one would be looking anywhere else for the next waltz.

Carnation blushed. "For my sister, I suppose I can."

He offered his arm. "At least you didn't break my nose," he murmured when she took it.

Tamsin slipped out of the ballroom, hiding a grin.

WHEN TAMSIN TRIED to open the door to the library and found it locked, she knew it was all going according to plan.

"Lord Stirling went in there with a bottle of brandy and demanded not to be disturbed," a younger footman informed her. "The master won't like it, but he was right angry."

"Oh dear," she said. "He does get cross."

"M-my lady," he stammered when she smiled at him.

"I suppose I ought to go home. Would you mind fetching me my cloak?"

She'd never had her cloak fetched so fast in all of her life. She was grateful for it when she stepped out into the cold rain. Thunder rumbled above her as she picked her way through the wet grass, around a large dog snoring happily under a bush, and toward the library window, just in time to catch a small boy with a dirty, tear-stained face.

"Hello," she said, smiling through the rain beading her eye-lashes. "You must be Simon."

Simon froze, right before he started to tremble.

"It's all right," Jack said, jumping through the open window. "She's with us."

Simon nodded. "All right." He widened his eyes at her. "You're pretty."

Henry grinned, joining them on the lawn and shutting the window quietly behind him. "Is there anyone who doesn't tell you you're pretty?"

She fluttered her eyelashes at him. "Someone has to pay attention to me, don't you think? Since my own husband won't?"

"You'll pay for that later," he murmured.

"Promise?"

"Definitely."

They hurried as the rain intensified and carriages gleamed like painted lanterns around them. Lightning flashed. "Wait," Henry ordered them suddenly. "I know this carriage."

They paused around a black, well-appointed carriage with no crest and no coachman waiting up on the box.

"It looks like all of the others," Tamsin said. "Doesn't it?"

Henry frowned. "There's something familiar."

Jack pointed excitedly to a small crack in the glass. "This is the same carriage the man who wanted you stolen from used!"

Henry stilled. "Are you sure?"

Jack nodded. "Positive."

"And I know I've seen it before." Henry shook his head, wa-ter flinging from his hair. "All the drivers are huddled in the stables. We'll never ferret out the right one."

There were over two hundred carriages waiting in the area around the Braithewaite house. And more than twice that many people inside.

"We'll never find the driver *or* the owner," Tamsin said, frustrated. They were so close now. The rain threatened to drown them, filling her mouth when she spoke. "But I'm sure I can get a copy of the guest list tomorrow."

She shivered. Simon sneezed.

Henry sighed. "Damn it. It'll have to do. Let's get you all inside and dry." He ushered Tamsin forward, twitching her hood more securely in place. "Your lips are turning blue."

"It's just rain."

"Still." He glanced pointedly at the boys. She nodded. "You know what this means, don't you?" he asked.

"No, what?"

"We now know that, at the very least, your thief is part of Society."

She narrowed her eyes, suddenly comforted. "And that's *my* territory."

Chapter Twenty-Six

WHEN THEY FINALLY reached the house and ushered the boys inside, Simon was immediately mesmerized by everything he saw. By the plaster molded into trailing vines, by the golden candlesticks, and even by the gleaming marble under his feet.

Jack, on the other hand, looked terrified.

"Don't touch anything," he whispered, yanking on his brother's sleeve when he wanted to poke a large potted fern.

Simon looked up at Tamsin, all skinny knees and elbows and wide blue eyes. "Do you have any more of those ices?"

Tamsin smiled. "I don't know. Why don't we go down into the kitchen and see?" She held out her hand, and when Simon took it, Jack might pass out or else spontaneously combust.

"Don't!" he blurted out. "He's dirty."

He wasn't wrong. Simon was covered in soot from the chimneys and mud from the garden. He pulled away, mortified. "Sorry, miss."

She crouched down. "I don't mind a little dirt."

"But you're a *lady*."

"That's true. But did you know that the other lady who lives here plays in the dirt all day long?"

"She does?"

"And she tracks it through the house on her boots and the hem of her dress. That lady who helped us with the dogs?

Sometimes there are leaves in her hair."

Jack frowned. "That can't be true."

"It absolutely is," she replied. "Priya is a horticulturist. She studies plants. She's a right mess."

"I heard that," Priya said drily from the nearest doorway.

Jack and Simon jumped in unison and then stepped closer to each other.

"It's all right," Henry murmured.

"There she is now." Tamsin stood, making her voice light and cheerful. She widened her eyes with mock shock. "Just look at her sleeves."

Priya frowned, glanced at her sleeves along with everyone else, and then sighed. "I was repotting some orchids."

"In the middle of the night?" Simon asked.

"Some plants prefer not to be fussed over during the day," she explained. "They like moonlight."

"Are you a witch?"

Henry choked on a laugh.

"Sometimes," Priya allowed with a wink. She did add, with a slightly more acerbic tone, to Tamsin, "How am I the witch when you're the one who collects skulls?"

The boys were in danger of having their eyeballs fall out of their heads while they tracked the conversation, the flicker of candlelight on gilt picture frames, the sound of clattering hooves on cobblestones outside.

"Lady Langdon, may I present to you Jack and Simon Nimble," Tamsin said.

"How do you do?" Priya's curtsy would have impressed the queen.

The boys bowed, jerkily, but very seriously.

"All right now, to the kitchen," Henry interrupted. "I want roast beef and hot chocolate."

"Roast beef?" Simon asked. "What's that?"

"Why, it's the best dinner a man can ask for. Add some potatoes and some buttered peas, and there's nothing better."

"I want to try it!" he said.

"You'd better hurry, or I might eat it all." Henry winked.

"Race you."

They took off, thundering down the back stairs, hooting. Jack followed at a slower pace, eager but clearly not accustomed to playing.

It broke Tamsin's heart all over again. "Do you think they'll mutiny if there are no ices?"

Jack shook his head. "Simon won't be any trouble, I swear."

"I was only teasing," Tamsin said. "But how do you feel about cake? Do you think cake will appease those wild men currently stomping about?"

He nodded, nearly smiling.

"Well, that's a relief," Priya said. "Henry *is* a lot of fuss and bother. I had no idea I could tame him with cake."

By the time they reached the kitchen, Jack looked less uncomfortable, and Henry and Simon were arse-deep in the cold storage. "Success!" Henry shouted, looking over his shoulder. "Jack, come and help me."

As they pulled out platters of cold roast beef, potatoes, and assorted cheeses, Priya went to the shelves of dried herbs. "If those boys don't have scurvy, they will shortly." She opened lids and sniffed various herbs. Tamsin only recognized mint. "Do you think they'd drink tea?"

"Strawberries," Henry murmured, joining them as the boys fell on the food. "I've seen enough scurvy on the ships. Limes or lemons would be better, but any fruit will help."

"I'll make a pot of chocolate to warm us up," Tamsin announced.

"You know how to cook?" Jack asked, shocked.

"Well, I can heat up milk, I am sure," she said. "Theoretically."

It took a little assistance, but they were soon sipping thick, warm chocolate, hair and clothes drying by the fire. Galahad, Priya's cat, wandered out of a dark corner, utterly delighting Jack, who tried to appear as though he were entirely nonchalant about the whole thing.

"I have a bag of candied lemon peels here," Priya said. "But no one in this house is brave enough to eat lemons, even sugared."

"I'm brave!" Simon insisted.

"Are you sure? Even the captain there has to be coerced."

"No, really, I'm brave enough."

"Excellent. You may have the bag, then. If you'll share with your brother."

Jack swallowed. "I don't have any money."

Priya tilted her head. "I don't want money. I'm grateful that it won't go to waste. I might have given up and just tossed them out."

"Oh." He petted the cat, who purred loudly in response.

"Why don't you sleep here tonight?" Tamsin asked quietly. "I'd feel better knowing you're safe."

"I can keep us safe."

"Of course you can. But why not rest, just for now?"

"We have to stay together."

"Of course you do," Henry said. "A captain never abandons his first lieutenant. There are rooms upstairs, or you can sleep right here by the fire if you prefer." It was no coincidence that Henry offered a place near the door.

Jack noted it too. "I guess that would be all right."

They settled into a pile of blankets, whispering to Galahad, who decided he quite liked the adoration and accepted it as his due.

"I've never had to work so hard to have anyone accept an invitation from me," Tamsin muttered as they left the boys to their rest.

HENRY WAS WAITING for her in her bedroom.

An oil lamp lent a soft glow, gleaming off the mirror, the gold threads in the coverlet, and the intensity of Henry's dark gaze as he tracked her progress into the room. The back of her neck prickled delightfully at the tension searing the room.

Especially when she closed the door and realized Henry had the silky green rope that usually held back the heavy drapes at the window. "I told you I was good with knots."

Desire bloomed swift and hot inside her. "How good?"

"You did ask for proof," he said, padding toward her. He'd already removed his boots, his coat, and his cravat. "And a captain never makes a promise he can't follow through on."

"And you did promise," she whispered. Nervous excitement bubbled along with the desire, an uncertain thrill that she found she liked very much.

"So I did." He narrowed his eyes. "You're still dressed." He motioned with his finger that she should turn, command in every line of his body.

She obeyed, arousal pulsing between her legs. She already felt exposed, swollen.

He unlaced the back of her gown, and she wriggled free. She wore a short chemise, one that barely grazed her mid-thigh, her stays, her embroidered stockings.

"Perfect," he said.

The lamplight touched the arch of his scarred eyebrow, his straight nose, the slice of throat and muscled chest exposed by his open lawn shirt.

"Come here, Tamsin."

She hesitated, mostly to see what would happen.

"Are you going to make me repeat myself?"

Oh my.

Why did that softly spoken question, laced with power, send quivers through the back of her knees? She approached him, licking her lower lip.

He watched her mouth, loosening the rope in his hands. His crooked smile was brief, his voice pure sin. "Good girl."

She considered throwing herself at him right then and there, but she did not want the game to end.

She already knew that she might go up in flames the moment that he touched her.

If he ever touched her.

He seemed content to let his gaze roam and ravage, to circle her slowly, with predatory grace. His breath was on the back of her neck, and she nearly squirmed even though he had yet to touch her.

He chuckled huskily. "Put your wrists together, my beauty."

She blinked at him.

"Now."

She lifted her arms, wrists pressed together. He finally touched her, fingertips barely grazing her pulse point, the backs of her hands, as he wrapped the rope around her. When she was secured, he finally kissed her, deeply, desperately, his tongue sliding along hers even as he tightened the knot that bound her with a single snap. It jolted through her, kindling little fires. She gasped.

"That's a Savoy knot…" He pushed her back against the post of the bed, tossing the end of the rope over the top and securing her there.

With her arms stretched out over her head, and her feet comfortably on the floor, she never would have considered the position to be so erotic. Her breasts jutted out; her back arched slightly. She was entirely at his mercy. And he was focused entirely on her pleasure.

He dragged his mouth gently over the swell of her breasts, pausing to nip, to lick, and then to pull her free of her stays. He sucked one nipple into his mouth, pulling rhythmically, tongue swirling.

She tested the knot, wanting to touch him.

"Ah ah," he scolded, glancing up at her with that wicked smile and the stern slash of his eyebrows. He lowered to his knees, never breaking eye contact, until he was between her legs. Her parted her thighs, and she made a little noise in the back of her throat, half moan, half gasp. He lifted her knee onto his shoulder, kissing the inside of her thigh, widening the space between them until he'd reached her center, and she whimpered.

He licked at her gently, flicking his tongue between her petals, over her bud, flattening it for a long swipe that had her squirming. He increased the pace and the pressure but never lost the rhythm even as he explored her. He dipped his tongue deep into her and then returned to licking small, tight circles around her bud before drawing it completely into his mouth and sucking until her breath stuttered. She couldn't keep up with the assault to her senses, the restraining silkiness of the rope, the stretch of her arms, the glide of his tongue, the feeling of being both powerless and utterly powerful.

When she fell into her climax, it was truly like falling. There was nothing to catch her but Henry's mouth and the waves of sensations that finally lifted her back up. She sagged, shivering with the delicious aftermath. Henry leaned back, wiping his face, looking utterly satisfied.

"Is it my turn yet?" she murmured.

"What makes you think I'm finished?" he drawled. It was a side of Henry she had only seen glimpses of before, hints. A sip here and there.

She would happily drink the entire bottle.

He unhooked her from the post, but he did not untie her. She pouted slightly, and he nipped at her lower lip. "Tomorrow you may have your wicked way with me," he teased, running his palms down her arms to restore the circulation. It tingled, not unpleasantly. "But today, today it's my turn." He gripped her chin gently. "Yes?"

She nodded.

He cocked an eyebrow, waiting.

"Yes," she said.

And that was all he needed. He pressed against her until she bent backward, the bed a soft landing. He stepped back only long enough to take off his clothes, before dragging an open-mouthed kiss from her ankle to her knee, gently scraping his teeth up her thigh, over one breast than the other. She squirmed and gasped, exquisitely sensitive.

He finally lowered himself into the cradle of her hips, jutting against her, sliding the tip of his shaft between her petals. She lifted her hips impatiently.

He chuckled, though it was strained, full of ragged self-control. "Patience, Tamsin."

"*Now*, captain." She was half begging, half commanding. And entirely successful.

His eyes gleamed, and that was the only warning before he plunged into her. Their moans tangled in the sweaty air. She stretched around him, and he thrust into her, again and again. She met every thrust until the bed rattled beneath them alarmingly.

A small vase fell off the nightstand. They grinned at each other once, like the old friends they were, and then the fire was between them, inside them, consuming them, burning like the new connections between them.

When he came with a groan, she followed, putting her bound arms around his neck, keeping him as close as she was able, for as long as she was able.

$$\text{\textbullet}\text{\textbullet}\text{\textbullet}$$

Chapter Twenty-Seven

I T WAS A measure of the toll war took on a man that he could not sleep, even after a night such as this one.

He'd wrung every glorious drop of pleasure from Tamsin, and she had done the same with him. He might live to be a hundred years old and forget his own name, but he knew he would never forget the vision of her spread naked, knots at her wrists and a playful challenge in her eyes.

He was ravaged, in the very best way. Exhausted.

But he still wouldn't sleep easy, unfortunately. Other visions tugged at him, floated to the surface from the muck of memories he tried to drown, but most nights they turned anchor and threatened to drown him instead. At least this night he could enjoy the soft silence of the house, of Tamsin sleeping peacefully a few feet away. He could stand at this window, roll brandy on his tongue, and feel a kind of comfort he'd not known before. It was the darkest part of the night; the moon was on the other side of the trees and only a few stars struggled through the fog. The rain had abated, and the very faint light silvered leaves and flowers. It was peaceful, nearly as restful as proper sleep.

And yet wrong.

There.

Just under the blanket of quiet, a sound that did not quite fit.

He stepped closer to the glass, peering into the shadows. He couldn't see Pierce, leaning against his usual tree. The sound had come from the front of the house.

Only the open window brought it to him, a muffled noise.

The hairs on the back of his neck lifted. He knew this feeling, the simmering tension when a ship was spotted through the glass, hazy in the mists, just a suggestion, a question, until it was too late.

He cursed softly and pulled the dagger from his coat, flung over the back of a chair painted in violets, even as he made for the door.

Tamsin sat up blearily. "What is it?"

"Stay here," he snapped at her. "Lock the door behind me."

He was already out in the hall and down the stairs by the time her bare toes hit the cold floorboards. He would have been confident on the ship where he knew his men would take orders.

No one in this madhouse was likely to follow an order.

He needed to be quick.

The front door was still locked, which was reassuring. Whatever he had heard came from outside. The house was not yet breached. He had no way of knowing how far his father was likely to take his tests, but attacking a woman's house put him far beyond the pale. Any woman's house.

The fact that Tamsin was inside only hammered the edge of Henry's anger to a killing point.

He unlocked the door, staying clear of the opening as he peered outside. No one dove for cover, and there was no hackney or horses waiting on the cobbles. His father's men had come on foot. He stepped out carefully, keenly aware of the breeze shifting the leaves, of the many dark corners created by Priya's jungle of a garden even in the front of the house, the flicker of the gaslights lining the street, a moan.

He turned his head sharply. Another moan, a filthy curse whispered by someone in pain. Not just someone. Pierce.

His first lieutenant lay sprawled by an urn thick with snapdragons. The ground beneath him was sticky with blood. His blood, if the knife sticking out of him was anything to go by.

"Gallagher," Henry said, keeping his voice low, his ears peeled for anyone waiting in hiding. He crouched by his friend, assessing the damage. "Fuck."

Pierce didn't open his eyes, but his mouth ghosted a smile. "You always did have a shite bedside manner, captain."

Henry was wearing breeches and nothing else. He didn't even have a handkerchief to help stop the flow of blood. He'd have to tear the bottom half of Pierce's shirt. "This is going to hurt like hell."

"It already does."

Pierce grunted when Henry shifted him, working as fast as he could. Pain dug white grooves at the sides of his mouth as he struggled to breathe.

Henry finally had a wad of cloth and could see about pulling the blade free. "How many were there?" he asked.

"One," Pierce answered, disgusted. "A woman."

Henry frowned. "The old bastard is sending women now?"

"Took me by surprise. It's an effective tactic."

"Which means there are more of them."

"Likely. Go on," Pierce said. "I'll survive."

The question of whether or not to leave the first lieutenant alone to possibly bleed out was rendered moot when Tamsin flew out of the front door, wearing a frilly dressing gown, and followed by Priya.

"I told you to stay inside."

She didn't dignify that with a response. Not that he expected her to, beyond expletives and name-calling. She came to a halt, her toes just at the edge of the pool of blood. She immediately ripped a layer of flounce off her hem. "Never mind, Mr. Gallagher," she said brightly even as her mouth trembled. "We've seen worse in Little Barrow. Antiquarians are always hacking off parts of themselves."

Priya rang the bell at the front door. "We'll have the footmen bring him inside."

"It's not safe out here," Henry said. "Wait inside."

"You can argue," she returned sharply. "Or you can go deal with whoever is trampling through my roses out back."

"Bleeding fucking hell."

"That too."

Candlelight glowed in an upstairs window, followed by another. The footmen were waking. "Go," Tamsin said fiercely. "We'll take care of him."

"I'm meant to take care of *you*," Pierce said, using his good arm to pull himself up via the urn. "I can get inside."

Tamsin and Priya immediately popped up on other side of him, helping him shuffle to the house. Henry waited until they were on the doorstep before vaulting over the decorative railing and sprinting down the lane to the mews and the gardens. The horses shifted in the stables, clearly awake and agitated. The garden, however, was still.

Until two boys exploded out of a lilac tree.

Jack waved a cast-iron pan, full of smug superiority and excitement. "We just chased a bloke through the garden! That way!"

"Stay back." Henry moved through the garden, roses brushing against his knees. Footprints glittered in the wet grass. A single set. They led to a low part of the fence where a broken pot lay on its side. He scaled the fence, but he knew as he looked down the lane that whoever had been here was long gone. The fog closed in tight.

"Mayfair is so exciting!" Simon said, as Henry dropped back to the ground. He wielded a fire poker proudly, and his hair stuck up all over his head. "I tried to stab him with my sword!"

With fear and fury burning like acid in his gut, Henry forced himself to smile. "Good lad."

Jack's bloodthirsty glee was, just like his gaze, far older than his years. "Who was it?"

"I don't know."

"What do they want with Lady Tamsin?"

"Nothing," Henry assured him. "Let's go back inside."

Jack didn't look convinced. He looked mutinous and incensed.

Henry knew exactly how he felt.

TAMSIN AND PRIYA managed to get Pierce inside and down the hall, trailing blood on the marble by the time two footmen thundered down the stairs. They took him the rest of the way into the nearest parlor, the one with the wallpaper of roses, before Priya sent them off for supplies.

Pierce lay on the settee, protesting. "I'm getting blood all over your needlepoint cushions."

"Hang the cushions," Priya said. She pushed him back down when he continued to struggle to get up. He hissed a breath out, jagged with pain.

Priya took a closer look at the dagger, her expression clinical. Tamsin was used to skulls and ghosts and things that went bump in the night, but seeing a dagger sticking out of someone's side made her feel pale.

She swallowed. "What can I do?"

"I'm going to pull it out," Priya said. "Be ready with the cloths."

"I can do it," Pierce protested. "This is hardly something a lady—"

"Hush," Priya said sharply. "Ready, Tamsin."

She lifted the clean sheets the footmen had delivered. They hovered outside, waiting for orders.

Pierce tried one more time. "Shouldn't you call a doctor— Argh! *Ifreann na Fola.*"

English failed him as pain made him clammy. Priya had clasped the hilt of the knife with a competent hand that betrayed no shaking whatsoever, and then yanked it out.

He clenched his back teeth. "Warn a man."

Tamsin rushed in with the cloths, pressing hard on the wound and trying very hard not to look too closely at the torn flesh. Blood pooled.

"You were lucky," Priya said. "It's not spurting. And I think the tip of the blade hit one of your ribs and got stuck there instead of sliding past to your lungs or your heart."

"Aye." His breathing seemed easier. "You've done this be-fore."

"I have a brother," she said drily.

"Does he get stabbed often?"

"You'd be surprised." She approached with a jar of vinegar.

"Hell no, you madwoman," Pierce choked.

"Do you want to get a fever and die?"

"I'll be fine. Get away with that."

"Don't be such a baby."

Their bickering was strangely soothing, and it was the most Priya had spoken to him to acknowledge his presence. Much more soothing was Henry filling the doorway, two muddy boys at his heels. Tamsin indulged in a sigh of relief when he winked at her then approached Pierce.

"You may as well get it over with. These ladies are obsessed with vinegar washes."

"Torture, you mean."

Henry grabbed a bottle of port from the side table and passed it over. "Here."

"I have laudanum," Priya said.

"Hate the stuff." Pierce took a very, very long swallow. Then another.

Jack and Simon crowded closer, curious. Tamsin winced at them. "Maybe you should…"

Too late.

Priya moved the cloths and doused the wound with vinegar. Pierce jerked, swearing in Irish, English, and another language Tamsin did not recognize.

"Gor," Simon said gleefully. "That's a lot of blood."

Pierce opened one eye. "You don't have to sound so happy about it, lad." He looked at Henry. "Did you get them?"

He shook his head, clearly frustrated.

"We chased a bloke through the gardens," Simon explained.

Pierce and Henry exchanged a glance. Tamsin narrowed her eyes. That glance again. Oh, Henry had some explaining to do.

"Now what?" Pierce muttered when Priya soaked the cloths in honey and water.

"Honey and comfrey will help ward off fevers and keep it from going foul." She motioned to the hovering footmen. "Please help Mr. Gallagher to the Ivy bedroom."

He scowled. "I'm not staying here. 'Tisn't proper."

"Don't be ridiculous," she said, barely looking at him. "You're not walking home injured or being jostled about in a carriage. You'll ruin my stitching."

"What stitching?"

"The stitching I'm going to do when our audience finds their beds." She pointed to Jack and Simon. "Wash your faces and your hands in that basin of clean water first."

"Yes, miss." They nearly saluted her. Tamsin hid a smile.

Pierce grumbled as the footmen helped him up. "Mind I don't bleed on the carpets."

When they were finally alone in a room strewn with bloody bandages and basins of dirty water, Henry scrubbed his face wearily. "You should go to bed too."

She raised both her eyebrows. "Like hell, Henry Talbot."

"What did I do? You're the one who ran outside against express orders."

"You're keeping secrets," she said, all steel and softness. "And it stops now."

Tamsin led him to her bedroom, where she sat on the edge of the bed, sheets rumpled and in disarray. Had that really only been a couple of hours ago? She hadn't known her body could feel those things. Could want what it wanted. And that there might be a safe place to play with that knowledge. She wanted to revel in it.

Instead, a man had been stabbed outside the front door.

Henry shut the door and leaned against it, bare chest damp with the last of the rain. His pant legs bristled with wet grass.

"What's really going on, Henry?"

"I've told you."

"You've told me there are men after you."

"Yes."

"Why?"

"I don't know."

"Who?"

"I don't know."

She made a sound of exasperation. "Please, stop lying to me."

He pushed a hand through his thick hair. "It's complicated, Tam. Dangerous. It's why you should never have married me. I did warn you."

"So you say."

He was startled. "You don't believe me?"

"Why would I? When you're lying to me."

"It's not that simple."

"It could be. If you let it."

He cursed under his breath and started to pace, all leashed power and anger and frustration. "Tamsin, please. Don't."

She was very aware of her thin dressing gown, of the torn ruffles, of the spot of blood on her hem. Pierce being sewn up by Priya down the hall. The scar on Henry's eyebrow, the newer one on his arm from those footpads. None of it made her feel as vulnerable as this conversation.

Priya wouldn't let Pierce's wound fester.

And Tamsin wouldn't let Henry's wound fester either.

"Tell me."

There was a long silence, heavy and fraught and sharp. And then he spoke, his head hanging down, hair tumbling over his forehead. "It's my father."

Whatever Tamsin had been expecting, it wasn't that.

"Your *father*? Your *father* sent men to stab you?"

"He has been since before I joined the Navy."

"But... Wha... *Why?*" Why would a parent do that? Her father wasn't exactly a paragon of fatherhood, but he'd never try to murder her, either. Shock was rapidly giving way to a kind of righteous fury that she was vaguely surprised did not set her own hair on fire.

"The same as always," Henry replied. "He calls them tests. As the next Earl of Culpepper, I need to be strong. Tough as iron."

"And unhinged?"

He nearly smiled. She hadn't meant to be funny. His father was clearly mad.

"You are strong. And kind and clever and honorable."

"It doesn't matter."

"It bloody well does!" Honestly, she didn't know how there wasn't steam hissing out of her, like a kettle on the boil. She desperately wanted to go to him, to touch him, but he stood so straight and sure that she knew he was afraid he might break. "Henry, I love you."

She'd said it before, though they hadn't talked about it. He looked just the same now as he had then. A flash of yearning, a devastating hunger. And then nothing.

Polite, bland nothing.

"Don't," he said, sounding more broken than she felt.

It was her own fault, really. She knew better. She couldn't fix this. Not like that.

She sighed, trying to smile through the pain and confusion prickling through her. "Never mind, Henry," she said gently. "I won't say it again. I know it's not fair when you don't want to hear it. I'm sorry."

"For God's sake, don't be *sorry*."

"I know you don't feel the same."

She could survive this. She could be brave. He did love her, in his way. And this kind of friendship and heat was a stronger foundation for a happy marriage than many of the aristocrats she knew. She was lucky, in her own way. The tears threatening to burn through her defenses would pass. Something could be sad and not inherently wrong. He had clearly suffered enough, and she wouldn't be the cause of one more moment's pain to him.

"You think I don't love you?" It was ripped from him, jagged and hoarse and utterly disbelieving. "Is that what you think?"

"I'm not an idiot, Henry."

"No, but I bloody well am." He crossed the room in two strides to clasp her shoulders and pull her to her feet. His eyes blazed. "Tamsin Bell, I've never loved anyone the way I love you, nor will I in my lifetime."

She stared. "Did you steal some of Pierce's port earlier?" She wouldn't give in to the giddy warmth caused by his declaration. Couldn't.

He laughed gruffly. "Only you would ask me that at a moment like this."

"Well, you're not yourself." She didn't want pity. She knew why Jack's face went sour at the thought. Why he fought so hard. She wanted Henry more than anything in the world. But she didn't want the lie. Not from him. "I'm strong enough for the truth."

"Are you?" He laughed again. "Because I'm not sure I am." He shook his head, gaze burning. "I love you, Tam. I always have."

"You… do?" She wasn't sure she could trust her own ears. She'd wanted to hear him say those very words for too long now. But she could, at the very least, trust the way he was looking at her. The way he touched her.

"Of course I love you. How could I not? You're fearless and generous and annoyingly beautiful."

She huffed a small laugh. "Is that your idea of a compliment?"

"Have you looked at yourself lately, woman? It's distracting."

She'd received enough compliments in her lifetime to know when one was honest, when one was spoken without expectations. This one made her blush. She hadn't blushed over someone telling her she was beautiful since she was fifteen years old.

He stroked her cheek. "I do love that blush."

It was probably wrong to feel so happy when less than half an hour ago a man had been stabbed nearly to death on the front step.

"Your letters kept me alive when I was away."

"They were silly chatter about dances and the new gaslights at Vauxhall Gardens."

"They reminded me that there were things to stay alive for. That you were here."

"I'm always here," she said.

"The least I can do now is keep you alive."

She stiffened. "I don't like *that*."

"Tamsin, my father relishes taking away the things I love. To keep me *strong*."

Understanding clicked.

"My nanny when I turned three," he continued. "He turned her out when I called for her after a bad dream. Then there was the stable master who snuck me barley candy. The butcher's wife in the village who wiped my tears. The kitchen cat."

"General Whiskers?" She was outraged all over again.

"He could never get rid of my grandmother, of course. Not his own mother."

She felt ill. "Persephone?"

He nodded once. "He would have tried, eventually, I think."

"And so, you left to fight Napoleon."

"And so, I left." His tone made her shiver.

"Well, he's not going to murder a viscountess, surely."

"No, but you've seen the men he sends after me. At some point, you'll get caught in the crossfire."

"I shan't." She could tell he didn't believe her. She ran her palms up and down his bare arms, to comfort herself as much as him. "Why didn't you say so before?"

"I didn't want you to see that kind of darkness."

She sighed. "Henry, although being the daughter of a duke has afforded me more protection than many others, I am still a woman in this world. I see the darkness every day. We all do. We see it and we bear it. And the Lord Eatons of this world, my own father, yours, my stepmother even, would have it break me. But I won't be broken. Not for anyone. So your father, such as he is, can do his worst."

Henry shuddered. "Don't say that."

She kissed him lightly. "He can't touch us. I won't let him."

"You can't stop him, love."

She kissed him again, gently, tiny nips, easing back slightly when he shifted, teasing them both. Until he finally pressed her to the door, aligning their bodies, his chest warm and strong, his mouth bold.

Henry loved her.

He *loved* her.

He tilted her head back, taking his fill of her, tongue stroking hers, teeth scraping along her throat, closing gently over her earlobe until she gasped. He was the first to pull away. His forehead touched her. "I should go."

"It's nearly dawn. You may as well stay."

He didn't say anything. True fear pierced her then. Daggers and shadows in the night meant nothing.

"Henry?"

"That was too close. You could have been hurt. You might be next time."

"*You* were hurt! You've already been stabbed and your face bruised, all in, what now, the matter of a week? Two?"

"That doesn't matter."

"Of course it does!" Her hands curled into fists. "I'll be paying your father a visit."

"Don't." It was a command, Captain Talbot at the helm. But Henry underneath, afraid for her. "Surely he's proven he has no compunction in hurting you."

"Your father is a horse's ass. And I have every intention of telling him so."

"You can't." He caught her shoulders. "Promise me you won't try."

She bristled.

"Stop protecting me, Tamsin."

"No. You first."

"Absolutely not."

"Then why should I? Because I am a woman? Or you are a man?"

"That's not it."

"What, then?"

"Because you are precious to me!" he burst out, sounding annoyed, and more than a little feral.

"Don't you think you are equally precious?"

He laughed. It was rough and cold, and she hated it. Hated what it meant about how he thought of himself. Not for the first time, she had elaborate revenge fantasies on how to make his father pay.

All of London, if need be.

They'd scorned him, then feted him, but they never saw him. His own father did not value him or respect him, not until Society had shown an interest. And even then, it was only a twisted sort of attention, more poisonous than paternal.

She wasn't having it.

But she knew Henry well enough to know that he would bolt this very morning if he thought it would keep her safe. Running had kept him safe for too long. She needed a little time.

"You can't go," she said softly. "Not yet, not like this."

"Not until we have your theft problem under control," he said. "But after that…"

She'd burn Vasilisa to ashes along with the rest of her collection before she'd let Henry's monster of a father drive him away. If nothing else, she would go with him. She couldn't tell him that either, not yet.

"Promise me you won't disappear," she said instead.

"I won't."

"Promise," she insisted fiercely.

"I promise." He kissed her again, swift, hard, hungry. "I love you, Tamsin."

"I love you too, Henry."

She waited until he was gone before seeking out Priya. She was in Pierce's chamber, mixing herbs in a pestle. "How is he?" Tamsin asked.

"Henry was just here asking the same. I've given him willow bark tea for the pain."

"It was like drinking bitter ashes," Pierce grumbled.

Priya raised an eyebrow. "As you see, he'll be fine." She read the icy determination in Tamsin's face before she'd spoken another word. "What is it?"

Tamsin lowered her voice.

"I need everything you can get on the Earl of Culpepper."

Chapter Twenty-Eight

T HE MIDNIGHT MARKET was a fine distraction, such as distractions went.

It was held in a different location each time, sometimes assembly rooms, sometimes ballrooms in the estate holder's house. Tonight, the address led Tamsin and Henry to an empty house on the end of a bustling street well out of Mayfair.

Carriages waited in the fog, and the eye-shaped brass door knocker that announced each market had been attached to the door. Henry knocked, keeping a wary eye on their surroundings and an arm around her waist.

She leaned into him, the ticking of a clock echoing in the back of her head. She had almost suggested they not come. Once this mystery was solved, he would leave. She felt it in her bones. He wouldn't be dissuaded. If she had mentioned it, he would have kept investigating without her.

And that simply would not do.

A man opened the door, accepting her invitation and then stepping aside to let them in. The main parlor was lined with glass-fronted cabinets filled with odd treasures collected to intrigue and confound. There were the usual books claiming to be grimoires, filled mostly with sketches no older than she was. But there were also crystal balls, Morris Men bells, curse tablets, and iron nails.

Customers milled through the space, monocles in hand,

whispering to each other about provenances and folktales and gruesome lore. Many of them wore masks to hide their features. It smelled like dust and old paper and incense.

Henry glanced down at her fondly. "Admit it, you prefer this to birthdays and Christmases combined."

"Well, of course I—Oh." She tugged him toward the corner cabinet, while trying to school her features not to betray her interest. Under a scatter of iron nails pulled from a gallows was a small box open to display a gold poison ring in the shape of a skull. Tamsin coveted it immediately. She would have bid on it right then and there if she'd been able to.

There were poppets too, but no Vasilisa.

She bit back disappointment. After all, she'd hardly expected to find her pilfered doll on display. Whoever had taken it had miscalculated. No one was likely to pay a single penny for it.

There were love spell curios, but no sign of Sir Wormwood. There were witch prickers used to find "witch marks" in Scotland, but no Miss Montague. Tamsin wondered why they were not here already.

Mirabelle was here, however, circulating and greeting everyone while making notes in a little book. She wore a very smart blue dress, her blond hair in a twist. "Lady Tamsin."

They exchanged curtsies. Henry bowed.

"I'm sorry Miss Stewart is missing this," Mirabelle said. "She had hoped to be back in time, but alas."

"I'm sure she's grateful for your help."

"Do look around. The bidding will start in half an hour."

Henry watched her walk away. "That wasn't at all awkward."

Tamsin grinned. "Imagine how I felt when I saw her at the Cabinet of Curiosities after I drugged her brother."

"Isn't it a bit odd that she's here?"

"I thought so too, but she's a friend of Miss Stewart, who is usually in charge of these events."

They had made it to a broken Gaulish pillar from France with a recess for a skull when a footman approached. "Lady Tamsin, you are invited to view a private collection upstairs."

She sucked in her breath. This was it. It had to be.

"This way, please." He went through to the hall and paused at the foot of the stairs. "I regret that the invitation is for Lady Tamsin alone."

"Like hell." There was no threat of violence in Henry's demeanor—there didn't have to be. The ocean tides crashed on the shore whether or not they were invited.

The footman seemed to realize the futility of arguing and bowed. "Of course, my lord."

They followed him upstairs, leaving behind the din of conversation and the clusters of chandeliers. The light was dimmer here, the air quiet with the quality peculiar to unoccupied houses. Henry was right behind her, guarding her back. She knew he had several daggers on hand. She had diamond hairpins.

Very long, very sharp diamond hairpins.

There was no conceivable reason why Henry's father might be caught up in this particular mystery, but she invited him to try. Just once.

They were taken to an upstairs room that had originally been a family parlor. There was no furniture left, but the walls were bright and cheery, painted with stripes. And on the mantel sat her childhood doll, a lit candle on either side of her.

Tamsin darted forward. There was no mistaking Vasilisa's blue frock, her braided yarn for hair. Tamsin felt her mother's presence all over again just looking at it.

She turned to smile at Henry over her shoulder, but the footman was between them, and then he was suddenly lunging for the door. He slammed it in Henry's face and turned the lock.

"Tamsin!" Henry yelled.

Tamsin stared at the very large footman who stood between her and the door. Her heart raced in her chest. "What are you doing?"

Henry continued to pound on the door. "If you touch her, I'll kill you."

"I don't mean to hurt you, my lady," the footman said. It would have been more reassuring if he hadn't crossed his beefy arms and stared over her head.

"Then let me pass."

"I'm afraid I can't do that."

She glanced at the window. It was too narrow for her to pass through. "Do you work for the Earl of Culpepper?" That made no sense at all. Even for one of his monstrous tests, this seemed unduly complicated.

The footman frowned, confused. She trusted that natural and involuntary reaction more than his words. "No, my lady."

"Who, then?"

"I can't say."

"You really should. Don't you think it odd that you were hired to jail a viscountess? And a duke's daughter?"

He paled, just enough to give her a twinge of vengeful glee. At least he wasn't trying to harm her. But he was far too large for her to have any hope of taking the key from him.

"I can double your fee."

"I'm sorry, my lady. I couldn't tell you, even if I knew."

"Blast," she muttered. Just like the man who'd hired Jack.

The door rattled with the force of Henry's entire body.

"You should probably let me go," she said mildly.

"Can't."

"You've made him cross."

The door shuddered and groaned under Henry's assault.

"I can handle a toff."

She smiled slowly. "Is that so?"

There was a curse from the hallway, a single moment of taut silence, and then Henry's boot connected with the door. Once. Twice.

The footman jumped and turned. Too late.

Tamsin stepped back prudently, all of the fear draining from her.

The door cracked and then smashed open, slamming into the wall. Henry surged into the room, icy rage curling his lip. His gaze flicked to Tamsin. "Did he hurt you?"

"No."

The footman raised his fists. They were huge. He might even know how to use them. But he had no idea he was facing not only Lord Stirling, but also Captain Talbot. And more importantly, Henry, her husband.

He didn't posture, didn't threaten. He didn't even bother sinking into one of the fighting stances he'd no doubt practiced with the other sailors and at Gentleman Jackson's when in London. He merely attacked, fast, precise. He punched the footman square in the face while also aiming a vicious kick at the other man's kneecap. There was a crack, a pop, and a spurt of blood.

The footman toppled.

Henry reached her before he'd even touched the ground, and the crash fluttered the hem of her dress. His eyes were wild as he caught her up against his chest. "You're all right."

She smiled up at him. "I'm perfectly fine."

"I should kill him."

"Sounds messy. Let's just go home instead."

He glared at the prone footman. "I have questions."

"He doesn't know who hired him—it was a man who hid his face, just like with Jack. And it wasn't your father."

"You got all that in the three minutes you were locked in here?"

"Did you doubt me?"

"Of course not." His kiss was desperate, a brand to reassure himself she was unharmed. "I'll come back for him."

Tamsin picked up the doll from where she'd dropped it. She checked the hem for the mark leftover from an altercation with her stepmother's bulldog. "It's definitely her," Tamsin said.

Henry put his hand on her lower back, as if he couldn't stand to not be touching her as they moved out into the hall. To not know she was safe.

"I'm glad." He frowned. "But why just give her back? Why now? Like this?"

"Good question. I'd have paid an embarrassing sum to have her back. Nostalgia is expensive. And why try to keep me in here?"

"It's not about the doll at all, is it? It was merely a lure?"

"I suppose it must have been."

"Which means you must have something else this thief

wants." He shut the door. "I'm going to find something to wedge against this so he can't get out and warn his master. Stay here." He stopped in the next doorway. "I mean it, Tamsin."

"Yes, yes."

He stayed where he was. "On second thought…"

"What?" She hurried to his side and peered into the room. This one had a single item set up on the windowsill: a grotesque metal mask with pointed ears and an elongated tongue.

"What in the devil?" Henry said.

"It's a scold's mask," Tamsin replied. "Used to punish gossips and witches during the witch hunts. And it has to belong to Miss Montague. Torture devices are her milieu."

"Luckily, she's not here yet."

"They mean to trap her as well. To trap all of us." She darted to the next room, just out of sight in the gloomy hall.

"Tamsin," Henry said, racing after her.

She pointed to the unassuming chunk of stone, a faded flower painted on the surface. "This must be a stone from Hever Castle, where Anne Boleyn's ghost pays a visit every Christmas. I'd heard a rumor Lord Chevril managed to procure one from her childhood bedroom. I'm a bit jealous, actually."

The next room contained a small doll, not unlike her own, but rather more primitive in style. "That is a love poppet." The poppet was sewn with red thread, an iron nail struck through its embroidered thread. "And it must belong to Sir Wormwood." When she picked it up to inspect, she froze. "Henry." She turned it over, straw stuffing poking into her palm. "It's been undone."

She turned Vasilisa over. The back of her had been sliced, the wool Tamsin's mother had used for stuffing missing in hunks. She hadn't noticed in the tumult.

"We have to get out of here. *Now.*"

"Someone is looking for something very particular," she said. "And it's not the poppet but what's *inside* a poppet."

"So it would seem. *Move*, love."

She narrowed her eyes. "I have an entire collection of poppets."

"I am aware of that."

She turned on her heel, swift as a lark.

"Oh, threat of bodily harm does nothing, but *that* gets you moving."

"I will show them bodily harm if they touch my collection." She paused at the top of the stairs. "Are you coming?"

He dragged a heavy chair covered with a sheet from one of the rooms then lodged it against the handle of the first door to keep the footman contained.

"We have to warn the others," Tamsin said. "And we have to get to my collection. They've only missed it because I'm not living in your house, and they must not realize it." Her eyes widened. "Persephone is storing it for me at her museum. You don't think they'd go there, do you?"

"I doubt it. For one thing, I guarantee Percy has set guards on the place."

"True."

"And Conall has set more she does not even know of." He blew out all the sconce candles, plunging them in gray shadows. "First, we get you out of here."

"What about the patrons downstairs?"

"They are here to muddy the waters and mask the true purpose. I don't think they are in any danger. Do you?"

"I suppose not."

"Come on, then."

His fingers curled around hers as he pulled her confidently behind him. "How can you see?"

"It's no darker than a ship's hull," he told her. "I don't want them to know we've gotten out. They may have set someone to keep watch."

She followed him gingerly. "Persephone was nearly murdered during her betrothal, Meg was attacked practically on her wedding day, so I suppose it's only fitting that we were locked up on our honeymoon."

"This does *not* count as our honeymoon!"

He sounded so disgruntled that she had to smile at him in the darkness. They crept down the stairs and then toward the kitchen stairs, ducking into small library.

Henry went straight to the window and poked his head out. "No one obviously watching, and it's not far to the ground. It'll do."

He slid out in one movement, all lethal grace. When Tamsin followed, he clasped her waist and helped her down. She finally took a deep breath, not realizing how tight her muscles had been while trapped upstairs, right down to her lungs. They stayed pressed to the wall, inching out toward the sidewalk.

The house spilled golden light and chatter, the patrons inside oblivious to what was happening around them.

Henry glared up at the other buildings. "Too many windows," he muttered. "But we'll have to risk it."

They darted out of the alley, toward their carriage, only to be interrupted by Lord Chevril, limping toward them.

"Lord Chevril, what happened to you?" Tamsin asked. Earls who wore that much scented pomade and shoes that tight did not generally walk from Mayfair.

"My bloody coachman didn't check the saddles properly, and the straps snapped. Carriage can't move and there were no hackneys to be had. I suppose I ought to be glad it's not raining."

"Your carriage?" Henry asked thoughtfully.

"What is it?" Tamsin asked.

"I don't know," he admitted, looking frustrated. "There's something in the back of my head, but I can't figure out what it is. There's a chart to navigate here, but I can't seem to figure it out."

When Lord Chevril raised his hand to knock, Tamsin winced. "I'm afraid there's more bad news, Lord Chevril."

"Eh?"

"You shouldn't go in there."

"I want my property back!"

"I know," she said. "I did too. And whoever stole from us counted on it and locked me in a room. Your stone is in there, upstairs, in a room with a sturdy lock."

"Devil… Beg your pardon, Lady Stirling."

"Does it feel at all haunted?" she asked. "Do you think Anne Boleyn might seek it out?"

"That is my hope. I have a scientist friend who is endeavoring to—"

"If we could focus," Henry interrupted.

"Eh?" Lord Chevril frowned. "Yours is quite the tall tale. Why should I believe you? This could be a trick."

"Look at the state of my dress, Lord Chevril." Tamsin showed him the dust marks and the tear in the hem from climbing out of the window. "Do you think I would be out dressed like this?"

He sniffed. "I suppose not."

"Will you stay and make sure Miss Montague and Sir Wormwood don't go inside?"

He nodded. "I suppose I must. Where will you be?"

"Following a hunch."

Chapter Twenty-Nine

THE PERSEPHONE MUSEUM had a new sign hanging over the door, and apparently Conall had won the discussion over the name. The curtains were still drawn over the windows.

Tamsin sighed. "Percy's gone to Little Barrow. I'd forgotten."

Henry withdrew a key from inside his coat.

"She gave you a key?" she asked. "I'm jealous."

"She wanted me to keep an eye on the place when she's away."

"Brilliant."

"She insisted I keep the key on me at all times, in case of museum emergencies. I didn't even know there was such a thing as museum emergencies before now."

She flashed him a grin. "You've been away for a long time."

"Apparently."

He let them into Persephone's favorite place, her own little word of sand dunes and jackal-headed gods and gold statues. Tamsin could not help a proud little nod at the lines of turquoise scarabs secured in a line on the wall, leading visitors to the various rooms housing the collections.

They also led, most unfortunately, to the end of a pistol.

Henry moved to block her before she'd closed her mouth on a surprised gasp. A very tall, very large man took up most of the narrow hall, his face set like one of the statues: unmovable.

"Museum's closed," he said.

"Glad to hear it," Henry said. "I am Lord Stirling."

The man did not move. "Lord Stirling has a scar through his left eyebrow."

Henry pushed his hair back, using his other hand to keep Tamsin behind him.

The man lowered the pistol. "Apologies, Lord Stirling," the guard said.

"No apology necessary," Henry said. "Northwyck's man, are you?"

"The countess hired me."

"Better and better." Tamsin skipped out from behind Henry, despite his warning growl. "I'm Lady Tamsin—that is, Lady Stirling."

The guard blinked at her. Henry muttered something about putting away her smile when they had work to do.

"And you are?"

"Er, George, my lady," the guard finally said, bowing. She thought he might be blushing. It was really quite sweet. "The countess has put your boxes together in a crate in the sorting room so they would not get mixed into the rest of the artifacts."

"How kind," she said, as though it had been his idea. "Thank you so much."

"This way."

Henry shook his head fondly when she grinned at him. "Has there been anyone suspicious about? Loitering?" he asked. "Trying to get inside?"

"No, my lord. No one except yourselves."

"You're sure?"

"Aye. There's a room for the guards to stay in when it's our shift. No one gets in or out. And the lower windows are barred."

"I'm beginning to think Percy has gotten paranoid," Henry said. "I might love that about her."

"I believe the bars were the earl's idea. The countess mentioned a moat of scorpions."

"Of course she did."

"Here you are." The sorting room was enormous and filled with chests and boxes and papers nailed to the wall, all covered with lists in Persephone's handwriting. George lit the lamps and led them to a deep crate under a back window. On the side, the words *Tamsin Bell, fragile* had been painted.

Henry's lips ghosted in her hair. "You're no such thing."

She leaned into his warmth for a moment. Then she smiled at George. "Thank you, George."

He backed away mumbling.

"I keep telling you to be careful with that smile," Henry murmured.

George stopped a few feet away. "I should be on proper watch, do you reckon, my lord?"

"After the night we've just had? Yes."

"Who knew dusty old things could be such a bother?"

Henry shook his head. "You have no idea."

Tamsin was already leaning on an iron crow, wedged into the crate, jumping on it to pop the lid. Her blood felt tingly. She was righteously indignant, angry, determined. And strangely excited. It was a heady mix. She jumped on the bar again.

The nails had groaned and loosened by the time Henry reached her. When he finished prying the lid off, the boxes beneath were neat and undisturbed. She let out a sigh of relief. He pulled out the boxes and chests for her, until she found the one containing the poppets. She unwrapped them and laid them out on a table.

"That is remarkably unsettling," Henry said.

"Some of them are meant to be," she agreed. "They protect, or they carry wishes. This one is meant to represent an enemy." The doll in question had its eyes and lips sewn shut with black thread. Henry shuddered. "You've been to war," she reminded him, amused.

"And that is just as unnerving as a French cannon, I assure you."

"I think she's sweet."

He shook his head. "That's because everyone thinks *you're* sweet."

"I am sweet!"

"How many times have you mildly poisoned my father?"

"Far fewer times than he deserves, I assure you."

She inspected the poppet, but nothing seemed out of order. No stitches were loose, no material obviously newer than the rest. She was looking for something far subtler than that, surely. She would have examined these items before purchasing them, after all. She might not be an expert with forgeries like Persephone was, but she knew her folklore.

The next poppet was bulky and badly sewn. It had come to her that way, but it was worth a closer look. She unpicked the stitches, wincing. "This is a part of history," she muttered. "Someone made this because they were desperate. They might have been hanged for a witch for their trouble."

And for her trouble, she only found straw that crumbled to dust when she touched it and a tiny braid of hair. Nothing worth this fuss.

"I'll put you back to rights," she promised, moving to the next.

The little doll filled with lavender was by the far the sweetest of the lot. There was nothing overly occult about it, nothing to suggest a curse or a trap for witches. She hadn't bought it specifically, rather it had been part of a chest Miss Stewart had set aside for her. There'd been a fair number of elf arrows and medieval rings and coins, as collected by most antiquarians, and this little poppet. She'd assumed from the lavender that it was a good-luck charm or some such.

But now she wondered.

A carriage clattered by, the sound rumbling gently through the floor. Henry frowned out of the window, distracted.

She pulled the thread loose, expecting more wool for stuffing and some lavender stalks. She did not expect to find something else nestled inside. Pieces of parchment folded small.

Her heart pounded in her chest as she pulled one loose. "Henry."

He glanced away from the glass. "You found something."

"I think it's a letter." She unfolded it carefully. The handwriting was flowery, faded to a dull brown. She sucked in a breath. "Henry, listen." She smoothed out the parchment gently.

"Dearest Holland, It broke my heart to give you the cut direct at the theatre last night. It has been months since I felt your lips on mine. And I have received every letter you wrote, felt the words engrave themselves on my heart. But I must be brave for both of us now. For all three of us. For you must know that my son is your son. But he must belong to my husband now, and to the earldom. He might never know himself as your child, but know, in your soul, that he is yours. That we are both yours. Always yours, L.

"There are dozens of love letters hidden in here. And 'L' could be anyone," Tamsin added. "That *is* frustrating. I don't know how we'll ever find out who his real son is, but I've heard of Mr. Holland. He was a minor baronet. He had no children," she said after a moment's thought. "Well, that he claimed publicly, I suppose. His house went to a distant cousin when he died, just a few months ago."

"How do you know that?"

She waved her hand dismissively. "He's in *Debrett's Peerage*. My stepmother insisted I memorize it when I was fifteen so that I might know all of the lords and their titles."

"That's quite the feat. Those volumes must weigh a ton each."

"I thought it deadly dull and useless." She wrinkled her nose. "But I suppose it had its use, after all. Don't tell my stepmother. And if I remember correctly, the house was sold off, contents and all, to pay the new baron's gaming debts. That must be how it found its way to the Cabinet of Curiosities. Miss Stewart often buys from estate sales."

"She might be involved. She could know the identity of this mystery baby."

"I doubt it. She gets boxes of odds and ends from all over England every week."

Henry whistled. "So our Mr. Holland is now an earl. That's quite the step up."

"Illegitimate."

"Exactly."

"I suppose that's why he's gone through so much bother. The housebreaking, locking us up. He knew someone had these letters in their possession."

Henry exhaled. "It's lucky he didn't know who it was had it exactly," he said. "There are many who would kill to keep this kind of secret."

He was right. If the child had grown up to be an aristocrat, that kind of inheritance was worth thousands of pounds, thousands of acres of land, power in Parliament. Social clout.

Another carriage went past. Henry's head whipped toward the sound. The noise of the wheels seemed to shake something loose in him, to solidify whatever had been distracting him. "Son of a bitch," he whispered.

Tamsin glanced up from the letter. "What?"

"I know who's behind it. I know who Mr. Holland's illegitimate son is."

"That was fast. Who?"

"Eaton."

"ARE YOU SURE?" Tamsin asked, yet again, on their way from the museum to Priya's townhouse. "There's no question the man is a jackass, but…"

"I'm sure." His jaw was tight, and he'd tucked Tamsin up against his side. She snuggled into his warmth. "I knew there was something about that carriage the night of the Braithewaite ball. A small, distinct crack in one corner of the window. Jack remembered it. And I knew I'd seen it before." He kissed her hair as if he couldn't help himself, and she wondered how she could be so annoyed and agitated and happy at the same time. He *loved* her.

"And?"

"And I saw that same crack in the window of the carriage Eaton used to abduct you. The very well-heeled, expensive, but strangely anonymous carriage."

"That's why he pushed the betrothal. He wanted to get his hands on my collection." She straightened. "Mirabelle showed an interest as well, the one time she paid me an unexpected visit. *After* the duel."

"And she had access to all of the Cabinet of Curiosities."

"What do we do now?" Tamsin asked as the carriage slowed.

Priya's street was quiet and dark, as dawn hovered just on the edge of London.

"I'll talk to Eaton."

"Think he'll be reasonable, do you?"

"Not exactly."

"We need a better plan than that." She eyed him wryly. "Such as an *actual* plan."

"I want you far away from all of this."

"It's too late for that now," she said, emerging from the carriage.

"It's not."

"Actually, it is," Eaton snapped, his arm shackling Tamsin and squeezing tight. She squeaked. Then she cursed the way only a Cinderella could curse.

Henry stepped down, hands held out appeasingly. The rest of him was not in the least appeasing, from the tautness of his muscles to the fury smoldering in his eyes. He looked more like a pirate than a ship's captain in the king's Navy. "Eaton, let her go."

"I don't think so," Eaton said. "Not yet."

"I'll eviscerate you if you hurt her." It was a promise, nearly pleasant and polite for its ferocity.

"I want her collection of oddities," Eaton snapped. "You'll get it for me, and then maybe I'll let her go. Maybe."

Her collection of oddities was safely stored in Persephone's museum. Except for the small chest of poppets on the seat of the carriage, waiting to be sewn back together. Eaton had a lot to answer for, not the least of which was the unfortunately necessary desecration of rare, folkloric relics.

Eaton aimed a pistol at the coachman who was trying to sneak down off his perch. "Inside the coach," he ordered the man. "Or I'll shoot you dead."

The coachman did as he was told, locking himself inside. There would be no help from that quarter. When Henry shifted, the pistol was trained on him.

"Don't move."

Tamsin's heart stopped. She squirmed, but the band of Eaton's arm was too constricting, and he was too strong. She wore useless silk shoes that would do no damage whatsoever, even if she managed to strike him somewhere helpful. She had no weapons of her own, only diamond hairpins and a reputation for charm and vivaciousness on the dance floor.

A reputation for being flighty and pretty and entertaining.

She could use that.

She could talk.

"Why do you want my museum?" she asked, hoping to distract with some chatter, at least long enough that they could figure out how to stop him. "I didn't think you cared about witch nails and fortune-telling cards."

"*I don't.*"

"Then what is it?"

"Never mind," he said, shaking her. Her teeth snapped together.

Henry snarled a warning. "Eaton."

"*Give me what I want.*"

The flintlock pistol moved again, the cold metal pressing into her temple. She froze, breath strangling in her throat.

"*Stop.*" Henry's command lashed out, the whip of a captain accustomed to being obeyed.

Eaton paused, despite himself, but he did not lower the pistol.

"Eaton, you can have whatever you want. Just let her go."

"I need those poppets. This is your fault, you bitch. You didn't need to make everything so damned difficult."

"Well, I *am* a Cinderella," she said drily.

"Tamsin," Henry said quietly. "Don't."

Talking obviously wasn't helping.

But chatty, social butterflies didn't just talk.

They also swooned. Gracefully, to show how delicate they were. Coyly, to offer a glimpse of an ankle. Or, as she'd seen Meg do often enough, to extract themselves from unpleasant social situations. And Eaton would no doubt expect her to fight. She had poisoned him, after all. Just a little. And then she'd knocked him unconscious.

So, she didn't fight.

She simply met Henry's coldly furious face and then dropped, swift and sudden.

She made herself as unwieldy and heavy as she could. She shifted slightly with every compensation Eaton tried to make, like a particularly obnoxious octopus. If she could have grown extra limbs with which to trip him up, she would have done so gladly. He grunted, swearing.

He didn't let her go, not right away. But it gave Henry just enough time to slam his fist down on Eaton's wrist, cracking it like a flower stem. Eaton roared in pain, and the pistol clattered to the ground. Tamsin reared up, smashing the back of her head into his face.

It hurt.

A lot.

And it was entirely worth it.

He yelped and stumbled back, and she was finally free of him. She was quite smug about it, actually.

And then a shot rang out, shattering the shadows.

Eaton's double-barreled flintlock pistol lay on the ground. The shot had come from somewhere else.

The smell of gunpowder, the strange vibration in the air— she'd remember it always. The hiccup of time, where it slowed down and sped up.

And Henry jerking back, hitting the carriage with a violence that rattled the window. He slid to the ground, blood smearing the paneling behind him. The horses reared and took off at a gallop.

"Henry!" Tamsin didn't understand why she wasn't flying through the air, why she wasn't at his side already. He clutched his right arm, cursing between his teeth. He was alive.

She still wasn't at his side.

It took too long to realize that she wasn't frozen in shock. Instead, Eaton had hold of her again. He lunged, face contorted with blood and rage. His hands closed around her throat. This wasn't a promise, a threat to get what he wanted. Her breath caught. She plucked at his hand, but it did her little good. Pain and fear made it difficult to move. Her throat burned.

And then a second shot rang out.

Eaton dropped her. The second bullet from his pistol caught him in the thigh, and he crumpled.

"I told you not to touch her," Henry said, dropping the weapon.

Tamsin stumbled to him.

He touched her face. "Breathe, Tam. Slow breaths."

That was when she realized she was gasping but getting very little air. She drew in a slow breath, every part of her trembling.

"You need a doctor," she finally said, hoarsely.

"As long as he doesn't give me another vinegar rinse."

She smiled, though her eyes were annoyingly blurry.

"Don't cry, Tam."

"I'm not crying." She absolutely was. "Your arm."

"Just my arm, nothing vital," he assured her. "But we should move. I don't know who fired that shot."

She helped him up and managed to get him up the walkway just in time for Mirabelle to barrel around the corner. "What did you *do?*"

Henry propped himself up, smearing blood on the white column. "Tamsin, get behind me."

Obviously, Tamsin did no such thing. "That's a lady's pistol," she said. "My father gave me one when I was younger. It's too small for more than one shot. She's not a threat."

"I don't need a pistol." Mirabelle's pretty face contorted. "You shot my brother!"

"Regrettably, only once. And what did you do to Miss Stewart?"

She scoffed. "She's fine. Her friend didn't really send a letter asking for help, but nothing's happened to your precious Miss Stewart. Which is more than I can say for you."

"Interesting," Tamsin said. "Because I have a letter too. A whole packet of them, actually."

Mirabelle froze in the act to trying to reach her brother, moaning pitifully on the ground. "*What?*"

"Yes, we found the most interesting reading material inside one of my poppets."

"Give it to me."

"Oh, I don't think so. You tried to murder a viscount. My *husband*." Tamsin hadn't known how much vengeance could boil inside her.

Henry was still trying to nudge her safely inside. His blood dripped onto the ground at her feet. She stood her ground balefully.

"My brother is an earl," Mirabelle sputtered. Earls could get away with almost anything.

"Not according to your own mother."

She laughed, and it was a hateful sound. "My mother was *weak*. She should never have told anyone in the first place, let alone again on her deathbed. She and my father couldn't have sons, you see. Only daughters. She couldn't leave well enough alone with her lie; instead she sent that stupid doll to *that man* as a keepsake, and then he died shortly after her and his house was sold off before we could get inside. Thought herself in love, didn't she? As if that matters more than my brother's life, his *title*. And you, *you*, thinking you're so much better than him."

"That's because she is," Henry said. "She's worth twenty of your brother. Of you. A hundred times, even."

Mirabelle tossed her useless pistol aside and pulled a dagger from her reticule. "We'll see about th—"

She did not finish her threat.

A thin china vase painted all over with ivy leaves fell from above and struck her on the head. It broke, and she crumpled with a small mewl of surprise.

Pierce leaned out from his window, his bandage white in the gloom.

"That's the bloody woman who stabbed me."

Chapter Thirty

TAMSIN WAS ONLY mildly disappointed that Eaton was expected to recover full use of his leg.

She didn't tell the doctor that, of course. Or the magistrate and the watch, who had been called in to take both Eaton and his sister away. Mirabelle would have a headache for a few days and a scar in her hairline, but she'd also be just fine.

Still, they had tried to murder a viscount and a war hero, as well as a viscountess. And as Eaton was about to be revealed as illegitimate, his title would not shield him from consequences.

"What if no one believes us? Or the letter?" Tamsin asked. It was full morning now, the doctor having been and gone and breakfast trays delivered. She nibbled on a bun, hungry and yet completely without appetite. Her fingers shook. "I feel odd."

"It's the adrenaline," Henry told her, propped up in bed, a clean white bandage around his wound. Priya had checked the doctor's work. Twice. She'd added more honey and sent up a pot of willow bark tea. She'd insisted Tamsin's regular tea be liberally laced with honey as well, to ease her throat. "It keeps you fighting, but once it runs out, it takes you down."

"I don't care for it." She sipped from her cup.

"Your neck," he said gently, furiously even as his touch was whisper-soft. "He's left red marks."

"She took an entire chunk of your arm," she pointed out. "That's rather more pressing."

"It really isn't."

She laced her fingers through his and kissed his knuckles. "She might have killed you."

"Lucky for me, those tiny pistols are not exactly reliable at a distance."

When Tamsin shivered, he pulled her closer. She climbed very carefully into the bed with him, snuggling against his good side. She laid her head on his bare chest, the steady beat of his heart soothing the wisps of panic still fluttering through her. She willed her racing pace to synchronize with his.

"Do you really think they'll deport Eaton and Mirabelle for this?"

"I do," he said, stroking her shoulder, down her arm. "Pierce will corroborate what he heard, as will the coachman." The coachman had eventually returned, along with the nervous horses and a fine story to tell at the pub. "And I intend to talk to the actual heir of the Eaton earldom. I expect he'll work hard to make sure this isn't swept under the rug."

"That would be the second cousin, a Jonathan Dunham."

He smiled briefly. *"Debrett's?"*

"Debrett's."

"You're safe now," Henry murmured when she shivered slightly. "I'll make sure of it."

She did not find the comfort in his statement that he intended. She knew he was thinking of his father now, of the men who would come to test him. She went cold.

"You promised you wouldn't leave without saying goodbye."

"And I shan't."

"You shan't leave at all."

"Love…"

"No," she said firmly. "You're going to stay right here until your arm is healed."

And then they would just see.

Eaton hadn't won. And neither would his father. She'd make sure of it. Somehow.

"And if you insist on going, then I'm going with you."

He stilled. "Your whole life is in London."

"I don't care about London."

"You care about the Cinderellas." He sounded torn, worshipful. "I can't take you from everything and everyone you love. It's selfish. And I'm not worth it."

"I'll decide that for myself, thank you very much," she replied fiercely. "And you're right about the Cinderellas at least. I do care about them, but I can visit them from Scotland or France or wherever." She tilted her face up to his. "Your father is not all-powerful."

He smiled. "No, but I'm beginning to think you are."

She huffed at the compliment, refusing to let it sway her. "Do you know why I keep searching for ghosts, Henry? Why I want to believe in them despite what it makes people say about me?"

He shook his head. "Why?"

"Because it's nice not to be alone. When I was little, I was hoping to see my mother. I haven't been that picky in years. I've lived for many years in a house full of people hired by my stepmother who aren't allowed to really talk to me. I'm not welcome at home beyond the occasional family meal for appearances. Persephone lives in Little Barrow, Meg is in Perchance-upon-the-Sea, and Priya is not fond of visitors, even when she loves them. And everyone else only knows *Lady Tamsin*."

He frowned. "You're lonely."

"I have been, yes. So don't leave me alone, Henry Talbot."

He kissed the top of her head. "I love you, Tamsin."

"I love *you*, Henry," she returned. "And I'm keeping you."

She waited until he had nodded off before easing from the bed. She adjusted the curtains, fussed with his blanket, and felt her wobbly tears dry to stone. He was safe. They were together.

And she intended to keep it that way.

She kissed him softly before leaving, and he smiled, still asleep.

When Tamsin closed the door behind her, Priya waited in the hall, a single piece of paper in her hand. "What's this?" Tamsin asked.

Priya smiled.

"Consider it a wedding present."

FOR THE NEXT two days, Henry and Pierce roamed the house like disgruntled, caged lions, all grumbles and glares.

Priya said it was because they were healing.

And annoying.

Jack and Simon returned to the house, lurking on the sidewalk until Tamsin marched outside with meat pies and the lure of a story about a gunfight that had happened right where they were standing. After devouring lunch, they asked to see Henry, and then demanded to see his wound. It was still red and thick with congealed blood, which thrilled them.

When Henry was well enough to prowl to the library, trying to find something he had not read yet, Tamsin went for a walk.

A long walk.

She had to tamp down the fear that he would be gone when she returned. That he would find the first ship out of London and run away, as he'd done before. That she wasn't enough to keep him here.

She told herself that she had to trust him. Trust that he had heard her.

She took Crow with her because Henry had hissed through his teeth in pain trying to jam his wounded arm into his coat, flatly refusing that she should go alone. The afternoon was bright and warm and full of blooming flowers by every door. A perfect day for war.

The Culpepper townhouse was like every other townhouse in the square, imposing and stately and meant to intimidate.

Tamsin was not intimidated.

This was a battlefield she knew well.

She pulled the bell, smiling at the butler who promptly answered. "Good afternoon. I am Lord Culpepper's daughter-in-law, Lady Stirling."

The butler bowed. "Your ladyship. I'm afraid the earl is not at home."

She knew perfectly well that he was. She'd sent Juniper ahead to discreetly check with the housekeeper. She also knew at a glance that the butler was very proud of the pin through his necktie. It was shaped like a peacock, with a single tiny diamond eye. Everything else about him screamed of a man who upheld proper etiquette with heavy dignity.

"Sturgeon, isn't it?"

"Yes, your ladyship."

"If you don't mind my saying so, that is a very striking pin," she said. "I quite admire it."

"Thank you, your ladyship."

She tilted her head. "Would you mind very much telling me where you found it? I should like to get something similar for Lord Stirling."

He straightened, preening ever so slightly. Crow, standing silently behind her, snorted. Sturgeon narrowed his eyes, sensing mockery.

"Please forgive him," Tamsin said. She leaned in conspiratorially. "He sneezes whenever he is around lavender beeswax polish. You must keep this house very clean indeed."

Sturgeon inclined his head, mollified. "Indeed."

Her stepmother insisted on lavender beeswax polish in obscene amounts. Tamsin had once seen Beryl slide down the hall as though she were skating on the Thames in winter. The Chester butler had started his own line of polish, and it had become quite fashionable and the mark of a proper aristocratic household.

"And your pin?"

"From Boddington's, your ladyship. On Bond Street."

"Excellent. Thank you." She tilted her head. "Is the earl really not at home? Even for family?"

He hesitated.

She smiled. "I suppose it would be quite rude of me to simply push past you. And you could not do much to stop me, as it would not be polite."

He almost smiled back. "I certainly could not catch up to you by the time you reached the third door on the right."

"Thank you." She beamed at him and promptly sailed away.

"The earl is not… gentle," Sturgeon added.

"Don't let the pretty face fool you," Crow murmured. "That

one's a bruiser."

"I heard that!"

HENRY FOUND HIMSELF at the docks, where the ships were packed so tightly together, he could have walked across them to the other bank. His arm hurt like the devil and his mood was no better.

Mudlarks roamed, searching for lost pocket watches, trinkets, the teeth of dead men—anything that might fetch a price. They avoided him, the glowering, brooding earl with blood on his sleeve and the dark eyes of a pirate.

Men shouted back and forth, loading and unloading the decks. The ever-present gulls wheeled overhead. The smell was thick and awful but familiar: mud, unwashed bodies, fish. Nothing like the clean salt spray of the ocean he was considering. There was no Navy ship to take him away this time, only regular passenger ships who did not need another captain on board, only his coin. But they could take him anywhere, from India to Iceland to Fiji. People dreamt of such voyages. God knew he had, for years. Anything to get away from his father.

When he was eight years old, he'd been sure it would be pirates. At thirteen, Persephone had convinced him a sail down the Nile would be best, but he had to promise to take her along. At not quite twenty, he'd chosen the Navy, the day after his father sent a man to break his leg if he could not show the "gumption" to stop him.

He'd felt so free stepping on that ship for the first time. Terrified but excited. Starting as a midshipman, despite not having attended the Royal Naval College. His title and their need made it simpler for him to shadow the officers, rising in the ranks over the years. He'd had the courage to face Napoleon and his armies but not his grandmother, nor Persephone. He'd left them letters, running in the night like a coward.

And now here he was again.

Worse than a coward, he was betraying Tamsin by just standing here.

But he didn't know how else to save her.

She was no kitchen cat, but his father was likely to show her the same consideration. His men would show her none at all when in the grip of a fight. And he already knew she would not consider her own safety, not if it might save him or Jack or any of her friends. She was fierce and loyal and brave. All the things he had never been.

He would suffer the loss of her in his life if it meant keeping her safe. He would choose that misery every day if it meant she could be free to live her life.

But she wanted to live that life with him.

She'd offered to leave with him. She would say that she should be at his side, watching the trunks being packed onto the hull. She'd made him promise he would at least say goodbye. But if he said goodbye, he'd never have the strength to carry his plan through. He could not look into her blue eyes and cause her pain.

But this would cause her worse pain.

He was a coward.

Not like her. She was perfectly willing to take on his father and his men. And she'd do it while wearing dancing slippers and smile brighter than a summer's day.

His father would win again.

That alone would infuriate her.

And she would think he did not love her, as if the very air in his lungs wasn't less important to his survival than she was. She was everything.

She was the woman whose letters had kept him sane.

A woman who chose to smile even when she felt broken.

A woman capable of making her own decisions.

A woman who was strong enough to ask him to stay when too many people she loved had walked away.

"Ticket, sir?"

A woman he would do anything to keep safe.

Anything.

"Sir?"

TAMSIN DID NOT bother knocking on the library door, instead marching inside, wearing her most charming smile. The one the

Earl of Culpepper was not wise enough to fear.

He was at the sideboard, pouring brandy into a crystal glass. He was surprised. "You were not announced."

"This won't take a moment."

He stayed standing, and she knew exactly what he was about. She'd seen him do it before, looming over people to intimidate them. He'd towered over Henry, sneering.

She couldn't help the frisson of anxiety that Henry was even now booking passage to France, or the Americas, Italy.

She forced herself to stay calm. She raised an eyebrow with the perfect aristocratic ennui that suggested she was bored of the earl's attempt to make her nervous. "Your son was recently shot, saving my life."

"I heard."

"And yet you did not visit him."

"He's obviously not dead." He waved away any concern. "I sent a man to check."

"Yes," she said pleasantly. "About that." She reached into her reticule, the one embroidered with pink roses, and pulled out a piece of parchment. "You're not going to do that anymore. Not only is it grotesque, but it's unnecessary."

"Watch your tone with me, miss."

"That's Lady Stirling to you. Your son is already strong. He's also clever and kind, not that you ever cared about that."

"He can't be that strong, if he's got a woman fighting his battles for him."

"Reginald Caesar, you're embarrassing yourself," Henry's grandmother snapped, walking into the room as though she owned it. She wore several ropes of very large pearls, enough to make any mermaid proud. A cloud of perfume wafted around her. "More to the point, you're embarrassing *me*. Please forgive my son, Lady Stirling, though he does not deserve it." She gestured imperiously at her son. "I'll have a brandy."

"Mother, this has nothing to do with you."

"If it has to do with my grandson, it has to do with me. Brandy. *Now.*"

Muttering, the earl poured her drink and handed it to her.

Lady Culpepper turned to Tamsin. "You have come to say something? Pray, don't let me interrupt."

"Yes." She faced the earl again. "I don't know what's made you cruel for all of these years, and I don't care. It ends now."

The dowager countess smiled. "Oh, I *am* enjoying this little visit."

The earl did not look remotely cowed. He leaned back in his chair and steepled his fingers, unimpressed.

"I know I am not the first to say this to you," Tamsin continued. She laid the parchment on the heavy oak desk between them and smoothed it down. "But you will listen to me, because I am the first to also have this at my disposal."

He scoffed, glancing down.

He stopped scoffing, stopped glaring, stopped making any noise or movement of any kind for a long, glorious moment.

Lady Culpepper leaned forward, intrigued. "What is it?"

"It a guarantee, Lady Culpepper," Tamsin said, not looking away from Henry's father. "A guarantee that the earl will treat his son with respect, and if he cannot manage that, he will, at the very least, remove himself from our lives."

The earl was turning red. "You little—"

"Ah ah," Tamsin interrupted him. "I am not finished."

He choked on his anger.

Tamsin remembered every broken bone Henry had suffered as a child, every bruise, and wished Meg were here to paint a portrait of that particular shade of red. She would take it to the modiste and have an entire gown made from the color.

"I'm afraid your son has many debts and secrets, Lady Culpepper," Tamsin added. "And this is, of course, not the only copy. Several have been delivered among friends and barristers, all sealed. Should anything untoward happen to Henry, or myself, or our loved ones—anything at all—those letters will not only be opened, but they will be published in the *Times*. Immediately."

He swallowed, now pale. "I'd be ruined."

"Yes."

"You would take down the noble title, this earldom, for my son?"

"I'd take down the entire country for your son."

"Well, you did take down a traitor," Henry said mildly, leaning in the doorway. "I suppose Britain is the next logical step."

She wanted to run to him. She hadn't been sure he wasn't already somewhere she could not follow. "Henry."

He raised his eyebrows. "You've rendered the earl speechless. I admit to not knowing that was possible."

"Here now, boy," the earl thundered, standing so suddenly that his chair hit the wall behind him.

Henry only smiled at Tamsin before flicking a glance toward this father. "No."

"See here—"

She tapped the letter. The earl subsided, glowering.

"I'll take that." Lady Culpepper snatched the paper away.

Panic rose in her son's face. He pointed a finger at Henry. "Are you going to hide behind their skirts? Are you going to let them do this?"

"Certainly," Henry said calmly. "When they are so very good at it."

Tamsin could see him fighting his natural inclination to placate his father's temper, to hide from the threat, but she was sure no one else could. He looked every inch the naval captain, something his father would actually respond favorably to.

Tamsin slipped her arm through Henry's, holding on tightly. "I believe we're done here, Lord Culpepper."

THEY LEFT HENRY'S father sitting at his desk, staring at the place where the letter had sat. His grandmother patted Henry's cheek. "You've married well, my boy." To Tamsin she added, "I'm only sorry I never thought of it earlier."

"As am I," Tamsin admitted.

"I do believe I shall leave for Little Barrow tomorrow," the dowager countess added cheerfully, or as cheerfully as her naturally icy, severe demeanor allowed. "Come and visit me soon."

"I will, Grandmaman."

"You as well, Lady Stirling." She sailed upstairs, calling for her maid.

Henry was stunned and so damn proud. He'd never seen anyone push back against his father with such ease. The earl had the gift of flustering everyone within eyesight. He sent the maids out of the house in tears at least once a month, and once, the butler himself.

"Thank you, Sturgeon," Tamsin said to that same butler. "You were very helpful."

He bowed. "Lady Stirling."

"Did he just smile at you?" Henry asked, once they were out on the front step. The sun gleamed off freshly polished ironwork, glass windows, bonnets, and silver walking sticks. Mayfair was awake now and ready to be entertained.

"Of course he did."

"I can count on one hand the number of times that dour old man has smiled at me in my entire life."

"She's prettier than you," Crow said drily from the bottom step.

"True."

"And probably cleverer."

"Also true. As to that, it seems we shall no longer be needing your services." Henry could scarcely believe it.

"I am glad to hear it," Crow said. He inclined his head toward Tamsin. "Lady Stirling, it's been an honor."

"Thank you, Crow," she said. "You shall have to join us for Christmas dinner." Crow blinked. So did Henry. She frowned. "What?"

"I was only doing my job, your ladyship."

"You stayed up all hours of the night to protect me from harm," she said firmly. "The least I can do is feed you roast goose once a year."

Henry loved her all over again. She collected rare people just as she collected rare artifacts. He didn't know how he'd never seen it before. He'd known there was sharpness and steel under the sparkle, but he hadn't realized how expertly she could wield it. Deeply generous or fiercely protective. She'd make a hell of a ship's captain. That, he had already known.

Henry grinned. "You may as well give in now, Crow."

"Aye, sir." Crow bowed his head smartly and walked away, whistling.

"How did you know where I was?" Tamsin asked Henry. The square bustled around them, carriages passing to and fro, footmen rushing by with packages, sidewalks being swept clean, visitors arriving for tea and gossip.

"I knew you'd be here. After all, I explicitly told you not to come."

She wrinkled her nose. "Don't be cross. Your father drank all of the brandy, and I didn't get a single sip."

"Well then, you've clearly suffered enough." He tilted her chin up. "Did you really just blackmail my father, one of the most feared and brutish men in London?"

"With a little help from Priya." She smiled at him brightly. "You didn't underestimate the Cinderella Society again, did you?"

He kissed her lightly, right there on the front step, where everyone could see them. He felt the stares even as he heard the whispers.

"Why, Captain Talbot, you will scandalize Mayfair."

"I have to keep up with you lot, don't I?"

Her mouth turned serious. "I was afraid you'd gone."

He wanted to tell her it had never crossed his mind, not since she'd begged him not to, but he wouldn't lie to her. Not here. Not now, when she'd cleared the path through the shadows and muck of his past.

"I went to the docks," he admitted. She stiffened, just for a moment, and he hated himself all over again. "But I couldn't do it. Even though I thought it was the only way I knew to protect you."

"What made you stay?"

"You." He caught her gaze, willed her to believe him. "How could I not fight as hard as you were willing to fight? How could I let you think for one moment that anything or anyone was more important than you—and especially that man?"

Her breath caught, her lips parting. He wanted to kiss her, desperately, deeply, until she melted in his arms. But he wanted her to hear him first, to believe every word he said.

"You're everything to me, Tamsin. And I don't regret choosing to do anything to protect you, but I do regret each and every shred of a single second where you might have thought I wanted to be anywhere but at your side."

"You're staying?" she whispered. "Truly?"

"I'm sorry I made you doubt me. Us." He kissed her again, the kind of kiss guaranteed to turn gossip into scandal. He poured every ounce of love he had for her into it, every need and want and desire, until their breaths tangled, until she gasped once. "I won't ever do that again. You are stuck with me for as long as you want me." He leaned closer to whisper to her, letting the words tickle her ear in the way he knew made her squirm, "And when I die, I promise to haunt only you."

She giggled once, startled, and it was like sunshine. "Now that *is* romantic."

"I see the lady in you, Tamsin, and I see the woman. And I love them both."

"I see the captain in you, Henry, and I see the man. And I love them both."

He kissed her again; he couldn't help himself. "We should get married again," he teased. "Those sound like proper vows."

She grinned. "I'm still not obeying you."

He grinned back. "Thank God for that."

They finally left his father's house, walking out of the shadow of the hulking building and into the bright bustle of the square.

"Do you know?" Tamsin asked. "Blackmail makes one hungry."

"Gunter's is not far from here."

"A capital idea."

Naturally, they ordered lemon ices.

With extras for the two boys watching them from up a tree.

Epilogue

CHRISTMAS AT THE Stirling London townhouse that year was a mad affair.

It was loud, crowded, and entirely too much.

In other words, perfect.

Holly branches were tied to every door with red ribbons, wreaths of pine hung from the windows, and mistletoe crowned every dark and secret corner. Henry wasted no time in pulling her under that mistletoe every chance he got.

A quick trip down to the kitchen to see how they were getting on resulted in his pulling her into his study.

She went willingly, laughing. "There's no mistletoe in here."

"There are no people here either," he said, nuzzling her ear. "A sailor knows when to strike."

"Captain Talbot," she whispered against his cheek. His hands tightened on her waist, and he captured her mouth instantly, flaring heat between them, as she knew it would.

"You've filled the house to bursting," he said, stroking his palm down her lower back, clutching at her dress. "Are you happy?"

"Yes." She dug her fingers into the thick hair at the nape of his neck. The light glinted off her new wedding ring, the gold poison ring from the Midnight Market. She still did not know how Henry had managed to procure it, and he refused to tell her. "And you, Lord Stirling? Are you happy?"

She knew he was. He had unpacked all of his books, which vied for space with her relics. He'd bought roughly a hundred more since they'd moved into his townhouse, which was fortified like a small castle, despite the mild behavior from his father. She loved finding him sitting by the fire in his bedroom, light gleaming off his chest, a book in his hand.

She liked to distract him with kisses, small, teasing nips, just as she did now until he groaned and pushed her against the door.

"I'd be happier if you weren't wearing so many damned clothes."

He slipped his hand between her thighs, even as she reached for his hardness pressing deliciously against her. He dragged his mouth across the column of her throat, biting down gently until she moaned.

"This is the only Christmas present I want," he said, pulling at the ribbons on her neckline.

Someone rang the doorbell.

"Ignore it." A love bite on the swell of her breast to convince her.

A crash sounded from outside.

"Damn it."

And then a shout from the other side of the door: "I don't know where she's gone."

"And I've just remembered why I hate Christmas," Henry murmured before bending to suck the tip of her nipple into his mouth, once, twice. She gasped, then swore when he pulled away, and put her dress to rights.

Warmth tingled and throbbed through her body, in her breasts, between her legs. Building. Waiting. Impatient. *"Captain Talbot."*

He smirked. "This party was *your* idea."

And he would tease her through every waking moment until they finally reached the bedroom. And she would love every minute of it.

She rose on her toes to speak softly in his ear. "I've new curtain sashes. Very jolly."

He sucked in a breath. She was the one smirking when she

slipped out of the study.

Persephone grinned, holding an armful of the kitchen cat that she'd been chasing down the hall. "I don't want to know what's got that look on your face."

Tamsin winked. "Why do you have the cat?"

"In ancient Egypt they sometimes wore gold collars," Persephone explained. "I thought he might like to be festive." General Whiskers the Second did not look festive. He looked resigned. Glum, even. "But apparently not." Persephone sighed before kissing the top of his head and releasing him to chase cookie crumbs in every decorated parlor.

Persephone and Conall had arrived, with Persephone's grandmother in tow, as well as Priya and the Duke of Pendleton, who could not understand why all of this madness was not happening at his estate in Little Barrow, which had seventy available bedrooms.

Henry's grandmother arrived just before Meg and her duke, and his siblings and their adoptive father George.

Pierce and Crow had also accepted their invitations, mostly because they had no earthly idea how to refuse.

Jack and Simon were getting more and more comfortable, and by the end of summer they were sleeping in the bedroom Tamsin had set aside for them, with two beds near enough each other for comfort, and far away enough from each other for some independence. They still went into neighborhoods that made Tamsin nervous for them, but by Christmas it was mostly to convince other orphans and pickpockets that if they lined up at the kitchen door, they would be fed meat pies every day at lunch, no questions asked. Tamsin had hired a second cook for the express purpose. And when some of the neighbors began to grumble at the success of her pack of wild children, the Duke of Pendleton and the Duke of Thorncroft, along with the Earl of Northwyck, showed up to help hand out meat pies. On the day Dowager Countess Culpepper stood in her pearls with a basket of muffins, the entire neighborhood retreated behind their curtains in defeat.

Although Tamsin would not have minded a ghost or two at

the supper table, there simply was no room.

"There you are," Priya said, coming down the main stairs. The banister dripped with more pine boughs, brought in from the Stirling country estate. "You're flushed. What have you been— Do you know something? Forget I asked."

Tamsin grinned. "What do you need?"

"The Cinderellas are taking tea in your private parlor."

"They are, are they?"

"Yes, and you're late."

Priya led the way back up the stairs, past a line of portraits of ghostly ladies. "Pierce is outside teaching the children very inappropriate sea shanties."

Tamsin laughed. "They must have gotten tired of carols."

Her private parlor was filled with the things she loved: a witch bottle filled with strange substances, a rowan cross bound with red thread, poppets with iron nails through their hearts, and a child's doll. Also, the women she loved best in the world: Persephone, Meg, and Priya.

"Did you hear about Miss McKinney?" Priya asked without preamble. "Someone's been sending her dead pigeons."

"That's dreadful," Persephone said. "Why?"

"Because she is the sole heiress to the family fortune and someone wants to scare her into giving up the house. So I think it's time the Cinderella Society opens its doors to new members. Don't you agree?"

"How do you mean?" Meg asked. "Are we putting notices in the paper?"

"No, we shan't need to. I already have a list of ladies who might benefit from our expertise."

"We have expertise now?" Persephone scoffed, adding honey to her tea. "Last I checked, I was ruined and only tolerated because I am now a countess."

"And I collect poppets," Tamsin put in helpfully. "Does she need a curse?"

"Or a scarab beetle?" Persephone added.

"There they go," Meg said to Priya over the mound of her very pregnant belly.

Priya rolled her eyes. "This is not about antiquities."

Persephone was in very great danger of pouting. "Oh."

"Not everyone has a duke for a godfather and sisters at their back, as we do," Priya pointed out.

Meg got misty. "What a lovely thing to say."

Priya pointed at her. "Don't."

"Don't what? Agree with you?"

"Don't cry," she said. "Women carrying babies always cry. You've cried three times already today. Have some more cake instead."

Meg shrugged. "I can't argue with that logic. Though this baby currently trying to kick my spine might disagree."

"When Meg tears up, Priya tears up," Persephone whispered to Tamsin. "Have you noticed?"

"Can we get back to the matter at hand?" Priya asked. "I can ferret out any pertinent details which might help us. And Meg can teach them how to steal."

Meg perked up. "I think I like this finishing school."

"Persephone can show them how to watch what people do instead of only listening to what they say."

"I can also show them how to properly work a barrow. You wouldn't believe the bathtub corners left by some so-called antiquarians at the new dig in Norfolk."

Tamsin bit into a slice of gingerbread cake. "I don't know what I could teach them, but you know I'll help."

"What do you mean by that?" Priya demanded.

"I have no skills, Priya," Tamsin said. And for once, she was so happy it did not bother her overmuch. "Not like the rest of you. These ladies will already know how to dance and how to curtsy."

"Bollocks to that, Tamsin Talbot," Priya said.

Tamsin blinked. "Merry Christmas to you too."

"You do so much more than you think we notice. It's insulting, honestly," Priya grumbled. "I'll wager you can tell me more about a person by the way they dance than anyone else could fathom. Say, for instance, Miss Howard."

Tamsin shifted under the force of her friends' collective

stares. Unable to ignore the dare, she pictured Miss Howard.

"She will not dance because she has a slight limp no one else notices."

"And Lady Tansy?"

"She dances every dance and wishes she was a wallflower instead, but her mother will not allow it."

"Lord Chevril."

"Lord Chevril only dances the quadrille because he thinks it shows his calves to the most advantage."

"There, you see?" Priya said. "You know all that, and they think they are being clever and discreet. You know how to camouflage yourself better than anyone. And since you also happen to *know* everyone, it won't be the least bit odd or out of the ordinary for someone needing our help to approach you."

"That's true," Meg agreed.

"So it's settled."

Tamsin smiled, amused, and more than a little touched. She hadn't thought of those things as gifts or abilities. It was rather nice. "I suppose it is. I have a suggestion for our first new member."

"Who's that?" Priya asked.

"Carnation."

"Your stepsister?" Meg asked. "The one who wears pink?"

"Yes. I think there is far more to her than meets the eye."

"Excellent. And she is a spinster."

"Is that a requirement?"

"I think spinsters shall be our secret weapon," Priya explained smugly. "No one sees them or cares to see them."

"True."

"But we shall arm them," Priya lifted her flute of champagne. "To the Cinderella Society."

"To the Cinderella Society!"

"And better yet, to the Spinsters of Mayfair!"

About the Author

Alyxandra Harvey lives in an old stone house with her husband, multiple dogs, and a few resident ghosts who are allowed to stay as long as they keep company manners. She likes chai lattes, tattoos, and books. Sometimes fueled by literary rage.

Author of The Drake Chronicles, The Witches of London, Haunting Violet, Red, Love Me Love Me Not.

Twitter: AlyxandraH
Instagram: alyxandraharveyauthor